Praise for

THE SEAMSTRESS OF SARDINIA

'A delicate novel of a woman's formation and emancipation.'
—Simone Mosca, *la Repubblica*

'Bianca Pitzorno's most political book: it has a female protagonist, it is written by a woman, and I would like men to read
it, above all.'

—Nadia Terranova, *Robinson*

'Pitzorno is an icon. . . . [This novel] is yet another confirmation.'
—*Corriere del Ticino*

'A compelling storyline like a feuilleton, yet touching on contemporary issues that have to do with women's emancipation.'
—*Cosmopolitan* (Italy)

'Pitzorno is one of the greatest Italian writers. . . . [This] is an
extraordinary novel. . . . Only a wise hand could draw the parallel between sewing and writing without making it trivial:
Pitzorno succeeds in her most "political" book.'

—*la Repubblica*

THE SEAMSTRESS OF SARDINIA

THE
SEAMSTRESS
OF SARDINIA

A NOVEL

BIANCA PITZORNO

HARPER PERENNIAL

NEW YORK • LONDON • TORONTO • SYDNEY • NEW DELHI • AUCKLAND

HARPER ● PERENNIAL

This is a work of fiction. Names, characters, places, and incidents are products of the author's imagination or are used fictitiously and are not to be construed as real. Any resemblance to actual events, locales, organizations, or persons, living or dead, is entirely coincidental.

First published in Italian as *Il sogno della macchina da cucire* by Bompiani, Giunti Editore S.p.A., 2018.

First published in English by The Text Publishing Company, 2022.

THE SEAMSTRESS OF SARDINIA. Copyright © 2022 by Bianca Pitzorno. English translation copyright © 2022 by Brigid Maher. All rights reserved. Printed in the United States of America. No part of this book may be used or reproduced in any manner whatsoever without written permission except in the case of brief quotations embodied in critical articles and reviews. For information, address HarperCollins Publishers, 195 Broadway, New York, NY 10007.

HarperCollins books may be purchased for educational, business, or sales promotional use. For information, please email the Special Markets Department at SPsales@harpercollins.com.

FIRST U.S. EDITION PUBLISHED 2022.

ISBN 978-0-06-327169-2 (pbk.)

22 23 24 25 26   LSC   10 9 8 7 6 5 4 3 2 1

THE SEAMSTRESS OF SARDINIA

In loving memory of

Signora Angelina Valle Vallebella, our summer landlady and the only seamstress in Stintino, who had a beautiful treadle sewing machine and worked with the door open onto the piazza, Largo Cala d'Oliva as it's known, and who pierced the village girls' ears with a red-hot needle and a cork—she plaited my hair every morning in her courtyard full of hydrangeas in bloom;

and Signora Ermenegilda Gargioni, the most intelligent and creative woman I have ever met, who left our loving hearts behind two years ago, and who, even after going blind, continued to use her treadle sewing machine up to the age of ninety-seven;

and Giuseppina Friedfish, whose real surname I cannot remember, who after the war was hired by the day to come to our house to sew for us, and who turned so many old coats for us, and made me so many little smocks for school, with pleats down the front and cap sleeves, and made my brothers so many piqué overalls, and when I was five years old showed me how to sew my first few stitches and patiently explained the fundamentals of sewing, including the use of a hand-crank machine;

and my grandmother Peppina Sisto, who taught me to embroider both in white and in colours, and who, when she saw me using a needle without putting on a thimble (as I always did and continue to do), would complain to my mother, predicting that I would go on to become an unruly woman;

and all the modern-day seamstresses of the Third World, who sew for us the fashionable rags we buy for a few euros in cheap department stores—each working over and over on the same piece cut by somebody else, in an assembly line, for fourteen hours straight, wearing nappies so as not to waste time going to the toilet, and who, after receiving a pittance in wages, are burnt to death in giant prison-factories. Sewing is a beautiful, creative activity, but not like that, *not like that.*

The stories and characters in this book are the fruit of my imagination.

However, every episode has its origin in a real-life event that I learnt about from stories told by my grandmother, who was of the same generation as the protagonist, from letters and postcards she kept in a suitcase, from newspapers of the time, and from the recollections and anecdotes that make up our family vocabulary. I reordered events, filled in the gaps, invented details, added in surrounding characters, sometimes changed the stories' endings. But occurrences of the kind described here did take place once upon a time—even in the best of families, as the old adage goes.

The seamstress paid by the day, the *sartina*, was a frequent presence in bourgeois houses up to the time of my early adolescence. All the more so in the post-war years, when everybody was forced to 'recycle' and reuse clothing and fabrics in new forms. It was not until later that industrially produced linen and clothing came along, as well as ready-to-wear fashion, and then the big designer brands. When low-cost clothing started appearing in department stores, rich people who cared greatly about elegance, or who wanted to stand out, continued to get their clothes made to measure, but by renowned dressmakers at true couture houses.

The era of the sartina was over.

The aim of this book is to ensure that they are not forgotten.

My Love, Light of My Life

I WAS SEVEN years old when Nonna began entrusting me with putting the finishing touches on the garments she sewed at home for her clients, during those periods when she had no jobs that sent her to work in other people's homes. She and I were the only members of the family left alive after the cholera epidemic that had taken from us, indiscriminately, my parents, my brothers and sisters, and all my grandmother's other children and grandchildren—my aunts, uncles and cousins. How the two of us managed to survive, I've never known.

We were poor, but that had been the case even before the epidemic. All our family ever had was the strength of the men's arms and the dexterity of the women's fingers. My grandmother and her daughters and daughters-in-law were well known in the city for their skill and precision in sewing and embroidery, and for their honesty, cleanliness and reliability when they went to work in domestic service in the homes of the upper classes, where they showed grace and competence as maids while also taking care of the wardrobe and linen. And almost all were good cooks. The men worked as day labourers—masons, removalists, gardeners. In our city there were not yet many industries offering work, but the brewery, the oil mill, the flour mill and the endless excavation work for the aqueduct often required non-specialised labour. As far as I can recall we never went hungry, though we often had to move house and huddle together for a while in squalid hovels or *bassi* in the old part of town when we couldn't afford to pay the rent on the humble flats that people of our class usually lived in.

When the two of us were left alone I was five and my grandmother, fifty-two. She was strong, and could have earned a living as a maid in one of the houses where she had worked as a young woman and left a good impression. But she would not have been allowed to keep me with her in any of those homes, and she did not want to leave me in one of the orphanages or charitable institutions run by the nuns. There were several in our city and they had a dreadful reputation. Even if she had only worked days as a maid she would not have had anyone to leave me with. So she took a gamble that she would be able to support us both with her sewing work, and she did so well out of it that I cannot recall wanting for anything during those years. We lived in two small rooms partly below ground level in the basement of a noble *palazzo* in a narrow cobbled street of the old town, and she paid the rent in kind, by cleaning the entrance hall and four flights of stairs. My grandmother spent two and a half hours on this task every morning, getting out of bed before dawn, and only after putting away buckets, rags and broom would she start on her sewing.

She had set up one of our two rooms in such a smart and seemly way that she was able to receive clients when they came by with an order or, occasionally, for a fitting, though in most cases she would go to their houses, with tacked-up clothes over her arm and pincushion and scissors tied to a ribbon around her neck. On those occasions she would take me with her after a thousand exhortations to sit quietly in a corner while we were at the client's house. This was because she had nobody to leave me with, but also so that I could watch and learn.

My grandmother's speciality was full sets of linen for the home—sheets, tablecloths, curtains—but also shirts for men and women, underwear, and baby clothing. In those days there were few department stores selling such items ready to wear. Our biggest rivals were the Carmelite nuns, who were especially skilled at embroidery. But my grandmother also knew how to make day and evening wear, jackets and overcoats for women. And also, by reducing the measurements, for children. I always went around smartly dressed, neat and clean, unlike the other little urchins who lived in our laneway. But despite her age, my grandmother was considered a sartina, a little seamstress, someone to go to for simple, everyday items. There were two true, important dressmakers in the city who, in competition with each other, served the needs of wealthy, fashionable ladies, and who each had an atelier with various employees. They received catalogues with patterns, and sometimes even fabrics, from the capital. It cost a fortune to get something made by them—the kind of money Nonna and I could have lived on for two years or maybe more.

And then there was one family, the lawyer Provera's, that went so far as to order the wife's and daughters' ballgowns and other dresses for special occasions from Paris. A real extravagance, because it was well known that regarding everything else, including his own wardrobe, Avvocato Provera was extremely mean, even though he boasted one of the largest fortunes in the city. 'More money than sense,' my grandmother would sigh. In her youth she had worked for the wife's parents. They too were extremely wealthy— for the wedding they had bestowed on their daughter Teresa an extraordinary trousseau worthy of an American heiress, all of it straight from Paris, along with a princely dowry. But evidently their son-in-law was only disposed to invest in the elegance of his womenfolk. Like all gentlemen, the lawyer went to a tailor for his clothes, but the work of a tailor was utterly unlike ours: the textiles, cuts, sewing techniques and apprenticeship rules were all very different. No woman was ever admitted to that trade, perhaps because modesty forbade women from touching men's bodies to take measurements—I don't know—but that was the tradition. Two completely separate worlds.

My grandmother was illiterate. She had never been able to allow herself the luxury of going to school and now, although she would have liked to, she could not offer me the chance either. I needed to learn quickly to help her, then dedicate all my time to work. The alternative, as she often reminded me, was the orphanage, where, yes, they would teach me to read and write, but I would be living as though in a prison—suffering the cold, eating poorly—and then, at fourteen, when they sent me on my way, all I would be able to do was work as a maid, living in somebody else's house, my hands in cold water all day, or burnt over the stove or a hot iron, doing exactly what I was told, day in, day out, with no prospects and no hope of improving my lot. Whereas by learning a trade, I would always be able to maintain my independence. The thing she feared most, my grandmother admitted to me many years later, just before she died, was that if I went into domestic service living under the same roof as a family, I would be molested by the master of the house or by his sons.

'I'd be able to defend myself!' I declared defiantly. Only then did she tell me the tragic story of her cousin Ofelia. When her master propositioned her, Ofelia rejected him, slapped him in the face and threatened to tell his wife. As revenge and in order to pre-empt any accusation, he took a gold cigar case from the drawing room and hid it in the little room where she slept. Then he got his wife to accompany him on a search of the maid's humble possessions and upon their 'discovery' of the cigar case the girl was fired on the spot and sent on her way without a letter of reference. The lady of the house told all her acquaintances about the theft. News spread and after that no respectable family ever wanted to employ the 'thief'. The only job Ofelia was able to find was as a scullery maid in a tavern. But there too the drunk patrons made her life difficult, making unseemly demands, fighting over her, getting her mixed up in brawls. One evening she was arrested, and that was the beginning of the end. Due to the prostitution laws brought in by Cavour and Nicotera, police regulations were extremely strict. They put her under surveillance and, after the third brawl, which was no fault of her own, Ofelia was forced to register as a prostitute and go to work in a bordello. There she fell ill and a few years later she died in hospital of the French disease.

For my grandmother, recalling that story was like reliving a nightmare. She knew how fine the line was between an honourable life and a hellish one of shame and suffering. When I was a child she never spoke to me about it—in fact, she did everything she could to keep me ignorant of sex and its dangers.

But very early on she began giving me needle and thread, and a few scraps of fabric left over from her work. Like any good teacher, she introduced it to me as a game. I had an old papier-mâché doll in a terrible state. I had inherited it from one of the cousins who had died; she had been given it by the lady her mother worked for. I loved this doll deeply, and it pained me to see it all bare and covered in scratches. (My grandmother had removed its clothes one night and hidden them.) I was eager to learn how to make this doll a shirt at the very least, a headscarf, then a sheet and later an apron. My aim was an elegant dress with pleats and lace trimmings, but this was not easy and in the end my grandmother completed the job.

But in the meantime, I had learnt to sew perfect hems with tiny, identical stitches, without pricking my fingers and getting blood on the light white cambric of baby clothes or handkerchiefs. By the time I was seven hems were my daily task. I was happy to be told, 'You're an enormous help.' And the number of garments my grandmother could complete in a week grew from one month to the next, and so did her earnings, albeit modestly. I learnt how to do hemstitch on sheets, monotonous work that allowed my mind to wander freely, and pulled thread embroidery, which required more attention. Now that I was older my grandmother would let me go out alone—to buy thread from the haberdashery, to deliver completed garments—and if I stopped for half an hour on the way back to play on the street with other girls from the neighbourhood, she would not complain. She did not like leaving me home alone for too long, however, and when she needed to spend the whole day sewing at a client's house she would bring me along, on the pretext of needing my help. That kind of work was advantageous because if it was a dark day we could use all the candles and gas lamps we needed without worrying about the cost. And at midday we would be given lunch, meaning on those days we would also be saving on food. It was always a good lunch—pasta, meat and fruit, far better than our usual meal. In some houses we had to eat in the kitchen with the maids, while in others the meal was served just to the two of us, in the sewing room. We were never invited to eat with the owners.

Usually in those wealthy, elegant homes there was, as I said, a dedicated sewing room, well lit, with a large table for stretching out and cutting fabric, and often there was even—marvel of marvels—a sewing machine. My grandmother knew how to use one—I don't know where she'd learnt this—and I looked on fascinated as she moved the treadle up and down in a rhythmic motion and the fabric slid quickly under the needle. 'If we had one at home,' she would sigh, 'just think how much work I could take on!' But we both knew we'd never be able to afford one, and in any case there wasn't the space.

One such evening, as we were putting everything away at the end of a day's work, in came the little girl for whom we were sewing a white confirmation dress, spurred on by the lady of the house. She was a girl of about eleven, like me. She timidly handed me a rectangular parcel, nicely wrapped in thick grocer's paper and tied with string. 'They're children's chronicles from last year,' her mother explained. 'Erminia has read them over and over, and a new

12

one arrives each week. She thought you might like them.'

Before I spotted the stern warning in my grandmother's eyes, the words had already slipped out: 'I can't read.'

Signorina Erminia looked down at her shoes in embarrassment, her face twisted with sadness like she was about to cry. After a moment's hesitation, her mother collected herself and said with an easy smile, "That doesn't matter. You can look at the pictures. They're so beautiful.' And she handed me the parcel.

She was right. When I got home and opened the package, spreading the contents out on the bed, they took my breath away. I had never seen anything so beautiful in all my life. Some of the illustrations were in colour, others were black and white, but all of them fascinated me. What would I give to be able to read the writing underneath! In bed at night, with the sheet pulled over my head, I cried a little, trying not to let Nonna hear me. But she did. And the following week, after we finished our work in Signorina Erminia's house, she said to me, 'I've made a deal with Lucia, the haberdasher's daughter. You know she's engaged to be married in two years' time. I've promised that we'll monogram twelve sheets in double back stitch for her, and in exchange she'll give you two one-hour lessons a week. She studied to be a schoolteacher, though she never got her diploma. I'm sure you'll learn fast.'

But it took me almost three years, because Lucia had little experience and I had little time to practise. I continued helping my grandmother, with more and more difficult tasks, and whenever we went to people's houses to sew I had to miss my lessons. To begin with, because I didn't have a primer and I didn't want to cost Nonna any money, I asked Lucia to use pages from the children's chronicles in our lessons, and she agreed. 'It's better that way. It won't be as dull.' She was twenty, but she had a child's love of riddles, tongue-twisters and facts about strange animals. The rhymes in the chronicles were funny and made us laugh, but they weren't the kinds of words people use every day. After a few months we had to borrow a schoolbook. I was happy to learn and very grateful to my make-do teacher. I asked my grandmother to leave the embroidered sheets to me: I wanted to do them myself. I finished them the night before Lucia's wedding. And in exchange for the following year's lessons I sewed twelve little tops in various sizes for the baby she was expecting. I also made an embroidered gown inspired by those worn by the king's little daughters, the princesses Jolanda and Mafalda. On display in a shop window I had seen a photograph of the queen holding them in her arms. When Lucia's baby, a lovely little boy, was born just after my fourteenth birthday, she said to me, 'That's enough lessons. I don't have time anymore. And besides, you've come far enough to be able to continue on your own.'

So that I could keep up my practice, she gave me her own little 'newspapers', which she no longer had the time even to leaf through. They weren't actually papers but opera librettos. Some were so well-thumbed that they fell to pieces as soon as you turned a page. I had never been to the theatre, but I knew that every year a bel-canto company came to town and performed the latest melodramas. It wasn't just the upper classes who went along, but also shop-keepers and some artisans who could afford a seat up in the gods. I knew some of the arias because our clients sang them in their drawing rooms, playing the accompaniment on piano.

I read those librettos like they were novels and discov-ered to my amazement that every single one of them spoke of love. Passionate loves, fatal loves. It was a topic to which I had not yet given much attention, but from that moment on I began listening in with greater curiosity to the con-versations of grown-ups around me.

During that time there was a lot of talk—in the homes of prominent families, in cafés frequented by gentlemen, but also in our little laneway and the nearby streets and the market stalls—about a story that bore some resemblance to those in Lucia's melodramas. Signor Artonesi's seventeen-year-old daughter had fallen head over heels in love with Marquis Rizzaldo and wished to marry him despite her father's opposition to the match. My grandmother and I knew the Artonesi family, who lived a few streets away in a large apartment on the first floor of an elegant and noble palazzo. There were many such buildings in the old town, alongside hovels which had once been the stables but which, now that the use of horses and carriages had diminished, had become the dwellings of the poorest and most desperate people. On several occasions the Artonesis' housekeeper had summoned us to the home to sew. She had been in charge ever since the lady of the house had died in the great epidemic, leaving behind her only daughter, protagonist of the much-discussed love story. We had seen the signorina grow up and had sewn various pinafores for her home use, as well as a few summer dresses in embroidered muslin. Her name was Ester and she was the apple of her father's eye. He was unable to deny her anything, not even the most extravagant request. Not only had he recently bought her a splendid grand piano, shipped from England, but he allowed her to take lessons at the riding school, which was frequented almost exclusively by men, and by a few young ladies accompanied by their husbands. In town, it was rumoured that Ester Artonesi did not ride side-saddle but straddling the horse, and that she wore a pair of trousers under her skirt for this very purpose. Despite the protestations of the housekeeper and their female relatives, the girl's father forgave her complete lack of interest in sewing, embroidery, cooking and everything else relating to the management of a home. And when Ester took a notion to learn foreign and ancient languages, he called in an elderly spinster of Tunisian background to give her French lessons twice a week, as well as the American journalist who had been living in our city for many years for English, and a priest from the seminary for Latin and Greek. In addition, ever since she was little Ester had had a science tutor to teach her botany, chemistry and geography, and who explained to her how various recent inventions worked. She enjoyed these lessons and never skipped them. (I adored her because once, when we were working at her house, she had come in with her science teacher so that my grandmother and I could hear him explain the mechanism behind their new German sewing machine. He had taken it apart completely, told us the name and function of each of the parts, let us touch them, and then slowly put it all back together showing us the cogs one by one and explaining to my grandmother how to lubricate them. I was eleven at the time and it felt like I was witnessing a miracle.)

'He wants to raise her like she's a boy...' the women in the family whispered in vexation. Signor Artonesi's sister-in-law even said to him resolutely, 'You know when Ester gets married none of this will be of any use to her. You're spoiling her.' But he shrugged his shoulders and suggested she take an interest in the education of her own daughters, who had begun giving themselves airs.

Signor Artonesi could get away with this sort of eccentricity and disdain for convention, as well as so much expenditure, because he was very rich. He owned huge sections of land sown with wheat, barley and hops, but unlike other major landowners in the area he had initiative and did not simply limit himself to collecting the takings from sharecroppers come harvest time. He also owned and managed several mills where the harvest from other farms was processed, as well as a large brewery, the only one in our region. He often brought his daughter along on his inspection rounds.

'You'll be in charge of all this one day,' he would tell her.

His sister-in-law, the girl's maternal aunt, would correct him: 'Her husband will be. Unless by indulging her so much you end up making a spinster out of her.'

This was unlikely, I always thought, because Ester Artonesi was not just a rich heiress, she was also very beautiful. She was slim, there was a rare elegance and grace to her movements, and her face was so sweet and expressive as to enchant even the most surly and indifferent of men. Many suitors buzzed around her, but she was able to keep them at bay. Kindly, and without ever causing offence, she had a way of making it known to them in a few words that they had best keep their distance. For this, too, I admired her. In those days, I found all men—and their sentimental sweet-talking—ridiculous. Some things could only happen, and some mawkish, cloying words could only be spoken, in the world of melodrama.

When I heard that Signorina Ester had fallen in love with Marquis Rizzaldo, whom she had met at the riding school, I could not believe it. First and foremost, at thirty the marquis seemed like an old man to me. My grandmother found nothing strange about it, however. To the woman who sold us needles and thread she pointed out that the marquis, although not as rich as the Artonesis, had a considerable fortune of his own, so there was certainly no risk he was a dowry hunter. What's more, he had an old and respected noble title, and because of the epidemic he was now the last of the family line. It was logical that he was keen to marry and bring an heir into the world, perhaps start a large family, while he was still fairly young. The age of his chosen bride presented no problem to my grandmother and her acquaintances—they had married at around sixteen.

But Signor Artonesi, who had hitherto indulged so many of his daughter's whims, was unwilling to support her in this choice. He had taken against the marquis right from the start, though he could find nothing specific to say against him. He thought Ester too young to become a wife and run a household. 'You have no experience,' he told her. 'You have so much to learn.'

'Guelfo can teach me,' she would stubbornly reply.

'All I ask is that you wait until you come of age,' her father insisted. 'And if you haven't changed your mind by then I'll give my permission.'

'Four years! Do you want me to wait till I'm dead? In four years' time I'll be an old woman. And in the meantime, Guelfo will look for someone else. You've no idea how many girls are circling him. And anyway, by the time I come of age I'll no longer need your permission.'

We knew the tone of these exchanges because their housekeeper related it all to us. She also told us about the passionate letters that arrived at the Artonesi home every day along with bouquets of flowers. And about the days

Signorina Ester spent shut up in her room crying because her father would no longer let her go out alone, and those accompanying her on outings had orders to prevent all contact with the marquis.

One day the girl came into her father's study white as a sheet and without saying a word handed him a letter she had just received. 'If I can't have you, I'll kill myself,' it said. 'My life has no purpose without you.'

'If Guelfo kills himself, I'll do the same,' Ester said, in a calm tone that frightened Signor Artonesi, who resigned himself to receiving the suitor and had a long, private talk with him. The result was that the youngsters could consider themselves officially engaged, but they must never meet alone. The marquis could visit Ester's house, go there for lunch every Sunday, accompany her and her father on their visits to the mill and the brewery, and—in the presence of her aunt and female cousins—take her to city balls during Carnival or to have a hot chocolate at the town's most elegant café, the one on the main street, frequented only by the upper classes and known as the Crystal Palace due to its large glass windows. But the two must never try to be alone together: they must always remain within sight and earshot of a witness. They were free to write privately to each other, however. As for the dowry, Signor Artonesi undertook to assign his daughter a very generous annual income, without granting her ownership of any of his properties. 'She will inherit everything after I die. It's as though it were all hers already,' he said, and the marquis was too embarrassed to protest. The engagement was to last two years, to put the couple's mutual affection to the test. Of course, to break it off once it had been officially announced and the city had been informed would have caused a scandal. But Signor Artonesi was more concerned with his daughter's happiness than her reputation, and he did not fear people's judgement.

Signorina Ester began preparing her trousseau. Her fiancé would have preferred her to order everything ready-made from Paris, like the young ladies of the Provera family, but she didn't trust catalogues. For her most elegant dresses she turned to both the city's ateliers, so that nobody would get jealous. 'Let's hope those pretentious dressmakers notice that the girl is still developing and don't design everything to fit her right now,' my grandmother observed sceptically. She was proud, though, that the young lady had come to us for her linen and undergarments.

During those two years we set all our other clients to one side—though this would later prove to have been very unwise—and focused only on the Artonesis, working on handkerchiefs, sheets, tablecloths and curtains in our own little home, and doing everything else in their sewing room. My grandmother made the future bride's night-gowns, slips, daywear and some exquisite little shawls edged with St Gallen lace that been ordered specially from Switzerland. And day by day I, too, learnt how to sew the finest pleats, the most minuscule buttonholes, and tiny ruffles and frills. And, like Signorina Ester, I continued to grow taller. After all, there were less than three years separating us.

We were paid punctually and generously, we were able to save on meals, and they treated us courteously: if only that kind of job could last ten years, or more! After a few months, I plucked up the courage to ask Signorina Ester if she might lend me some of her novels, and she not only agreed but enthusiastically guided me in my reading. She subscribed to a magazine called *Cordelia* and every week she passed on to me the issue she had just finished reading. For her part, she continued her lessons in music, languages and the sciences, but with less application than before. This in part because her fiancé had pointed out to her, fondly it must be said, that he considered such things an eccentricity, even a childish fancy.

If my eyes had not been so tired when I came home of an evening, I could have learnt many useful things in those two years, along with some my grandmother considered damaging. 'It's no good getting grand ideas and wanting things you can never have,' she would say whenever she saw me sighing over a novel. But one thing I learnt for sure: love was a beautiful thing, and any sacrifice in the name of love was painless. Sentimental men were not in the least ridiculous, as I had thought previously, and the marquis Guelfo Rizzaldo was the model lover, ready to give up his life for his Ester, as she was for him. I dreamt that I, too, would meet a man who loved me so deeply, a handsome and kind young man. I found the coarse compliments I received on the streets from errand boys offensive and irritating. I knew that sooner or later I would have to settle for one of them; I was not so deluded as to expect a Prince Charming to come my way. But in the meantime, it cost nothing to dream.

Time passed, and Signorina Ester grew taller and gave me the dresses that had become too short for her, all still in excellent condition. My grandmother hastened to alter them to my size and to remove all ornamentation—buttons, fringes, lace, frog fasteners and other trimmings. 'You can't be getting about dressed like a little lady. You'd be embarrassing the person who gave you the clothes, as well as me for allowing it.' The fabrics were excellent quality, very different from those that we and others of our social class typically wore. Unfortunately, Signorina Ester could not pass on her shoes as she had delicate little feet, smaller than mine. We needed to get me new shoes every year because my feet were growing fast, and that was a not inconsiderable expense, even though we went to a humble laneway shoemaker. As for her hats and parasols, once she had finished with them Signorina Ester gave them to her cousins, who got them refashioned by a milliner. It would have been unthinkable for her to give them to me, because women of my class did not wear hats, not even those who were better-off, or very vain. And using a parasol would have been inconceivably audacious and arrogant—only ladies could do that.

~

Signorina Ester stopped growing shortly before she turned nineteen, as the engagement period was drawing to a close and the wedding day was approaching. She and the marquis had never stopped loving each other; there had not been the slightest cooling of their affections, which instead seemed to grow stronger and deeper every day. Just watching them made me feel like I was living inside a love story. Even Signor Artonesi seemed finally convinced he had found a son-in-law worthy of his daughter, one who could make her happy and protect her once he was no longer around.

The marriage was celebrated with great pomp, and the bride and groom were radiant—she looked like a fairytale princess and he looked like an actor in the theatre. The bride's aunts, try as they might, could find nothing to criticise. If anything, they were rather envious that their own daughters' marriages would never be so sumptuous.

The young bride now had the title of marquise, but because she was not yet twenty everybody began to call her 'la marchesina'. I found it hard to address her using her noble title because I was too accustomed to thinking of her as my adored signorina. The reader will forgive me, then, if in continuing to tell her tale I do not always manage to give its protagonist the title that is her due, and sometimes 'Ester' might even slip out, as though she were a friend. But this does not mean that I was not aware, and do not remain so to this day, of my own place and of the enormous distance that separated us socially.

My grandmother was a little worried because, having finished the Artonesi trousseau, just one week before the
wedding, we now needed to find more work and new
clients. We had set aside some money, and I dreamt of being
able to put down a deposit on a sewing machine. Nonna,
however, insisted on saving every penny for leaner times
ahead, and it was true that we had not yet found any new
clients.

But she did not need to worry about this for long, poor
Nonna. The new marchesina was not yet back from her
honeymoon when one afternoon my grandmother, who
was letting down the hem of one of my winter dresses,
dropped her head to her chest, let out a long sigh and died.
'A sudden stroke,' said the doctor, who had to give permission for her burial. 'Her heart was worn out.'

Most of what little money we had set aside went on her
funeral and the cemetery, because I did not want her to
have a pauper's grave like the rest of my family.

Now I was truly on my own. I had a trade under my
belt, but no work in sight. I did not need to worry about
lodgings. The owner of the building, who had come downstairs to pay her respects, though she did not come with us
to the cemetery, had said I could stay on provided I continued to take care of the cleaning with the same dedication
as my grandmother. But what about everything else? Once
our savings were all gone, how would I pay for food, soap,
candles, paraffin and coal? I could not ask for help from my

childhood friends, who now worked in laundries and seedy taverns: they were all very poor and, even slaving fifteen hours a day, could still barely feed their children. Wouldn't it be best, the other women of the neighbourhood suggested, to abandon my aspirations to independence and get a position as a housemaid for a good family? At sixteen and a half, they said, I was too young to live alone. I thought about the story of Ofelia, which I had only recently heard, and about how hard my grandmother had worked to teach me her trade. It would have felt like I was betraying her wishes.

I came up with the strictest of economies and managed to get through a few more months. I went out every day and did the rounds of our clients from times past, asking if they might have work for me. I was embarrassed to persist when they said no, that these days they used a different sartina. I was also too embarrassed to turn up at the Artonesi household, let alone to Signorina Ester and her husband's new home. What could they possibly need, given my grandmother and I had produced dozens of spares of every article of clothing we had made, enough to last them for years? To make matters worse, the American journalist, the one who gave Ester English lessons, and whose linen my grandmother had always taken care of, had returned to her homeland for a few months to visit her sister.

Every day I looked in the drawer at my little nest egg, watching it become more and more meagre. I had already

pawned the clothes Signorina Ester had given me, as well
as the few sheets my grandmother had collected over the
years, both for our own use and so that I could have some
kind of a trousseau, and also the little gold chain from her
christening, and the coral earrings she had left to me when
she died. I had sold the few books I had to a junk dealer,
along with Erminia's children's chronicles, the issues of
Cordelia, and any of the opera librettos that were still in a
good-enough state. Reading would have helped to pass the
time, especially now that I had no sewing work to tire out
my eyes, but I needed every last penny. Luckily, I had been
able to hold on to the two little rooms in which I lived,
otherwise—what with my constantly wandering from one
house to the next in search of work, and my walks through
the fields on the edge of town to gather chard, thistles,
chicory and other edible greens—I'd have been at risk of
getting arrested for vagrancy.

Yet I refused to resign myself.

My stubbornness was rewarded. Just as I was about to give
up, after a week in which I had eaten nothing but plain
pasta and wild chicory, the Artonesi's housekeeper came to
see me. 'The marchesina wants to talk to you,' she said. 'Go
straight to their house. You know the address, don't you?'

I was astonished. What on earth could Signorina Ester
need?

Naïvely, it had not occurred to me that, in addition to
dozens of blouses, nightgowns and petticoats, the bride

would soon require a whole other kind of wardrobe. Not that I was ignorant of the ways of the world, but her love story had always seemed to me so poetic, so ideal, so disembodied, that my heart refused to dwell on the physical aspect of its 'joyous consummation', as the romance novels by Delly put it, and that this might lead to tangible consequences. I had never stopped to think about the fact that even the queen had brought into the world two little princesses and an heir, though every shop in town displayed a large picture of our sovereign holding her three little children all dressed up in their lace finery. I was more focused on the lace and the little bonnets than on how their wearers had come into the world.

I have to confess that, being a silly little romantic, I felt slightly miffed at the news that my signorina Ester was expecting a baby.

She, however, was ecstatic. She was glowing when she received me in the parlour of the large, beautiful villa where she lived with her husband.

'You must sew me the loveliest layette that's ever been seen,' she said. 'For the baptism we'll be using Rizzaldo family heirlooms—a christening gown and *porte-enfant*— it means a lot to Guelfo. It's yellowed a little with age, so you'll need to help me whiten it up. Guelfo wanted to order everything else from the Carmelite nuns, because of the embroidery, you know? It's a tradition in his family. But I told him I preferred to go to my trusted seamstress.'

I looked uncertain: I hadn't understood.

'That's you, silly!' She laughed and embraced me. She was as slim as ever to look at but on close contact I could feel her belly bulging a little, despite her bodice.

'Are you available?' she asked. 'There's a lot to do, so you'd need to start straight away. I'm going to require some things for myself, too—looser, more comfortable clothes, things to wear around the house. Can you start as soon as tomorrow?'

I didn't have the courage to tell her that I hadn't worked in four months, that I was desperate and her request would rescue me from the verge of starvation.

We agreed that I would go to her house to sew. 'That way maybe you can teach me. I'd like to make something too—I don't know—a bonnet, a pair of mittens. It would make Guelfo so happy. Up till now I've been a bit of a disappointment to him on that front.'

This suited me perfectly. Above all because I'd be given lunch, which meant a significant saving. But also because I'd have company, if not always Signorina Ester's, because she often went out in the carriage to pay visits and go shopping, then her maids'. Several circulated in the home— I'd not managed to count them all—each in a nice uniform with a starched apron. There was also a gardener, and a lad to look after the horses and carriage. If I'd had to work back in my own neighbourhood I'd be doing it alone and in complete silence—I could hardly burst into song on my own! When my grandmother and I used to sew at home it was different: we would talk, she would tell me about when she was young, she would teach me things, I would talk about what I'd been reading, she would grumble. Every so often one of her friends would come by to ask some advice about a sewing job and would stay to finish it off at our place. But those times were over.

Signorina Ester said I could move in to the villa if I wanted—there was plenty of room. But I didn't want to do that on principle. Not because I feared any sort of inappropriate behaviour by the marquis. How could he, when he was so besotted with his wife? But because I wanted to be considered a worker, an artisan, not a maid. Even though keeping my humble quarters meant getting up before dawn every day and spending two hours cleaning the stairs, I had somewhere I could call my home.

Signorina Ester had learnt organisation from her old science teacher. From France she had acquired, with the help of her Tunisian teacher, a magazine full of designs for all the clothes a baby needed from birth to age two, divided into three-month blocks, and she had sketched out a work plan. So we began working on twelve little tops in the smallest size: they were tiny. I say, *we* began, because she helped me with the simplest tasks, as I had done for my grandmother when I was five or six, and rarely left the sewing room. According to the magazine, these little tops were not to be made from new fabric—not even the finest cambric or 'egg skin' percale. The only suitable fabric was the linen of old bedsheets that had been washed over and over again for years on end until they became extremely soft. And all the stitching had to be on the outside rather than the inside, so that it didn't irritate the newborn's very sensitive skin. No embroidery, no buttons or buttonholes, only light silk ribbons sewn on with loose stitches that would not cause the slightest crinkling.

Naturally, Signorina Ester also had a sewing machine in her new home, but she didn't know how to use it, and neither did I for that matter. But in any case, the magazine said that all the garments for a baby's first year had to be sewn by hand.

Every so often the marquis came into the room, and he delighted in seeing his wife with needle in hand. 'You're becoming the perfect little wife,' he would say to her, 'and you'll make a perfect little mother.' If he was feeling playful he would sing, 'Dear little wife of mine, dear little orange blossom.' I felt annoyed when I heard these words. I had read the libretto of *Madama Butterfly*, which was all the rage that season, and I knew that the character they were attributed to—the American naval officer Pinkerton—was not an exemplary husband.

The marquis was even happier about his wife's pregnancy than she was. He had already decided that the baby would be called Ademaro, after his father and the ancestor to whom the family line could be traced back.

'What if it's a girl?' she would ask, to tease him. But his smile never faded. 'We'll call her Dianora, after my mother. And we'll get straight to work so that Ademaro arrives nine months later to join her. And then Aimone, and Filippo, and Ottiero...There'll be no shortage of sewing work in the years ahead,' he added, turning to me. 'My greatest wish is for a large family. Our greatest wish—isn't that so, Ester?'

His wife would blush with embarrassment, mostly because of that 'we'll get straight to work', but she didn't protest, as I hoped she would, about the names. Surely Signor Artonesi deserved to see his own name passed down through the generations too, I thought. But it seemed that Signorina Ester was no longer as attached to her father as she used to be. She only had eyes for her husband.

Their great fairytale love continued without a single dark cloud or disagreement, the slightest argument or hint of annoyance. I had little experience of life and none whatsoever of marriage. But with my grandmother I had gone into the private homes of many families, and I had never come across an atmosphere of such complete harmony and mutual adoration.

When his wife, at around the five-month mark, had some minor health complaints the marquis took fright; he was more distressed than the lady herself, immediately calling the city's most renowned doctor to her bedside. From the start of her pregnancy, Signorina Ester had been cared for by an elderly midwife who had brought into the world all the children of the city's most prominent families, but that was not enough for the marquis. Contrary to the advice of the midwife, who said that what the expectant mother needed was a little movement—short daily outings, on foot, not in the carriage—Dr Fratta decreed that the young lady must take to her bed and stay there until the delivery. Signorina Ester did what she was told, but unwillingly, because she became easily bored when left alone, and she had been strictly forbidden from tiring her mind through reading or writing. Moreover, her back ached, and she felt the need to move, she had pins and needles in her legs, but the marquis would not accept the slightest deviation from the doctor's orders. Fortunately, however, he had not forbidden sewing.

'The man's an animal! He might be good at treating pneumonia but he knows nothing about women's problems,' the midwife muttered under her breath, out of the marquis's earshot. The rest of us women paid her no heed. It was well known that doctors and midwives did not see eye to eye, and we thought she was probably envious.

We transferred all the equipment and the fabrics from the sewing room to the master bedroom on the first floor and continued our work there. 'Just as well you're here to keep me company,' Ester would say to me. Unlike in other noble homes, when the husband ate lunch out—which happened often—she never sent me to eat in the kitchen, but instead asked me to keep her company. She seemed to have read my mind—she didn't want me to call her 'marchesina', as the maids and the gardener did. 'To you, I'll always be Signorina Ester, like when we were little girls in my father's house.'

She confided in me a great deal. Sometimes we would

laugh and joke together. One time we discovered that, due to some strange connection of tubes, the flue of the newly installed cast-iron heater in her room communicated with the fireplace in the parlour on the ground floor and, if you opened the smoke duct, you could hear everything that was said in that room. At the time of day when we knew one of the maids would be cleaning out the ash and setting the coal in the fireplace, and the other would be fluffing up the cushions on the couches, we would listen in on their private conversations. One time we heard them flirting with the gardener, who had brought in fresh flowers for the vases. Another time we learnt that the younger of the two was being courted by the grocer's errand boy, and she was asking her colleague's advice on how she should respond. When left alone to dust the numerous knick-knacks and clean out the corners of picture frames, the older one—we would never have suspected this—liked to sing the latest tunes under her breath, and a couple of times she even tapped out a few notes on the piano. It was clear she was playing with just one finger, hesitantly, but they were the right notes.

To tell the truth, I felt a little embarrassed to be listening in on my peers and workmates. I wouldn't have liked to have someone eavesdropping on me. But there was no malice in my sweet employer—this was simply one of the few sorts of entertainment left to her—and the maids were reliable girls, well brought up and trustworthy, and we never heard them say anything inappropriate or rude, anything they could not have repeated in the presence of others. If they spoke of Signorina Ester and her husband it was always with respect. The marchesina seemed to inspire in them an affectionate protective instinct. She had earned it by treating them in an exemplary way, and it gave her great pleasure to see this confirmed by her eavesdropping. After a short while I forgot my scruples. But the pastime soon lost its appeal because, with the lady of the house relegated to the first floor and receiving visitors there, nobody went into the ground-floor parlour anymore.

The preparation of the baby's clothes was proceeding well. Signorina Ester kept getting bigger and bigger; to me she was looking somehow swollen—an unhealthy kind of swelling. The midwife continued to mutter disapprovingly and even the doctor began to look worried. Yet he still would not allow the marchesina to get out of bed.

The due date was approaching. Signor Artonesi came by every day to visit his daughter and would go home looking troubled. I had agreed to stay overnight at the villa, sleeping in the dressing room alongside the marchesina's bedroom. Her husband had moved into one of the guest rooms, though he sat by his wife's bedside all day long, holding her hand, brushing the hair from her forehead, kissing her with great caution, reading her the newspaper. He kept telling her how eager he was to finally see the face of the fruit of their love. And he thanked her for this enormous gift. 'Light of my life, you cannot imagine how much I admire your courage, your patience, your strength of spirit. What would I do without you, my love? You are the only reason my life has a purpose.'

His wife's face would light up with pleasure upon hearing these words, and she would forget about her physical discomfort and all her fears regarding the impending birth, about which she understandably felt a certain apprehension.

I must confess that I was afraid for them both. I had heard many stories of unsuccessful deliveries and they were all flooding back to me now. If anything bad happened to Signorina Ester I was certain the marquis would not survive it. He would shoot himself, or jump off a cliff. And little Ademaro would be left orphaned. Or perhaps he too would die due to complications during the birth. For the best, I imagined, poor little soul. All three of them in the same tomb, united in a single embrace.

The midwife came by every day and when I confided these thoughts to her, she was amused but also a little angered. 'Don't be a bird of ill omen,' she said. 'The marchesina is doing well; everything's in working order. She'll suffer a little, that's to be expected. But it's pain you forget as soon as you hold the baby in your arms.' She had explained to me the signs that meant I had to send for her at once. The doctor, on the other hand, had cut down on his visits because he needed to stay by the bedside of an important man who had fallen ill—someone more important than the marquis—who it was expected would soon reach the critical point when he would either die or pull through.

'The labour is always long with a first birth,' he had told the future father by way of reassurance. 'To begin with, the midwife will suffice. She has a lot of experience. She'll know when it's time to send the carriage for me.'

Finally, her labour began, shortly before dawn one Thursday in February. I sent the stable boy and within half an hour the midwife was by the expectant mother's side. 'You must be patient,' she told Ester and her husband, who had rushed in from the guest room in his dressing gown, his hair all sticking up. 'I suspect this young lad, or little lady, will not grace us with their presence before nightfall. And that's if things move quickly—it could take longer. Be strong, marchesina. Think of all the people strolling up and down the Corso of a Sunday morning, or a dance during Carnival, when the theatre is packed to the rafters, think of any big crowd. Just think—all of us came into the world in the same way.'

Signorina Ester was in a lot of pain, but her labour showed no sign of ending. The midwife suggested she sleep between contractions, so she could gather strength. The marquis had been driven out of the room because his anxiety and constant pacing by the bed were only causing more trouble. Lunchtime passed, then dinnertime. In each case, the midwife calmly went downstairs to the kitchen to eat, telling me to relax, that nothing was going to happen while she was away and that if I didn't want to come down myself she would bring some food up for me. I couldn't stomach anything. I couldn't believe how, in the breaks between contractions, Ester found the strength to talk, even to laugh. She asked me to open the wardrobe and show her the smallest tops and pants. 'We were wrong to make them so small,' she said. 'It feels like a giant is making its way through my belly, unable to find the way out.' At times she panted and moaned and bit on the sheets, and at times she would doze. Then she would wake up with a shriek, squeeze the midwife's hand, and apologise for worrying us. She would ask after her husband. 'Don't tell him how much I'm suffering,' she insisted. He would knock on the door from time to time, and if things were quiet the midwife would let him in; otherwise she would order him to leave. 'Out! This is not men's business.'

Signor Artonesi came by to get news. His daughter was resting and he lightly kissed her forehead, which was beaded with sweat, and returned home. Night fell. Like Ester, the midwife and I allowed ourselves to sleep a little during quiet moments, but sitting up in our chairs—we never once lay down. Through the windows we saw the sun rise. Every so often the midwife would lift the sheet and say, 'Be strong, marchesina, you just need to be patient a little longer.' At eight, her husband knocked and stuck his head in. 'Still nothing?' Signorina Ester was screaming at that moment, so she didn't hear him. He quickly retreated.

Midmorning, I heard the wheels of the carriage on the gravel outside. Just then, miraculously, things had gone quiet. The marchesina was sleeping peacefully. The midwife had gone into the dressing room to wash her face in the basin and tidy up her hair a little. I looked out the window and saw Dr Fratta stepping out of the carriage with his bag, and the marquis going to meet him. Had he called for the doctor without telling us, frightened by the screaming, or had the doctor come of his own accord? I saw them step through the French doors and into the parlour.

I don't know how the idea came to me, what guardian angel or wicked genie put it into my head. I ran over to the bed, dipped a cloth in the jug of water and wiped Signorina Ester's brow, and she sweetly awoke. I put a finger to my lips. 'Shh!' Let's listen in.' I tiptoed to the heater and opened the smoke duct. The two men's voices resounded clearly, loud enough that the midwife hurried out of the dressing room and looked around, astonished to find nobody else with us in the room. I gestured to her to keep quiet as well, pointing to the heater. The doctor was saying, 'From what I hear, the situation is critical and I'll need to intervene. There's no time to lose.'

The midwife snorted dismissively. Just a few minutes earlier she'd told me, 'I'll go and wash my face while the marchesina is sleeping. There's no rush. The baby is on its way, and in the right position, but it could take another hour or two. Stay calm, everything's going well.'

So what critical situation was the doctor talking about, when he'd only just arrived and hadn't even seen anything yet? 'From what I hear...' What had he heard, and from whom?

'Go on up, then!' the marquis urged him. 'My wife...'

'Exactly, *your wife.*' The doctor interrupted him, his tone very serious. 'Forgive me, but I'm obliged to ask you something.'

'Come! You can ask me on the stairs, or up in the bedroom. Let's go.'

'No, marquis. You and I need to talk in private, where no one can hear us. Especially not your wife.'

At this, Ester sat up in bed, her eyes wide.

I stared at her, willing her to be silent.

'I'm listening,' the marquis said impatiently.

'It could be—I'm saying it's possible, and we need to be prepared for this—that the situation has reached a point where it will no longer be possible to save them both.'

Ester looked at the midwife in alarm, seeking confirmation. With a mixture of lip movements and gestures, the midwife reassured her. 'It's not true. He's mad. Everything's fine. Stay calm.'

We heard a stifled moan from the marquis.

'It will be necessary to choose,' the doctor went on. 'And only you can do it. I will respect your decision. Do you want your wife to live or your child?'

'*I* have to decide this? Me?' His tone was incredulous.

'Who else?'

A long silence followed.

Ester relaxed back onto the pillow, smiling. She had no doubt about her husband's reply. *My love, light of my life. My life has no purpose without you*—I could read the words in her eyes.

The midwife made a face.

Downstairs, the doctor was insistent. 'Marquis, I will not go to your wife's bedside until you tell me what I must do. I repeat: mother or child?'

'How long will you give me to think about it?' was the anguished reply. Up in the bedroom, the smile on the marchesina's lips faded a little, then revived.

'Three minutes, no more,' the doctor said.

'Sorry, I need to know one more thing. Will my wife be able to have any more children?'

'I fear not. I will have to cut in various places to extract the baby. This kind of bloody birth damages all the reproductive organs.'

Silence. I can't say how those three minutes passed. I thought about the doctor's bag, his surgical instruments. I was terrified. I could already hear his murderous footsteps on the stairs. The midwife had moved to the head of the bed, behind the marchesina, and lifted her up under the arms, whispering: 'Push! There's no time to lose. If the doctor comes in here I have to do what he tells me.'

But Ester seemed relaxed and confident. *My love, light of my life, what would I do without you?*

Finally, we heard a cough, and the marquis's voice came through hesitantly. 'If it's a boy, I'll have an heir. And if it's a girl, as a widower I can always remarry and have more children.'

'So...?'

'Whereas, if I choose my wife, I give up the chance to

have heirs—today, if the baby that's lost turns out to be a boy, and forever, because she won't be able to give me any more children…'

'Don't beat around the bush, marquis. I need a clear answer: whose life should I save, your wife's or the baby's?'

A brief silence. The marchesina had gone whiter than the sheets. With each of her husband's words, a veil of incredulity had spread across her face.

'The baby's,' the marquis replied.

'All right. I will now go up. Do you want to come with me and give your wife a kiss? It might be the last time.'

'I haven't the courage. I'm going out. I'll go for a ride and come back this evening when it's all over.'

I heard the sound of his footsteps as he went out the French doors and headed for the stable, then the sound of the doctor picking up his surgical bag and making for the stairs.

Ester let out a cry but there was no longer anybody in the parlour to hear her.

In anger, I slammed the smoke duct closed and looked around for a heavy object I could hit the doctor on the head with as soon as he stepped into the room. The midwife, who was of a more practical bent, ran to the door and bolted it, before returning to the bed. I realised that Ester had not, as I had thought, cried out in fear of the doctor, or in disappointment at the marquis's betrayal, but because a sudden, violent wave of pain had whipped through her belly and lower back.

The midwife urged her on. 'Deep breaths! Push!'

The door handle turned. From the bedside table I grabbed an alabaster lamp in the shape of a lily, which had a square base in heavy black marble. The doctor was rattling the handle from the outside. 'What's going on? Let me in!' The light wood of the door was beginning to splinter.

I'll kill him rather than let him get his hands on my signorina Ester, I thought.

'Come on, marchesina, push!' said the midwife.

'Open up! Let me in!' the doctor kept shouting, banging on the door.

The bolt gave way. I raised the lamp. He entered with his bag of surgical instruments.

'Have you all gone mad? Out of the way, you snotty little girl! Let me through.'

I blocked his way, ready to hit him on the head with the marble base.

I believe I would have his soul on my conscience today if at that moment the room had not resounded with the midwife's triumphant shout—'Well done! Here it is!'—and straight afterwards a baby's cry.

I lowered the lamp. Disconcerted, the doctor stopped in his tracks.

'Is it a boy or a girl?' the young mother asked, exhausted.

'It's a girl.'

'No heirs for Marquis Rizzaldo. Not today, and not ever,' said Ester, and despite her exhaustion she was overcome by an attack of hysterical laughter. Then she fainted, laughing.

There was chaos in the bedroom. The midwife had cut the baby's umbilical cord, wrapped her up, still covered in muck, and handed her to me, while she hurriedly tried to revive the mother for the last bit of pushing. The doctor placed his bag on the floor and bent over it but, still holding the baby, I kicked it out of the way before he could open it. 'Don't you dare!' I shouted. At that moment the door opened and a maid led Signor Artonesi into the room. I put his granddaughter in his arms and ran to the bedside. After some shakes and slaps from the midwife, Signorina Ester was coming back to her senses. She recognised her father. 'Babbo!' she cried. 'If Guelfo comes back, don't let him in.'

'But…what?'

'The marchesina is delirious,' the doctor said.

'Now then, let's have a look at this placenta,' mumbled the midwife, oblivious to the consternation around her. 'Good, everything's fine. As for you'—she turned to the maid—'what are you waiting for, standing there with your mouth open? Go downstairs at once and bring me more hot water.'

'Don't let him in,' Ester repeated. 'My husband. I don't want to see him. I don't ever want to see him again.'

And she kept her word. While we women busied ourselves washing and dressing the baby, Signor Artonesi spoke in hushed tones to his daughter.

'When will she be able to get out of bed?' he asked the midwife, pointedly ignoring the doctor. 'I want to bring her home with me.'

'You're going to kill her!' the doctor exclaimed.

'Since you didn't get here in time to do so yourself,' the marchesina commented. I would never have thought her capable of sarcasm in her state, all sweaty and overcome by exhaustion.

'It's best she doesn't get out of bed for a few days,' the midwife advised.

'We won't be getting her out of bed,' her father said.

In half an hour he had her transport organised. He sent a lad to ask two burly men from the brewery to come in the firm's delivery wagon—the large one, drawn by two horses. In the meantime, he dismissed the doctor with a few sharp words and a cheque. Signorina Ester was carefully transferred onto an armchair that the two workmen lifted without difficulty, carried down the stairs and loaded onto the wagon. We climbed on board as well—the midwife holding the newborn baby, Signor Artonesi never letting go of his daughter's hand, and last of all me, clutching the satin-lined basket decorated with lace and ribbons that held all the baby's clothing. At her father's house Ester would still have her full wardrobe from when she was a girl, but the baby needed clothes and it would have been a terrible waste, I thought, to leave the results of our seven months of work behind at the villa.

A few hours after we arrived, the marchesina was sleeping

in the bed that had belonged to her mother, the midwife was changing the baby in the little room alongside and I was preparing to return to my own humble neighbourhood, when we heard a loud knocking on the main door that led onto the street. We peered out the window. As was to be expected, it was the marquis. It was only later that I learnt, from the stable boy, about his astonishment, his incredulity, when he returned to the villa to find the bedroom empty. He could barely understand what had happened, and he never found out the reason why. Ester always refused to meet with him, to speak to him, to explain the reason for her flight. Signor Artonesi did not wish to receive him either. Instead he sent his lawyer, a wily fox who found a way to refuse all the abandoned husband's demands and turn them against him. I don't know how he did it. In those days, a wife could not leave the conjugal home without suffering the consequences, much less keep the legitimate offspring of the marriage. But thanks to her father's support and money, Ester Artonesi managed it. Perhaps if instead of a girl she had borne a son, her husband would not have resigned himself to letting her take him, and would have fought longer and harder.

What most tormented the marquis, even more than his wounded pride, was not knowing why his young wife's immense love had suddenly transformed into deep hatred. The only possible explanation was that the pain of labour had made her go mad.

The only ones who knew the truth, other than the lady herself and probably her father, were the midwife and I, but neither of us breathed a word about the matter. The midwife was old and had already seen it all, but for me the disappointment was bitter. To discover, and in such a way, that true love was nothing but deception, that it existed only in novels, that men were all selfish traitors like Pinkerton, destroyed any illusion I might previously have entertained. You could trust nobody. My love, light of my life, without you I can live just fine—better, even.

Signorina Ester reinvented herself. She never let the marquis see the girl, who was named Enrica after Signor Artonesi and not Dianora after her paternal grandmother. She travelled far and wide with little Enrica, a long way from the gossip of our small city, and met all sorts of people I could never even imagine. When everybody in town was abuzz with the scandal of the Provera family's Parisian dresses, she was in Brussels, and when she got back she said people really were stupid to care so much about something as silly as that.

La Suprema Eleganza

IN THE EVENTS leading up to the scandal of the Parisian dresses I too played a not insignificant part. This was purely by chance; it was Queen Elena's fault or, if you prefer, it was because of her and the visit she made to our city as her husband's representative. I had never done any work for the Provera family until then. No sartina in the city ever had. Nor had either of the grand ateliers. As was widely known, the mother and two daughters had their clothes delivered every season from the sumptuous Atelier Printemps in Paris, much to the envy of all the other ladies in town. And a poor relative of the lawyer's, Signorina Gemma, took care of their linen, it seemed. The family had taken her in out of charity, and she was known to be skilled in embroidery and darning.

So I was quite astonished when the haberdasher told me that Signora Teresa Provera had dropped by to ask her to recommend a sartina who was highly skilled but economical. By this stage I had made something of a name for myself among the more modest families in town, in part because when she came back from one of her overseas trips Signorina Ester had brought me a beautiful gift as a sign of her gratitude: a portable hand-crank sewing machine from Germany. It had no treadle and no table; instead it came in a little case with a handle. Black and shiny, with golden decorations and embellishments, it was beautiful. It was not easy to use, because you had to turn the crank with your right hand, so only one free hand remained—and to make matters worse, it was the left—to guide the fabric under the needle. But after practising on old sheets I had learnt the basics. The important thing was not to go too fast.

Now the mothers of middle-class families and well-off shopkeepers would ask me from time to time to sew not only their bedlinen but also simple clothes for themselves and their children. They would bring me the fabric, choosing from the cheaper options. Partly because that was what they could afford, and partly because they didn't trust me with costly fabrics—what if I ruined them? But all told, I had become almost as skilled as my poor grandmother. I earned enough to live on and to be able to allow myself some small luxuries, such as membership of the lending library, where I borrowed the novels I enjoyed so much and the magazines that kept me informed about the world. This desire to know not just what was happening in our city but across the country and even overseas had been inspired by the early travels of 'my' signorina, the marchesina Ester, as she was still known throughout the city, despite the separation. I wanted to be able to follow her at least in my thoughts, to be able to listen to the stories she told on her return and not be left speechless like a fool.

Every so often I would borrow a fashion magazine. There were some that, in addition to patterns, published short sewing courses in instalments. I read those pages eagerly, in the hope of learning something I didn't already know, but they were aimed at bourgeois women who sewed to pass the time—the explanations were rudimentary and obvious, and taught me nothing new. I had even managed to redeem my grandmother's chain and coral earrings that I'd pawned. I had a tin for the few coins I was able to put aside each week, so that I would be able to afford a seat up in the gods at least once or twice during the opera season. To avoid the temptation to use that money for day-to-day needs like pasta or needles or a piece of coal, I kept the tin in my bedroom, hidden behind a small plaster statue of the Virgin that had belonged to my grandmother, in a recess in the wall that she used as a little altar of sorts. It was so high up that I needed to stand on a chair to reach it. In the top of my chest of drawers I kept savings to be used for daily shopping and emergencies, a modest sum that grew or shrank in accordance with how much work I had, but which thus far had given me peace of mind during the brief periods when no lady or family required my services.

I didn't have a sweetheart, even though my well-established business and financial situation, albeit modest, made me an excellent catch for a bachelor of any age in my social class. And I had received numerous proposals, both directly and through the matchmaker who circulated in all the city's neighbourhoods and the countryside and nearby villages as well.

However, I was naïve enough to continue to think of marriage not as an arrangement but as the realisation of a dream of love, and on this front I had been burnt by Signorina Ester's recent experience. If a neighbourhood boy I had known since childhood stopped me on the street and complimented me, made eyes at me or proposed a Sunday-afternoon stroll along the avenues of the city that were appropriate for people like us, I would be on my guard and respond brusquely, putting him in his place. And if it seemed to me on the way to work that some middle-class youth, student or minor official was following me, or even just looking at me a little more attentively than usual, I would change my route. I knew to expect nothing good from them, nothing but deceit and shame. I had read about it in novels and seen examples with my own eyes. Solitude held no fear for me. All my dreams, desires and plans for the future related to work, the progress I was making with sewing and design, and the expansion of my clientele.

Nevertheless, to be called upon by the Provera family, of all people, was the last thing I expected! Their impoverished relative must have fallen ill, I thought, or could no longer see too well, and they needed me to do the trim on some pillowcases, or to darn some old shirts. Unlike his wife and daughters, the lawyer, as I said, and in keeping with his renowned avarice, cared very little indeed about his own elegance and went around in shirts with frayed cuffs that moved the entire courtroom to laughter.

I accepted because I had no work at the time and above all because I was bursting with curiosity. No outsider, or at least none in my acquaintance, had set foot in that house. The Proveras had no domestic help, apart from a young maid who came from the country, Tommasina. She couldn't even speak Italian, and on the rare occasions when we'd run into her out and about, barefoot in the warmer months, and always carrying various bags and parcels, it was impossible to exchange even a few words with her. We wondered whether she took care of all the housework single-handedly— cleaning, cooking, washing, grocery shopping. Or perhaps she had some help from that poor relative they'd charitably taken in. That would explain the uncharacteristic generosity the lawyer had shown in welcoming the woman into the family: meals, lodgings but no salary, and in exchange a capable seamstress and a trusted maid. Signorina Gemma also left the house rarely and, above all, never gossiped.

In the laneways of our neighbourhood, however, there was no shortage of gossip among those who worked as seamstresses, milliners, washerwomen and shopkeepers. The same was probably true of the upper-class and aristocratic families, many of which were related to the Proveras, but we had no way of knowing this.

In accordance with the haberdasher's instructions, I arrived at eight in the morning. Their house was in the centre of town, on Piazza Santa Caterina, opposite the church. It was an elegant building, two storeys high, which overlooked a large cobblestone courtyard protected by a high wall. The only access from the piazza was through a wide driveway that day and night was kept hidden behind a large locked gate, so passers-by could never see in.

At the moment of my arrival it happened to be open because a farmer's cart drawn by a donkey had just passed through, so I followed it inside and did not need to ring the bell. The sharecropper had tied the animal to one of the iron rings built into the wall and was unloading a large basket of artichokes when a modestly dressed middle-aged woman hurried out of the house. Frowning, and without saying a word, she closed the heavy wooden gate. 'Why the rush, Signorina Gemma? I could've closed that,' said the farmer.

'You needed to do it sooner,' she replied. 'Can't you see that any impertinent little servant girl can come in off the street and start nosing about?' Then, pointing to a small doorway she had left open, she said to me, 'Get out of here at once, girl!'

'I'm the seamstress,' I said, more amused than offended. I was looking around with great curiosity. 'Signora Provera told me to come.'

'The seamstress! So how come you didn't bring your sewing machine?'

'I didn't think it necessary,' I replied. Although it was portable, it wasn't light, and I'd thought that for a few trims and some mending it would be useless.

'Well, from tomorrow you'll need to bring it with you,' said the woman who, from her name, I'd been able to identify as the poor relative of the family. 'Now, since you're empty-handed you can help us carry these baskets up into the house.'

In addition to the baskets, the cart contained sacks and saddlebags full of fruit, carrots, potatoes, beans, chickpeas, chicory, chard and other vegetables the sharecropper had brought from a nearby field that the lawyer owned. He came with the cart twice a week, I later learnt, and provided the family with everything they needed. That was why you never saw the Proveras' maid walking through the streets with bags of groceries. Even the meat they ate—chickens, lambs, goats—was brought in from the country. That morning the provisions seemed more than abundant for a family of six. 'We'll be eating well,' I thought to myself. But Signorina Gemma soon shot down that hope. Seeing that I was carrying no package, she said sourly, 'Didn't you bring your lunch?'

I was speechless. Never before, not once, had I gone to sew in the home of an upper-class family and not been given my midday meal. Nor had this ever happened to any other sartina. We would often exchange accounts of the kind of cooking, the recipes, the abundance, variety or monotony of the meals in each family. Clearly, this custom was not followed in the Provera household. Perhaps they were not even aware of it, since they weren't in the habit of bringing workers into the house.

Feeling annoyed, and carrying a basket of pears I would not get to taste, I made my way up the stairs to the residence. Gemma led me towards the kitchen. Through an open door I could see into the dining room, where the family was finishing breakfast—the three women in house clothes and the lawyer ready to go out. In the kitchen, a very young maid stood nibbling a piece of stale bread. Signorina Gemma told her off. 'Haven't you finished yet?' she said in dialect. 'Go on, take some feed down to the chickens, and then you need to clean the sewing room before we get to work.'

The large French doors of the kitchen opened onto an external staircase that ran down the rear façade of the building and led to a bare garden, as large as the courtyard at the front but without paving. Perched on the lower branches of a few orange and pomegranate trees, or pecking around in search of worms, were many chickens—forty or fifty, a number you would normally only see in the country or on the outskirts of town. At the end of the garden was the henhouse—a construction that ran the whole length of the outer wall. In those days, it was not yet forbidden to keep courtyard animals like hens and rabbits in city dwellings, but people only had enough for their own personal needs, six or seven animals, ten at the most, so that the smell and the noise didn't disturb the neighbours' peace and quiet. The Proveras' chicken coop was so big that I wondered who on earth ate all the eggs, enough to feed an entire boarding school.

But that was not the last of the family's peculiarities. As soon as the lawyer left, the lady of the house summoned me into the dining room, where her two daughters were still cleaning away the dishes from breakfast which, judging by the number of plates, mustn't have been too abundant.

We had already agreed on a daily rate in our communication through the haberdasher, so all that remained was for me to learn the nature of the work I was to do. However, after sending the two girls out and checking that the windows and doors were firmly closed, Signora Provera took my hands in hers and looked into my eyes very earnestly. 'Before you begin working for us, you must take an oath.'

'What do I need to swear?' I asked, disconcerted.

'That whatever you might see in this house, whatever conversations you might hear, or information you might learn—you won't go talking about it with anybody else.'

'I'm not a gossip,' I replied indignantly. 'There's no need for any oath.' And besides, what terrible things could I possibly hear about? What mysteries could a respectable and respected family be hiding? This was not a novel, after all. It was no secret that the lawyer was very mean—everybody knew that. But it was also widely known that he was very rich, so I wondered if they were worried about being burgled, and thought I might talk about valuables, jewellery and money I had seen and where they were kept, or about the best ways of getting into the house if you knew how to scale a wall or pick a lock.

'You can be sure I won't say anything to anybody,' I repeated.

But the signora was determined. 'Let's go over to the church,' she said, throwing a cape over her shoulders. 'You'll make your oath before the altar of the Lord.'

Then she summoned the poor relation and, one on either side, they escorted me down the stairs. The sharecropper must have gone back to the fields; the front courtyard was deserted and the gate barred. Signorina Gemma opened it using a large iron key that she kept tied around her waist, then locked it again behind us. We crossed the piazza and entered the church of Santa Caterina just a few metres across the square. There was nobody inside, but the holy light of the Eucharist burned on the altar.

'Here, before the consecrated host, you have to swear. The two of us will be your witnesses. Remember that if you break the oath, hell awaits you.'

It all seemed so ridiculous, like something out of the stories my grandmother used to tell about secret societies during the wars of independence. In fact, the Proveras—the lawyer in his youth, and his father before him—were renowned for being fervent followers of the republican Mazzini. But what did I have to lose? The prospect of going without lunch was a much greater preoccupation.

—

I took the oath. The signora told me what to say, and made me repeat her words exactly. When we returned to the house she handed me a piece of paper on which she'd written out the oath, and got me to sign it. She was astonished that I knew how to write. People of my station generally just signed with a cross, and I always wondered how the authorities could recognise that a given cross had been made by a particular person. She called her two daughters in to sign as witnesses, and that was how I learnt that the elder one was called Alda and the younger one was Ida. There didn't seem to be much of an age difference between the two, both still looked quite young, though they must have been over twenty. Pretty, but nothing special. Nothing like the enchantment my signorina Ester radiated. For one thing, their modest house dresses were somewhat worn out, like their mother's and their aunt's, and the style dated to several years earlier. Perhaps, I thought, when they went out—on the streets, to the public gardens, to the theatre, to parties and dances, visiting acquaintances—their Parisian style and the prospect of an impressive dowry made them seem like two great beauties.

Signora Teresa locked the document away in a drawer and heaved a sigh of relief. 'You will have gathered,' she said, 'that we called you here because of exceptional circumstances. It's an emergency. We are generally able to do everything ourselves, but on this occasion we haven't the time. The queen will be paying a visit to our city in less than a month.'

I had no idea what Queen Elena had to do with anything; it all just kept getting more peculiar. 'I've heard that you know how to cut clothes, as well as sew,' she continued, 'and that you own a portable German sewing machine and know how to use it. It's a lot faster, isn't it?'

'It depends. Certainly, for long, straight seams it is,' I replied, astonished at what she was asking. By now all the city's well-off families owned and used a sewing machine, even if only for hemming sheets and kitchen rags—a treadle machine, a model far more modern than mine and easier to use. Mine was one of the older ones; Marchesina Ester had chosen it for its size, knowing there was no room for a treadle machine in a home like mine. I thought Signorina Gemma had only asked me to bring it out of curiosity, to see how the hand crank worked.

In any case, when we moved into the sewing room I had confirmation that there was no sewing machine, treadle-operated or otherwise. Instead, on the large ironing table there were three bolts of exquisite heavy silk, each with bright floral designs, but in different colours and patterns, the likes of which I had never seen before. They were double-width, still rolled around thick cardboard. I calculated that each must measure about ten metres. More than enough for an elegant dress in the latest style, with a small train, drapery on either side and space behind for a bustle, as well as a cape and perhaps a little matching purse. Not that I had ever made anything of this kind, but I could work out how much fabric would be required based on the style. Alongside the three bolts of fabric were a measuring tape, a large pair of scissors, chalk and some patterns cut from heavy paper, which must have been based on fashion plates.

A fashion magazine with a French title was lying on the embroidery table. It wasn't hard to work out that I'd been summoned to turn those beautiful fabrics into one or more elegant dresses in the Parisian style.

'I don't have the skills,' I declared incredulously. 'The clothes I know how to make are a lot simpler. And I've never worked with silk before.' I knew it was very difficult to sew, slipping and sliding all over the place, and a nightmare if you had to work with it on the bias. 'You'll need to go to an atelier, to Belledame or La Suprema Eleganza.' I knew those dressmakers didn't only work with their own fabrics but also with those provided by their clients. I didn't dare ask, 'Why don't you just go back to Atelier Printemps in Paris?' It seemed like a real plunge to go from that house of marvels to me, a poor little sartina from L—.

'I don't have the skills,' I insisted. 'You'll have to find somebody else.'

'Don't worry,' Signorina Gemma said calmly. 'We have the skills. You just have to help us with the seams and the finishing touches. Today, luckily, it's just cutting and tacking, but tomorrow you'll need to bring your machine.'

And with a decisive motion she unfurled the nearest bolt of fabric, in shades of blue and green, and stretched it out on the table. It was a marvellous silk depicting cherry blossoms. The youngest of the ladies, Signorina Ida, approached it with a paper cut-out of the pattern and a pincushion, while her mother and sister began heating the irons. I could not believe my eyes.

I will recount to you here what I was able to discover and reconstruct day by day over the month that followed: the secret I swore never to reveal. A long time has passed now, and after the scandal broke the entire city found out about it, so I don't feel I'm breaking any promises.

In short, the Provera family had been lying for years. They had never, not once, ordered clothes from Paris. Instead, the women of the house had made them in secret, by hand, without even a sewing machine. And they had always done such a good job that nobody had noticed. After all, what was it my grandmother used to say when we would stop in front of shop windows to admire haute-couture dresses that had arrived from the capital? 'Who do you think made these, my dear, some goddesses in heaven? They were sewn by women like us, only more skilled and more expert.' Then she would sigh and add, 'And certainly better paid.'

The Provera household had once, many years earlier, had authentic Parisian dresses that could serve as inspiration. I learnt this later on from Signora Teresa who, secure in the knowledge I had taken an oath, did not hold back from confiding in me in moments of dejection. Dresses that were part of her trousseau when she married, a trousseau worthy of a princess that her extremely generous father had ordered for her from the most luxurious shops in all of Europe. Gowns for ceremonial occasions, balls, theatre, for summer and winter, jackets for stepping out in, and skirts, coats and cloaks, fine blouses for under- and outerwear. Every dress came with a corset, the right kind of wadding, and matching hat, parasol, gloves and shoes. It seemed as though there weren't enough days in the year, or hours in the day, to wear them all. They had arrived in large, sturdy cardboard boxes lined with embossed pale-blue paper bearing the words Atelier Printemps in gold, and others with the names of boutiques in Brussels and London. There were hardly enough wardrobes or rooms in the house to store them all. The newly married lawyer Bonifacio, a young man at the time, was proud to step out with a wife who was more elegantly dressed than Queen Margherita and her ladies-in-waiting. But when they returned home and, without the help of a maid, she would have to unhook and unlace everything herself, he would say to her sarcastically, 'Enjoy them while they're in fashion. Because I'm certainly not going to buy you anything new. Not in Paris, or here in town.'

Thanks to her husband's avarice, poor Signora Teresa, who in her parents' home had been accustomed to living in abundance and luxury, had to adapt quickly to a regime so strict that she spent half the day on the couch crying. There was no risk of embarrassment about being heard by the maids, because there were none, apart from a barefoot little servant girl confined to the kitchen, the daughter of one of the lawyer's sharecroppers, whose entire salary consisted of lodging and meals, the latter quite meagre.

Lunch and dinner for the master and mistress were also frugal. The bride's cousins and nieces stopped accepting invitations after constantly being served a soup whose only ingredients were two leaves of chicory, half a clove of garlic and a great abundance of water, without so much as some pasta or a drop of oil, followed by a small mouthful of boiled meat with a potato, then a piece of fruit, usually old and wrinkled.

But most humiliating of all for the young bride was not having so much as a penny for her own use. 'What do you need money for? What would you do with it?' the lawyer would ask. All the food, along with wine and oil, was brought in from his landholdings in the country and thus cost nothing. At the local store, where from time to time they inevitably needed to purchase candles, soap, needles, kitchen utensils, salted cod and other minor essentials, he had opened an account which he would settle once a year in person, after dedicating disproportionate attention to examining the list of purchases. And if he felt that the number of needles or candles used was even just slightly higher than in the previous year, his wife would have to endure a stern lecture about judicious management of the household.

In her father's home there had always been a silver dish

full of coins near the front door, and she and her mother would take a few on their way out, to give as alms, or as a tip, or to pay for a carriage or a hot chocolate at the Crystal Palace, and they didn't need to answer to anyone for what they spent. In the Provera household, all such expenses were considered superfluous, a true waste and a drain on the family fortune. The bride's dowry had been incorporated into her husband's estate, and invested in shares and new pieces of land. When he found out that his daughter had been left without even a modest income for her own personal use, her father offered to provide her with one himself. But his son-in-law took offence and refused. 'I'm perfectly capable of providing for my wife,' he protested. 'She wants for nothing.'

Needless to say, her husband had not opened an account for her at a textile store, nor did he allow her to frequent one of the elegant ateliers. 'That mountain of lace and ribbon your father bought you will last as long as you live. And so will all the gloves, and shoes and those hundreds of sheets and other linen.'

When the second daughter was born and the young mother needed more help than the servant girl alone could provide, the lawyer decided to offer a home to Signorina Gemma, an orphaned and poor second cousin in whom he had previously shown no interest. She had been living in an institution run by the nuns, where in exchange for board and lodging she carried out all manner of onerous household tasks. Signorina Gemma was happy to finally be part of a family, very fond of the two little girls, who called her aunty, and already accustomed to a spartan lifestyle, so she adapted without protest to the domestic restrictions imposed by her cousin. But unlike Signora Teresa, with whom she was as close as if they were sisters, she had rolled up her sleeves and looked around her for as many ways as possible to alleviate those restrictions. She had gradually increased the number of hens in the orange grove, always choosing good layers, and had found a way to sell the eggs, which every two days were taken away in secret and sold at the market. For the family's own use, enough eggs arrived on the farmer's cart along with the fruit and vegetables. She had also found a way to sell under the counter the odd bottle of wine or oil that they had come by in the same way. Having established his basic principles, the lawyer did not notice, or pretended not to notice, these little dealings, which nevertheless grew month after month, year after year, into a little nest egg that the two women could spend unchecked.

As for clothing, Signora Teresa's trousseau was indeed an almost inexhaustible reserve. The two little girls had baby clothes in white broderie anglaise like all the other children of noble families in the city. Except that theirs were made from their mother's dressing gowns and bodices, unpicked and resewn by Signorina Gemma with such expertise that nobody would ever have noticed. Once they had gone out of fashion, the signora's dresses were remade by the same able pair of hands, and others were reduced in size so the girls could wear them, and because the fabric was always high quality, and the trimmings, buttons and ribbons were removed and transferred to other garments, nobody ever recognised them. Signorina Gemma was also a skilled hat-maker—she had good taste and flair. Any hat that had gone out of fashion was taken apart, reshaped with a hot iron, decorated with new ribbons and silk flowers and wax fruit and embalmed bird's wings and feathers. She did the same with parasols, trimming their edges with new lace and ribbons and fake flowers that she'd salvaged from dresses. She was also extremely good at fashioning fake flowers from silk offcuts, curving the petals with little irons heated on the embers, and shining the leaves with melted wax. Avvocato Provera was aware of all this and gloated about the savings they were making, and that his wife and daughters continued to cut such a fine figure in front of their fellow citizens. So long as it didn't cost him any money.

With time, Signora Teresa, too, learnt to sew, though never as skilfully as her husband's cousin, who also taught the two young signorine as they grew older.

This work could have been done better, easier and faster, if there had been a sewing machine in the house. But that was the kind of object that was too cumbersome to hide in a wardrobe and too costly to justify to the lawyer. The nest egg was insufficient to permit them to purchase one outright; paying in instalments would have set tongues wagging.

The signorine grew older, and when the elder one turned twelve a minor family tragedy erupted.

The city authorities had decided to install a marble bust of Count Cavour in the atrium of the town hall. For the inauguration, they had planned a ceremony with a band, and girls dressed in white who would dance in and scatter flowers around the base of the monument. The girls had been chosen from among the daughters of the most prominent families in the city, and one of them was Alda Provera.

Despite his republican devotion the lawyer was proud she had been chosen, but Alda did not wish to take part. She threw a tantrum, crying and kicking up such a fuss that you could hear her all the way over in the church of Santa Caterina, her mother told me.

'I'm not going unless I get a new dress.'

'We'll make you one, don't worry.'

'No, I mean a real new dress. You can see that the white fabric of the ones we have in the wardrobe is all worn. Everyone will know it's an old dress that's been remade.'

After thirteen years of unpicking and resewing, cutting and remodelling, every garment in Signora Teresa's trousseau had been used over and over again. The fabrics were high quality, and the heavier ones were still in good shape, but the lighter ones had become threadbare; some had holes and were impossible to mend. And they were not to make her wear the better-preserved fabrics anymore either, Alda went on to say. By now they had done the rounds of too many parties and afternoon teas, and been seen at the theatre, in the public gardens and at the children's carnival.

'We can use the money we get from selling the eggs to buy three metres of cambric, muslin or broderie anglaise,' Signorina Gemma ventured.

'Where from?' asked Signora Teresa disconsolately. Only two shops in town sold fabric and both were owned by clients of the lawyer. Without a doubt he'd end up hearing about it, and there'd be a scene about waste and pointless expenses, and then he'd investigate the nest egg the women had put aside and, upon discovering that it was not so modest after all, he might even make them hand it over.

Alda was crying and Ida joined in out of sympathy. She was only ten but was vainer than her sister and suffered even more over never being able to step out with her friends in a brand-new dress. Their mother cried too thinking of their future, and about how her daughters would soon need to make their entry into society, attending balls and parties at which girls from all the best families would be on show trying to win the heart, if not of a prince, then at least of a wealthy husband of their own social class. How were Alda and Ida going to make the right impression if they weren't appropriately attired?

Signorina Gemma did not cry, but instead set her brain to work thinking up a solution.

Thanks to their secret trade in eggs, wine and oil, Signorina Gemma had come into contact with a few people who were involved in somewhat irregular dealings, always on the threshold of legality and quite familiar to the forces of law and order, but unknown to more well-to-do members of society. Not just roving salesmen but also people who salvaged and resold to the poorest families and humblest craftsmen all sorts of scraps, from butcher's bones to the horsehair out of rotting mattresses, bits of old furniture, rags and scrap metal. After asking around, Signorina Gemma had learnt that this underbelly of poor wretches had its own prince, who was actually not so poor himself because over the years he had found ways to expand his business, even going so far as to purchase an enormous underground warehouse in the small town of B——, thirty kilometres from our own. It was a dark cavern full of wooden shelves where he had amassed objects of every kind deriving from the failure of all manner of shops, from factories and, above all, from the demolition of houses, public buildings, hotels, manufacturing plants, first- and second-class brothels, and even decommissioned railway carriages. Not just objects, but also furnishings and structural parts of buildings, upholstery, railings, handles, gas lamps, windows, balustrades from balconies and terraces, steps, windowsills, and doorways in marble and in slate. He was constantly doing the rounds of the nearby regions on the lookout for new goods to acquire, covering an area of seventy or eighty kilometres in a large caravan pulled by four horses. His rounds would take him as far as the coast, to the port of P——, where he would buy up in bulk the load of merchant ships that had run into difficulties. Depending on the requests he had received from his customers, he would get sailors to bring him certain products from over-seas. All free of any checks by the authorities, without being registered, paying duty or going through the chamber of commerce. The man's name was Tito Lumia.

Signorina Gemma found out when he would be passing through our city and that brave and enterprising woman set out to speak to him in her shabbiest dress, with a shawl over her head. She asked whether his collection included any textiles and, when he said yes, explained that she needed fabrics of the highest quality, ideally from overseas, to be transported and delivered to a city address that was not her own, with the utmost discretion, so that she could make her selection and have the option of sending them back. And no one, but no one, was to hear about it. He would be further compensated for his silence. Perhaps Tito Lumia found the request unusual, but he accepted; it was no concern of his if there was something to hide—almost all his business dealings were a little suspect.

In this way, twice a year the Provera family had at their disposal silk, brocade, damask, velvet, organza and embroidered muslin, the likes of which our city had never seen. Some of the textiles were intended not for clothing but for upholstery. However, Signorina Gemma knew a particular technique for softening them that involved bicarbonate of soda and other household powders, and the aid of a hot iron. Sometimes she used the juice of plants to dye them, as was the custom in the villages. Nobody in the city could ever have imagined the presence of a laboratory of this kind in Avvocato Provera's central and well-to-do household.

Alda received her beautiful white muslin dress in time to dance and scatter rose petals at the base of the monument to Cavour.

Signorina Gemma had an ingenious idea to prevent anybody from asking which of the city's two dressmakers they had gone to for their gowns. Fortunately, the house was large, full of wardrobes and closets, and Signora Teresa had been able to hold onto the big boxes in which her trousseau had been delivered. She had looked after them carefully, protecting them from dust and mould, especially the sky-blue ones from Atelier Printemps in Paris, which she loved so much and which still looked new.

They chose one that was the right size for Alda's new dress, which they laid out among several layers of tissue paper. The servant girl working for them at the time was taken across to the church and sworn to secrecy the same way I was, and certainly took her obligation a lot more seriously than I did—after all, in addition to the fear of eternal damnation, she was afraid of losing her job. She was trained to utter a sentence in Italian in a clear and comprehensible way. Her task was to leave the house when it was still dark, with the blue box wrapped in a black shawl, and make her way down the darkest and narrowest alleyways, where well-off people never ventured, to the train station.

Here she was to await the arrival of the first night train from P—, the port city, which connected with the ship from Marseilles. She had to mingle with the porters unloading goods, whip the box out from under the shawl (which then went over her shoulders) and carry it home, balanced on her head for all to see as she made her way along the Corso just as the city was coming to life for the new day. She was required to go past the cafés, where the first customers of the morning were having breakfast, past the shops and tobacconists as the proprietors were rolling up the shutters, past the barber's, the pharmacy, the main entrance of the school—the blue box still clearly in sight—and to shout in a piercing voice to anyone who showed the slightest curiosity, as well as to those who showed none, 'Our signorina's dress has arrived from Paris!' She had to shout this the whole way home, where she would be received with a cup of hot milk and a small tip.

Naturally, a few of the people who saw her making her way along the Corso talked about it, and word spread throughout the city that Signora Teresa had followed her father's example by ordering her daughter's dress all the way from Paris, no less.

After this positive outcome, the whole business was repeated, in summer and in winter. Signora Teresa subscribed to a French fashion magazine that kept her up to date on the latest styles. They discovered that they could also ask Tito Lumia to procure paper patterns they could use to cut fabric to measure. Signorina Gemma directed all the work. She was the one in charge of cutting and tacking; the other three had become so good at sewing, finishing and applying decorations that their clothes looked like they'd been made in a real atelier with specialised workers. Naturally, everything had to be planned well in advance. The fabrics available from Lumia were not always appropriate and sometimes it was necessary to wait for new ones. The paper patterns were not always in step with changing fashions or easy to execute. But Signorina Gemma was an excellent organiser and the home workshop had never missed an appointment with a new season.

Every six months the servant girl would make her way back up the Corso yelling, 'Dresses have arrived from Paris for our signora and signorine!'

Now that three boxes were needed, balancing them all was going to be difficult, and too tiring for the poor girl, even with a ring of padding on top of her head, especially in winter, when the fabrics were heavy. But Signorina Gemma pointed out that there didn't actually need to be any dresses inside the boxes. Nobody was going to open them to check the contents during the short walk from the train station to the house. They could easily be empty but for scrunched-up tissue paper.

Frightened by the double threat of hell and unemployment, the servant girl never revealed the secret, not even after she had grown up and gone to work for another family. A new girl arrived from a village in the interior and she too had to take the oath. After that, Tommasina's turn came around. Tommasina was silent as the grave, not least because, apart from the sentence she had to say as she walked along the Corso, she didn't speak or understand a single word of Italian, and instead communicated in the thickest dialect that only Signorina Gemma could understand.

Up until then everything had gone smoothly. No one in the city had any suspicions about the ruse, and word of these clothes that arrived from Paris every season had spread even to nearby cities. Their fame stirred admiration and envy towards 'those holier-than-thou Provera hypocrites'.

It was the two daughters who got called that, because it was widely known that, once their early burst of adolescent rebellion was behind them, they had grown into timid, obedient girls—they were not capricious, they didn't read novels, when they attended social events they always dutifully kept their eyes to the ground, they didn't flirt with young men, and had never demonstrated the slightest inclination or preference. Their life was church and home, and the church was so close by that they didn't even need to go out for a short stroll to reach it. The only 'distraction' they allowed themselves was a two-week spiritual retreat with the Benedictine nuns at a convent in the mountains a few kilometres from the city. And they did not travel alone to get there: they were accompanied by their mother or their aunt. Such impeccable behaviour, along with their father's wealth and the prospect of a generous dowry, meant they had acquired many suitors among the city's well-to-do young men, and Avvocato Provera had received many discreet requests on their behalf. It was only because their father was aiming very high that neither sister was yet engaged, despite their age.

Among the city's men, by far the best catch of all was young Medardo Belasco, favourite nephew of the bishop. He had been brought up in his uncle's home and was very religious; in fact, the only reason he hadn't entered the seminary and taken holy orders was that he was the only male heir, and his parents, along with his uncle, expected him to carry on the family line. Next was don Cosmo, first-born son of Barone Vetti, who had attended the military academy in M—, and returned with the rank of captain and a greater knowledge of the world than that of his peers. Avvocato Provera intended him for Ida, while the young Belasco seemed to him the perfect husband for Alda. He had made some enquiries, without committing to anything, and had not come up against any objections or resistance. But he knew it was best not to rush things. The four young people needed to meet by chance—the girls had to make a good impression and find the boys their father had chosen for them neither disagreeable nor repugnant. Some years earlier, the engineer Biffi's daughter had run away from home rather than marry Count Aghiati, the man who had been chosen for her. This caused a tremendous scandal, not least because no one ever found out where she ended up, with whom, or how she was earning a living.

Alda and Ida had seen the two young men several times, but only ever at a distance—from the balcony, in church, at the theatre, at the public gardens—and had been seen by them. They had never exchanged so much as a word, though. They hadn't talked about them with other girls, nor had they heard any rumours or gossip about them. The sisters led such a sheltered life, each enough for the other, that they felt no need for friendships and did not spend time with their peers. When pressed by their parents, they said that they were in agreement with their father's choice and so, thus reassured, he went ahead with negotiations.

This was the point things had reached when high society— wealthy, aristocratic and bourgeois ladies alike—was abuzz with the announcement of Queen Elena's visit to our city. There would be a grand reception and ball in the vast frescoed hall of the prefecture. All the most important families had been invited and the unwritten protocol held that the ladies—dames and damsels, as they were described in the invitation—must all show off a new dress, never before seen. The city's two dressmakers were inundated but, even after employing extra workers, they could not meet the demand in the time available.

Some ladies took the train to G— which, being a larger city, had many beautiful shops and elegant ateliers. If there was not the time to produce new gowns, dressmakers there could at least adjust ones that had arrived from Turin or Florence.

The Provera household's four clandestine seamstresses flew into a panic. How was it possible, in a little over a month, to procure the necessary fabrics and produce three dresses worthy of being shown off to the queen and her ladies-in-waiting?

True to form, Signorina Gemma did not lose heart. Tito Lumia, after being advised of the urgency of the situation, miraculously managed to procure, in just a week, three pieces of silk in the most beautiful and original patterns. It was very heavy, perhaps originally intended for curtains rather than clothing, but it was good quality and Signorina Gemma's softening process would render it very easy to manage.

The problem of time remained. 'We're never going to be able to do this, even if we work day and night,' Signora Teresa lamented.

'This time we'll have to employ an assistant. And we'll use a sewing machine,' her husband's cousin declared.

This was why I had been summoned. Since there was no hope that my coming and going would pass unnoticed, Signora Teresa spread the rumour that her husband the lawyer, on a whim, had decided to get two dozen night-shirts sewn by machine. Initially, she had spoken simply of shirts, but Gemma pointed out to her that then his colleagues at the law courts would check whether her husband really was wearing new ones, whereas if they were night-shirts only his wife and family would ever be expected to see them.

~

That day, as Signorina Gemma had said, was dedicated to cutting and assembling the first dress, for the lady of the house. The different pieces of fabric were pinned then tacked together. I had never seen anybody work with such speed, confidence and skill as Signorina Gemma. Not a skerrick of fabric was wasted during cutting, and if pleats or darts were required the extra centimetres were calculated right down to the millimetre. Each piece of cut fabric was handled with extreme care so that the ends wouldn't fray (this is something that happens more with silk than with other materials: percale, for example, is much denser, even I knew that). But first, every single piece—sleeve, collar, various parts of the bodice and the skirt, sashes and drapes—had to be measured and fitted on Signora Teresa, before being basted, tried on again and, finally, sewn. For this operation, they were awaiting my hand-crank sewing machine, and I was asked to fit the finest needle possible. Signorina Gemma would have liked to use the machine for the pleats and darts as well, but I explained that the crank didn't allow you to sew close parallel lines. It would have been possible with a treadle-operated machine, which would leave both hands free to guide the fabric, though even that would be difficult with silk. They had to resign themselves to hand-sewing those details the same way they had always done, with the help of a measuring tape and an iron.

Lunchtime arrived, but work was not interrupted as was the custom in other houses. Tommasina brought in a teapot and slices of toast. One at a time, the four women stepped away from the table for a moment to gulp down a cup of tea, swallow a slice of dry toast, rinse their hands in the basin and return to work. I was not offered anything. 'You'll make up for it at dinnertime,' Signorina Gemma said. 'And tomorrow make sure you bring something you can eat quickly, because I won't be giving you a break of any longer than five minutes.'

When darkness fell, a beautiful pink opaline paraffin lamp was lowered over the table. The light from it was faint. They explained that they regulated the wick in accordance with the darkness of the fabric, and the material we were working with was light and brightly coloured. They were scrimping even on that little bit of paraffin, on the lawyer's orders.

They let me go when the Santa Caterina church bell sounded vespers. My eyes were hurting and so were my fingertips, only one of which was protected by a thimble. I feared we might still be going when the bell rang for night prayers. It was pitch dark as I headed home, with only a few gas lamps to light my way, and I was too tired to cook anything. I nibbled on a piece of bread and cheese, and heated up a cup of milk. I was sorely tempted to turn down the job, to stay home the next morning and send my neighbour's daughter Assuntina to tell them to look for someone else. But I knew I couldn't do it. Word would spread that I was unreliable, and nobody would ever call on me again. And also, despite the oddness of the situation, the excessive effort being asked of me and my offence at not being offered lunch, I knew I would learn a lot from the experience. I had never had a real sewing lesson: my grandmother had been my only teacher. And she knew none of the techniques used in the great dressmaking studios, which one could glimpse in shop windows and in fashion magazines, the likes of which she probably never even knew existed. I, on the other hand, had leafed through many, enough to know that Signorina Gemma was much more skilled than the rest of us *sartine*—she had perfect technique, sophisticated taste and perhaps even a special gift. If she had opened an atelier she'd have stolen the best clients from La Suprema Eleganza and Belledame. I would only be working in the Provera household a month—it was worth putting up with some hunger and a lot of hard work.

I couldn't keep my eyes open, but I had the strength to drop in and speak to my neighbour. She took in ironing but was terribly poor, always desperately in need of an opportunity to earn extra pennies. In exchange for a modest fee, I asked her to make me polenta and have it ready for me the next morning, sliced, toasted and wrapped in greaseproof paper, and to prepare me some dinner as well, maybe a soup of chickpeas and dill, which she could leave next to the hearth in the evening. And above all, I asked if for that month she could take care of cleaning the stairs and the entrance hall of the building, as she usually did when I was busy with a job. The envelope I kept in the top of my chest of drawers was nearly empty. For the first time, I was going to have to dip into the savings I kept in the tin. Never mind: it just meant I would not go to the theatre that year. I hoped the owner of the building would not object to this temporary substitution, but I just knew I would not be able to get up at four-thirty every morning and do needlework until vespers.

Finally, I collapsed into bed. I slept so deeply that the next morning I could not remember a single dream. All I could recall were occasional visual flashes, like the coloured pattern of the silk—not in the form of the dresses we were familiar with, but of Madama Butterfly's kimono covered in cherry blossoms, which I had seen in the theatre the previous year. That morning, when I saw the fabrics and those designs for the second time, they reminded me of illustrations and prints depicting Japanese figures and settings. I had admired them in magazines and in frames at Signorina Ester's house. For some time now, Marchesina Ester had told me, Japan had been very fashionable in Europe. The fashion was called Japonisme.

My sewing machine was greeted with great curiosity, and Signorina Gemma immediately learnt how to turn the crank in time with my rhythm, and taught her nieces to do the same, so that I could have both hands free to guide the fabric. In this way, the work proceeded quickly; more time was required, however, for the finishing touches—the trimming, ribbons, wadding, hooks and buttons, all operations that needed to be done by hand, very carefully and without rushing. We split the work. While mother and daughters did the trim on the first dress, Signorina Gemma and I cut and sewed the second, then the third. I was astonished and full of admiration at how, with just a few confident movements, she could line up the various pieces of material—some large, others medium-sized and still others very small—and pin them all together, tack them up and, after getting the wearer to try the thing on and be fitted, pass it all on to me to sew up. She would watch the path of the needle very closely, and when she took the garment back from me I would be amazed at how, as she delicately shook it out, those pieces of fabric would suddenly be transformed into a new and unique whole, in three dimensions, exquisite in every way. At the time, I would not have been able to use those words to describe this marvel, but I certainly had the feeling I was witnessing a miracle.

First, we would assemble the bodice; only after the sleeves and collar had been sewn on and checked would we move on to the skirt, trying it on one or other of the sisters, pinning it, tacking it at the waist, before finally sewing it on the machine. Perhaps in part because the fabric was so exquisite, to me it seemed like watching a flower bloom, one petal after another. And in my little fantasy, Signorina Gemma was like Cinderella's fairy godmother, transforming rags into a princess's gown with a wave of her magic wand. I was too proud ever to let my astonishment show; I always pretended I knew the next step in the process and how to carry it out. But in that month I learnt far more about dressmaking than my grandmother had taught me over many years or than I'd been able to pick up from magazines.

Every evening I returned home exhausted, lugging my sewing machine. I didn't dare to leave it at the Proveras' house. Someone—Tommasina, perhaps—might touch it out of curiosity and turn the wheel the wrong way, or bend the needle or the needle bar, and ruin the whole machine. I preferred always to keep it in my possession. Back home I would eagerly devour my soup, and some bread with whatever little accompaniment my neighbour had left for me on the hearth. I wondered how my four fellow seamstresses managed to get through so many hours on just a few pieces of dry toast. I found the snack of polenta and cheese that I hastily gulped down at lunchtime only gave me the tiniest amount of energy. But the satisfaction in the work we were doing made all the discomfort bearable.

Signorina Gemma had chosen three very similar designs, with just slight differences, particularly in the draping over the hips, the neckline, and the lace and ribbons. The girls' gowns had a bustle that protruded only a little. At the top, near the shoulder, the sleeves were puffed, as was the fashion, but then they narrowed at the elbow; the bodice formed a V at the front, and the full skirt flowed down over the hips. When the dresses were finally ready nobody would be able to tell they were homemade. And, as I had predicted, once they had their gowns on and their aunt had put their hair in rollers, and decorated it with feathers and ribbons in a kind of dress rehearsal, the two signorine truly looked like beauties. Their mother's dress was more modest, as was appropriate for her age.

Avvocato Provera, who had joined us in the sewing room to see the dress rehearsal, was gloating with satisfaction. Not worrying in the least about my presence—or perhaps he knew about the oath—he informed the girls that negotiations with the young captain and the bishop's nephew had come to a positive conclusion. Now Alda and Ida needed to win approval and favour from their future mothers-in-law who, along with their husbands and the bishop, were going to be attending the reception for the queen. And of course, the girls needed to win the admiration of their future husbands: not only would they be seeing the sisters up close for the first time, they would be in physical contact with them during the ball, albeit at a respectful distance. They would even be able to smell their perfume. 'Remember to take along mint or violet pastilles to suck on,' the lawyer urged them. 'Nothing disgusts a man as much as bad breath. And don't talk too much.' The two young men would feel the girls' hair on their cheek, admire the softness of their hands, their narrow waists, their white, sinuous necks. 'They can't not like you.'

The two signorine blushed at their father's words. I, too, might have imagined the dreamy magic of that first meeting—the birth of an attraction, the blossoming of love—but the story of Signorina Ester and Marquis Rizzaldo had taught me how many lies hide behind this kind of illusion. I looked at the girls in their beautiful Japanese-patterned gowns and thought of poor Madama Butterfly. Seduced, betrayed, abandoned, she took her own life. Signorina Ester had been saved by her father, but Cio-Cio San no longer had her father: he had killed himself to save his honour, just as his rejected daughter would go on to do. How would Avvocato Provera react if his two sons-in-law behaved badly towards Alda and Ida after they married?

I talked about it with my neighbour that night and, even though her husband was a drunk who beat her, she accused me of being too pessimistic. Neither of us could imagine how the story of the engagement of the two Provera girls would end.

By the time the gowns were ready, it was only three days until the reception. Signora Provera paid me the agreed fee without so much as a penny as a tip, and as I left she reminded me of the oath I had taken. My earnings were small compared to the huge amount of work I had put in, but I was happy because I couldn't put a price on all that I had learnt.

The following morning I got up early, even though I was extremely tired, and went down to the Corso, where I stopped outside the barbershop. I didn't need to wait long: along came Tommasina, barefoot, walking up the footpath with the big, sky-blue boxes balanced on her head, shouting, 'Our signora and signorine's dresses have arrived from

Paris!' Our eyes met as she passed me and I got the giggles but she remained impassive, showing no sign of having recognised me.

As usual, news travelled of the arrival of the 'dresses from Paris', and as usual, the curiosity and envy of the ladies who would be attending the queen's reception spilled out in the form of gossip and chatter about the lawyer's notorious avarice, which somehow allowed so much money to be squandered on his womenfolk's vanity.

But nobody, not even I, had any doubt that Alda and Ida would be the two most elegant damsels at the ball. Word had also spread through the salons of the successful outcome of the marriage negotiations, with people expecting the two engagements to be announced during the reception or, if court protocol forbade that, in the days immediately following.

The queen and her entourage arrived by train. The journey from the capital had been extremely long because every few kilometres the train had to stop to receive the well-wishes of the local population, who lined either side of the platform at small stations offering flowers and waving flags. In our city the shop windows displayed photographs of the sovereign surrounded by her little princesses and the young heir dressed in a sailor suit. We were all—from noblewomen to bourgeois women to humbler women living in the back alleys, and especially those of us who worked as dressmakers and sartine—curious to see how the queen would be dressed. We knew that on her arrival in Rome, as a young bride, she had been judged rustic and inelegant, and that her Savoy in-laws disdainfully called her 'the shepherdess'. Humble folk admired her, though, and in our city a large crowd lined the station platform to greet her and pay homage, and I'm not ashamed to say that I was among them. I must confess that in my naïveté I was proud that three dresses I had helped to make, that my hand-crank machine had sewn, were going to be seen by the queen, perhaps touched, perhaps admired by her: a shepherdess, yes, but one accustomed to wearing clothing made by the top dressmakers in Italy and indeed all of Europe.

The queen and her entourage stayed at the Hotel Italia, the most luxurious in the city. On the first day, she rested from the journey and received, in private, only the most important city authorities. The grand ball was planned for the following day.

It was only three or four days afterwards that I learnt what had happened at the ball. At first there had been attempts to keep the scandal a secret, and when the rumours began circulating they were muddled and vague. For some reason, the discovery that the Provera women's gowns were not from Paris, but had instead been made at home, seemed not just to be humiliating for them, but to constitute some kind of insult, causing deep offence to the queen and the other gentlewomen present. There was even talk of attempted lese-majesty, though in the end no legal action was taken against Avvocato Provera. But it was said that the family's reputation, and especially that of the two daughters, had been ruined forever.

For a while the news spread only in whispers. The main door of the Provera household in Piazza Santa Caterina remained barred. If the topic came up in conversation, relatives and friends of the family blushed and refused to talk about it. The only comment from anybody was a single word: 'Inexplicable!' But after the queen's departure, those present at the party began to speak more freely. Bachelors, not needing to explain themselves to wives, boasted of their own erotic exploits, passing on the spicier details, and neither the prefect nor other authorities were able to keep the press quiet any longer. Ten days after the fact, an especially bold satirical newspaper, one of those that never entered into the homes of people whose daughters were of marriageable age, published a long summary. It was from that newspaper that I finally discovered what had happened. I was astonished but also somewhat relieved because the reporter mentioned only in passing that the gowns were homemade, giving it little importance, and he did not mention my name but simply wrote 'using the services of a sartina'. I put the newspaper aside so that I could show it to Signorina Ester when she returned from her travels, and I still have the cutting to this day. It was the first time I had become involved, albeit anonymously, in a scandal, and it was not to be the last. But I will talk later about the second time. For now, I will limit myself to satisfying the curiosity

of you, my readers, about what happened that evening in
the frescoed halls of the prefecture.

Ceremony demanded that in the initial phase of the reception, the ladies who had just entered would separate from
their gentlemen and gather in the Hall of Nymphs, named
after the frescoes decorating it. This had been decked out
for the occasion as a dressing room, with mirrors and
dressing tables, where ladies would be able to take off their
coats and adjust their gowns and hair. Once everybody had
arrived and the gates of the prefecture had been closed, the
ladies would rejoin their respective husbands, fathers and
brothers in the hall of marine frescoes, and together they
would have refreshments as they waited for the queen to
take her place in the ballroom, ready to receive homage
from her guests, who would file past her one by one in
order of importance, so that they could be introduced. After
the ceremony the dances would begin.

In the dressing room, the news report related, when
Signora Teresa and her daughters took off their cloaks, the
three 'Parisian' gowns left the other ladies breathless with
admiration, surprise and, the chronicler maliciously insinuated, ill-concealed envy. The oldest and proudest of the
aristocratic ladies disdainfully observed them from afar
through their lorgnettes, but most of the ladies approached
them to look more closely, and to pay more or less hypo-
critical compliments. I imagined relatives and friends of the
family, aware of the marriage negotiations, would have

embraced Alda and Ida, whispering to each of them, 'You'll win him over for sure. Good luck!' And I wondered if the bishop's sister and Countess Vetti, the girls' future mothers-in-law, appreciated their manner, approved of the elegance of the two signorine's gowns and gave them some sign of benevolence.

Next, the reporter continued, the ladies joined their husbands in the hall of marine frescoes. The Provera ladies modestly entered among the last of the group. The bishop's nephew saw Alda, his eyes lit up and he was about to approach her, but his uncle grabbed his arm with an iron grip and held him tightly by his side. The bishop's face turned purple: he was incredulous. Captain Vetti—Don Cosma—who had been joyously heading towards Ida, had stopped in his tracks. Whispers of disdain and indignation flew from one gentleman to the next. The ladies, the three Proveras included, were baffled. And the gentlemen, the news report added, could not explain the reason for their disapproval.

At this point I wondered how all these gentlemen who had never picked up a needle in their lives could possibly spot something that had escaped the notice of their wives, namely that the three dresses were homemade, and why they took such offence, and why they could not explain it. People in high places, as my nonna used to say, were incomprehensible.

The reporter, having piqued his readers' curiosity, quickly explained the reason, which was much more serious than the one I had feared. Nobody had noticed that the gowns had been made at home and not in Paris. In fact, it was the very belief that they had been made in the French capital that fuelled the scandal.

What provoked the gentlemen's indignation was not the creation of the dresses, but the fabric, that beautiful silk, decorated with such exotic designs, over which our fingers had laboured for an entire month. Many of them had recognised it as originating from a famous house of sin, a celebrated brothel whose existence their sainted wives and—heaven forbid—the queen must never suspect.

It emerged later on—the journalist at the time did not know this, though I suspected it immediately—that, unbeknownst to the poor Provera women, Tito Lumia (probably unwittingly, since he was semiliterate and did not read the papers) had purchased from a French ship the remains of the fabric that a few years earlier had decorated the 'Japanese room' that was the pride and joy of the most luxurious brothel in Paris, Le Chabanais (I'm copying down the name from the newspaper cutting). All the men in Italy, in Europe, in the civilised world, knew the place or had at least heard of it. We women, on the other hand, were discovering its existence only now, in full prurient detail, from the pages of this satirical newspaper. It was the most famous bordello in Europe, frequented by millionaires, heads of state, the world's most fashionable artists and anybody who could afford—even just once, out of curiosity, as had been the case with some of our fellow citizens—the substantial minimum fee of five hundred francs. The heir to the throne of England had his own private room at Le Chabanais, with beautiful, specially made furniture and a gilded bronze bathtub in the shape of a ship with a figurehead. He would fill it with champagne and bathe in it with one or more of the 'residents' of the house. The other rooms, those intended for 'normal' clients, were themed: the Moorish room, the Indian room, the mediaeval, the Russian, the Spanish and, of course, the Japanese. The decor of the Japanese room was so elegant, so beautifully designed, that at the Paris Exposition of 1900 it had won first prize in the Decorative Arts category and a photograph of it had appeared in some illustrated magazines, though not those to be found in the homes of respectable families The curtains, the drapes, the upholstery on the furniture, the canopy of the four-poster bed—it was all made from that beautiful cherry-blossom silk in three different shades, the very stuff we used for the three Provera ladies' gowns. This silk, it was clearly specified during the Expo, was in a unique, original design, protected by patent.

How was it possible, the town's gentlemen wondered, as did the newspaper, that one of the most prominent and esteemed families in our city had come into possession of that fabric? Perhaps Avvocato Bonifacio Provera had a financial interest, some shares, in Le Chabanais? Perhaps, some even insinuated, when they left town on the pretext of going on spiritual retreats, the two signorine instead went to Paris to work temporarily in the world's oldest profession? And how come they had worn those sinful and compromising dresses in full sight of the queen? As a slight, an affront, to the monarchy? Perhaps the lawyer's fine republican and Mazzinian spirit had planned it all as a deliberate way of publicly insulting the head of state?

This, the journalist repeated, was what the gentleman present that evening in the marine-themed hall were asking themselves. Many of them had recognised the fabric immediately because, on a trip to Paris, they had seen it with their own eyes. These included His Excellency the most Reverend Bishop, who had himself succumbed to temptation. (The newspaper, not just satirical but also anticlerical, dwelt with particular gusto on this detail.) Just as, for the same reason, the queen's dignitaries, who had travelled with her from the capital, had also recognised it. The only person oblivious both to the existence of the brothel and the nature of its decor was the priestly Medardo Belasco who, unlike his uncle the bishop, took the sixth commandment very seriously. But just as he, and Captain Cosma Vetti, could never become betrothed to a young woman on whose head such a dark suspicion fell, so the court dignitaries could not allow the queen to be approached and offended by these three shameless women.

Two grenadiers in full uniform approached Signora Teresa and her two daughters and, unsuccessful in their endeavours to be discreet, ushered them out of the room. The lawyer followed them, unsure of what was happening. It was a bitter humiliation for them, but fortunately the queen was in the other hall at the time and was unaware of all these manoeuvres, so the rest of the evening went ahead as planned.

However, as was to be expected, behind the scenes all hell broke loose. As soon as the queen had left, the prefect and the chief of police called in Avvocato Provera to ask him the reason for the affront. The lawyer was astonished; as far as he knew, there was nothing incriminating in the least about the fabrics, they were part of his wife's trousseau which had indeed come from Paris, but about a quarter of a century earlier. He was in no position to recognise the material for what it was because, although he had been to Paris a few times on his own of late, his avarice—more so than his conjugal fidelity—had stopped him visiting a house of sin as costly as Le Chabanais. And he knew nothing of Tito Lumia or of the intricate web of lies that the women of the house had been spinning behind his back. All he would admit to was the trick with the boxes and the home-made creation of the ballgowns. As a lawyer he was aware that deceiving people, pulling the wool over people's eyes, was no crime. It looked bad, certainly. But he said, surely even the prefect and the chief of police had to admit that his wife's and daughters' gowns were more beautiful, more elegant, better made than those of all the other ladies. A stubborn man, he continued to deny that the fabrics were in any way offensive. The two functionaries were forced to adjourn and to summon the other gentlemen (though not the bishop) and ask them to testify, after which the prefect in turn admitted to them with a certain pride that he himself had visited the very same Parisian house of pleasure. This was not all. Avvocato Provera was shown the magazine containing the photographs of the Japanese room after it was awarded the prize at the Expo, as well as certain spicy barbershop calendars in which the exclusive design of the fabrics was clearly recognisable.

Here the newspaper article ended with a derisive little song attributed to university students, which relayed in verse a series of embarrassing little family scenes in which the city's noble husbands were forced to confess their dissolute indiscretions to their prudish other halves.

A couple of months later I found myself in the church of Santa Caterina for a funeral. Signorina Gemma was sitting in one pew, in full mourning dress. She had grown pale and very thin, and was unable to control the trembling of her hands—those hands that had once been so sure and confident as she wielded the scissors, cutting precious fabric to measure. She recognised me, greeted me, and invited me up into the house with her at the end of the ceremony so that I might greet Signora Teresa and her daughters.

'You're not going to scorn us like everybody else?' she asked me. 'After all, you knew our secret from the beginning—you could even be accused of being our accomplice. Thank you for keeping your oath, for not gossiping about it around town. You know how it all turned out, and the accusation that we knew the provenance of the fabric is truly slanderous. How could we possibly have checked where our supplier procured it from?'

I went up into the house with her and—miracle of miracles—Signora Teresa offered me a cup of coffee and biscuits. She and her daughters were dressed for mourning too, but they did not seem as despondent as Signorina Gemma. I noted the fabric of their black clothing—house clothes, but elegant, made of nice shantung that was soft yet stiff, of the sort I had seen in the windows of the city's best textile stores. The black hue was dense, uniform and with no greenish tints. The cut was excellent and the finishing perfect, as one might expect. All very different from the shabby little house clothes that I had become accustomed to seeing on mother and daughters during that month in which we worked together. But it was Avvocato Provera who held the greatest surprise for me. Nothing of this had leaked out in the city, but a few days after his second meeting with the authorities the poor man had an apoplectic fit that left him paralysed and mute in a wheelchair. He could understand everything, however. He recognised me, but when I greeted him he rudely turned his face to the wall. He had come into the sewing room where Signora Teresa was serving the coffee and biscuits, his wheelchair pushed by the servant girl. Tommasina, who was wearing a clean and respectable apron and sturdy little boots, was now trying to feed him, one little spoonful of coffee at the very least, but he kept his mouth clamped shut, shooting furious glances all around. I realised that he could not abide having to hand over to his wife the purse strings, and even having to watch her offer me that little bit of hospitality was like the fires of hell for him. His eyes lit up with anger whenever his gaze fell on the beautiful new treadle sewing machine that sat in pride of place by the window.

As she accompanied me outside, Signorina Gemma complained that Signora Teresa was a spendthrift; having gone without for so long, she did not understand the value of money and now wasted it, buying veal from the butcher in ridiculous quantities that they would never be able to get through, and giving away eggs to the orphanage. At church she put banknotes into the donation box. Once the household safe had been opened, and the tellers at the bank had verified all the savings and bonds, she had exulted to her daughters: 'We're so rich! What do we care for the city's gossips?' She was even planning to buy a motorcar. Not a horse and carriage: a motorcar.

'And is she planning to learn to drive it?' I asked with some trepidation.

'Don't be silly! She wants to employ a…What do they call it in France? No, not a mechanic, a chauffeur.'

I told Marchesina Ester about the visit when she returned to the city from one of her first trips away. She was indignant about the scandal and maintained that the two fiancés ought to have kept their word. If people wanted to make it a question of morality, she said, the two Provera sisters had not committed any sin; the lie about the Parisian gowns could be considered a joke—it was entirely harmless, and the four women had worked hard to reach the heights of all those other presumptuous and finicky ladies. Those dresses, in her opinion, were a guarantee that Ida and Alda would make model wives. If anything, the sinners were the gentlemen of the city who frequented brothels, including the prefect and the bishop. 'But that's not a question of morality—it's a case of hypocrisy,' she said.

My dear signorina Ester had some quite bizarre ideas about equality of the sexes, and about how men should not demand of women anything that they were not prepared to do—or refrain from doing—themselves. She would become indignant whenever she came to the last page of a novel published in instalments in the newspaper and it talked of 'fallen women' or 'sinful women redeemed'. She had given me a famous novel entitled *Mysteries of Paris*. It was very thick, and it took me almost a year to read it. She quizzed me on it and enjoyed discussing it with me. When she discovered that I been moved by the death of Fleur-de-Marie she said, 'Don't cry for her: get angry. She didn't choose that trade for herself. Why couldn't she get married and lead a normal life?' I reflected on her words. Since she had gone back to live with her father, Signorina Ester no longer spoke of love: she seemed to have eliminated it from her life. And for that matter, a young, separated woman could not even think of love. By law, she was still married to her husband—the most she could do was go back to him and hope to be forgiven. But I knew that my signorina would never do that.

When we learnt that Avvocato Provera had had a second apoplectic fit and died, the marchesina said to me, 'You know what would happen now, if the world worked the way it ought to?' And with that, she began to make up an ending to the women's story, as though she were writing a novel, but one that followed her own principles.

'All right. So, after the lawyer's death his wife, daughters and cousin would take their inheritance and disappear. Off to some distant land across the ocean. Not wishing to remain in a city that had treated them with such undeserved scorn. And for several years, nothing more would be heard of them.

'But then the American journalist who lives in our city, Miss Briscoe—you know, my English teacher—would return from one of her trips to the United States telling of a renowned French couture house in New York where the wives of millionaires and heads of state from all over the world lined up to get an original, unique garment made at an exorbitant price. The house was run by a mature lady who went by the name of…Let's see—how can we translate Gemma into French…Madame Bijou. She was assisted by a younger couturière, her daughter or granddaughter. This was Ida, naturally, and the establishment was actually Italian, but it sounded more chic to pretend to be French. Ida was married to a Hungarian pattern maker who worked for the company and played violin in his spare time. They had three beautiful, talented children who studied at the best school in New York. And Alda? In the throes of passion she had married a young Catalan painter, originally quite penniless. Spurred on by her, he had begun designing beautiful fabrics that he printed with a secret technique that he then patented. The designs on those inimitable fabrics were the secret to the success of the Bijou couture house.

'Alda and Mariano also had children. Actually…daughters. Four little girls with strong artistic inclinations—whether painting like their father, music like their violinist uncle, or dance…Shall we send that one to study with Isadora Duncan? And the youngest sang with the voice of an angel.

'Who have we left out? Madame Thérèse? Madame Thérèse went to live in the Bronx with Tommasina, and opened a school where they taught poor girls to cut and sew fabric, a kind of boarding house where the students received warm clothing, good food and also a little bit of an education, including instruction in sewing techniques. Mr Singer, the industrialist, admiring of the initiative, had given the school seven hundred and fifty of the latest model sewing machines. Hold on. The school was not reserved only for little girls. There was a section where every so often Madame Bijou would come and run courses, and where not just sewing classes but also food, lodgings and protection were available to prostitutes who wished to leave the streets and live an honest life.'

I laughed. 'Signorina Ester, I'm sorry, but you're too

much of an optimist, and also too romantic. In real life, unfortunately, that's not how things go.'

And in fact, the fears that Signorina Gemma had confessed to me turned out to be well-founded.

Signora Teresa was indeed bereft of any practical abilities, and unaware that since the time of her marriage there had been a great deal of inflation, so what to her seemed like an immense amount of money was indeed large, but not infinite. Thus, in a little over two years she squandered the entire fortune that her husband had accumulated through his great avarice. She did not keep in check the sharecroppers who robbed from her hand over fist, and she no longer had provisions from her landholdings but instead sent for them to be bought at the market and at the most expensive delicatessens in the city. She refurnished the entire house. But she spent very little time at home. Late every morning she would go with her daughters to take a hot chocolate at the Crystal Palace. They would not sit in one of the small internal rooms, like the handful of free, self-assured ladies did, but rather at one of the most prominent tables of all, one on the footpath, sheltered by the structure of glass and crystal that served as a kind of shop window, where the city's richest, most idle men would spend the day reading the paper, smoking cigars, talking of politics and tearing everybody else to pieces. She hoped, perhaps, that by putting the two girls on display like that she would be able to procure two new aristocratic fiancés for them. And since there were not many well-bred young men in the city, she also resolved to look beyond. She travelled far and wide with her daughters; she went to Paris and bought each of them a sumptuous trousseau from Atelier Printemps. She bought a motorcar, one of the very few in the city, and employed a driver, making him wear a uniform with a braided cap. She employed not one but two maids, dressing them in blue smocks with a white apron and a little cap. She employed a cook. Tommasina needed only to take care of the lawyer, and she did this with devotion until, as I said, he had a second attack and died. Signora Teresa and her daughters went to take the waters at an elegant spa. But to be able to pay for all these expenses she began selling off, one after another, her landholdings, apartments, store-houses, and then her state bonds. The estate was diminishing, not least because no one was working to replenish it. Tommasina ran away, taking with her ten silver spoons, two pearl necklaces belonging to the young ladies and a blue box from Atelier Printemps full of silk offcuts. When they found her a few days later she refused to reveal the name of the person to whom she had sold the stolen goods, so it proved impossible to retrieve them. Signora Teresa rained blows down upon the little thief and locked her in her room on a regime of bread and water, but refused to turn her in to the police. In the end, she had become fond of her and did not want her to finish up in a reformatory and after that, as always happened, in a brothel.

At that point Signorina Gemma, although she was

tormented by the unceasing tremor in her hands, took the reins of the family for a second time, and had a serious talk to the three women, putting an end to the crazy spending. The home in Piazza Santa Caterina had multiple mortgages on it and they would soon need to leave it, but the Proveras still had a small house in the country, not too far from the city, simply furnished but equipped with everything that was necessary. They retired there, taking with them the sewing machine which, on Signorina Gemma's advice, they had refrained from selling along with all their elegant new furniture. With great displeasure, Signora Teresa resigned herself to letting her maids, cooks and driver go, and retaining the services only of Tommasina. She was ashamed to sell the car and her daughter's Parisian trousseaus to her fellow citizens, but Signorina Gemma called for Tito Lumia, who bought the lot, as was his habit, though for a great deal less than all those luxuries had originally cost. But in one way or another, it was possible to put back together a small dowry for each of the girls. It was now a lot harder for the two sisters to find a husband. Other girls of their age and class avoided them, and their brothers kept a wide berth. Alda ended up agreeing to marry a rough shop boy from a nearby village who had been suggested to her by the matchmaker. Her husband did not allow her to host visitors, much less help out her relatives, and he constantly derided and humiliated her, criticising her refined tastes and meagre dowry.

Ida continued to live with her mother and aunt. If she had been less proud she would have looked for a position as a 'junior seamstress' in one of the city's two dressmaking studios. But she did not wish to be seen with a tape measure in hand, jotting down the vital statistics of the ladies whose salons she had previously frequented as an honoured guest and with whom she had exchanged pleasantries in the box seats at the theatre.

When I heard that mother and daughter had begun to take in sewing work, I was worried, as were all the other sartine in the city, that their great talent would prove stiff competition for the rest of us. But the Proveras were ashamed to do day work in the houses of families that previously they had frequented as equals, and they were neither willing nor able to receive wealthy clients in their humble little house in the country. So they only had access to a very humble clientele—country people, farmers who asked for repairs and mending, durable aprons and smocks, basic trousseaus consisting of sheets made of coarse fabric with simple edging and no embroidery. I learnt that Tito Lumia, working on behalf of a lentil wholesaler, had even got them to agree to sew a large consignment of sacks from thick hemp cloth. I wondered whether their beautiful treadle sewing machine with its gold decorations was strong enough to push the needle through such rough fabric, and if the needle would soon break, or whether needles existed that were much more robust than the ones I knew of. In sewing the scandalous silk, we had needed to fit my hand-crank machine with a very thin needle that could nevertheless be found in any haberdashery.

A Wounded Heart

I COULDN'T BELIEVE it. I couldn't believe that *l'americana*, Signorina Ester's English teacher, had done what Filomena claimed. It made no sense. She had been so full of enthusiasm when she told me that she was going away and had asked me to sew her a new corset, a special one, with little internal pockets between the whalebone ribbing where she could hide her money for the journey. She was happy, relieved to have finally freed herself from a tie that had been oppressing her and that in recent times had ruined her life. I did not know what this tie was, as she did not confide in me, but I could not help but notice that her mood had recently improved. I did know that she had already written to her sister in New York announcing that she would be arriving, because I had been the one who had gone to the post office to send the letter. I knew she had already bought tickets for the ship that would take her to Liverpool and for the transatlantic liner that three months later would take her from England to America; I had picked those tickets up from the travel agency. On the days when I went to her house to take care of her linen, she would also ask me to carry out little tasks like that. Her maid Filomena did not like being sent off on such errands as though she were some little servant girl, whereas I didn't mind since I was paid by the day—I was quite happy to stretch my legs every so often and take a look around the city. Filomena, for all her airs and graces, did not know how to read and displayed indifference, if not disdain, for her mistress's line of work. For me, though, that 'La Miss' was a journalist inspired great curiosity and enthusiasm. What a pity that none of her articles were ever published in the magazines that I sometimes borrowed from the circulating library. She wrote in English, and nobody in the city, except perhaps for Signorina Ester, was able to read her articles, which were published only in America. Seeing that I was interested in her work, she had recently told me happily that she had signed a contract with the Philadelphia newspaper she had been working for to write a series of twelve articles on some very old paintings with gold backgrounds that she had discovered in churches in the nearby countryside.

I was fond of La Miss, even though she was an eccentric woman and the best families in the city would not receive her into their homes, and instead gossiped constantly about her and said she was no good. They'd have felt this way about any woman without a husband, foreign or Italian, who had left the family home to travel the world and earn a living through work. If she had been poor, a sartina like me, a worker, a maid, they would have forgiven her this, provided she knew her place and did not expect to treat them as an equal. But La Miss considered herself their equal or perhaps, like a good American, she did not even realise that over here the distances between the various social classes and families were deep and insuperable. And that women were not permitted to behave with the same freedom as men. On her passport La Miss had got them to write 'professional'. She meant, of course, a professional in the field of journalism and art criticism; the police inspector had told people about this and all the gentlemen in town thought it very funny. For them, Signorina Ester explained to me, the word 'professional', when applied to a woman could only mean one thing—the oldest profession, a prostitute.

Ester, too, was fond of Miss Lily Rose. The Artonesi home was one of the few that had opened its doors to the young American when she had come to live in our city some ten years earlier. Signor Enrico had asked her to give his daughter English lessons, and that was how I had met her.

My grandmother was still alive then and we would often spend our days sewing at the Artonesi home. La Miss, who spoke perfect Italian, asked Nonna to go once a week to her house as well to take care of her linen. Sometimes I would go along too. La Miss rented an apartment in the modern part of the city, a nice place simply furnished but full of colourful paintings. She had painted some of them herself; others she had bought on her wanderings around the countryside and villages of the interior, visiting churches and sacristies. She painted as a hobby, whereas her profession was in art criticism and collecting, she explained to us. The articles that she posted to the newspaper in Philadelphia were about Italian painting, particularly that of our region, mostly older works, but also some modern art. After spending a few months going to her home, albeit just for short periods, my grandmother said, 'The city's gossips can say what they like: Miss Briscoe is a respectable woman. A true lady.' She pointed out to me that, regardless of the simplicity of her apartment and clothing, Miss Lily Rose must be a richer woman than she seemed. She travelled often, throughout our region and the whole of Italy, never worrying about the cost of transport. She went to the theatre. She subscribed to many Italian and foreign magazines and often, in nice weather, went to read them at the Crystal Palace, sitting under the glass alongside the rich idlers. Ladies, as I said, usually sat in the internal rooms and always went there in company, whereas La Miss sat alone reading, not worrying about all the curious people who stopped outside the glass to look at the gentlemen smoking cigars and eating ice cream. Once on a very hot day she saw a young lad dressed in rags squashing his nose against the glass, and called him inside. He was one of those little alleyway rascals who spent every morning with a basket on their back waiting among the market stalls for some gentleman to give them a few coins in exchange for carrying their shopping home. La Miss wanted to give him her ice cream, but a waiter ran up and rudely drove the little rascal away, giving the signorina a stern look of reproach.

Filomena went around telling everybody that her mistress ate meat every day of the week, even on Fridays because she was not Catholic, and this too was a topic for criticism and gossip. La Miss owned, and knew how to use, an expensive camera. The articles she sent to America were always accompanied by images of churches, paintings and landscapes, photos that she had taken and printed herself in a little room of the apartment set up for the purpose. She also had a bicycle, on which she rode around the countryside in search not only of artworks but also to gather herbs of every kind, which she would dry out between two pieces of paper and place carefully in a large notebook, writing their Latin names alongside. No woman we knew of, regardless of her class, rode a bicycle. Not even Signorina Ester, when she reached an age where she asked for one, had been permitted to have a bicycle.

I studied with great curiosity the clothes that La Miss wore on her excursions: she had certain puffy skirts with a central fold that opened out wide with each step like a man's trousers, short enough to completely reveal her ankles. Later on, when I moved from hems and seams to making simple garments, I became obsessed by those skirts. I would have liked to get my hands on one, lay it out on a table, understand what pieces it was made up of, how many darts it had and where. Did patterns exist with outlines that I could trace onto some fabric? Guessing the source of my curiosity, La Miss told me one time that she bought them ready-made in Paris at a large department store that sold everything required for the sport of men's and women's cycling. If I wanted she could show me one laid out, and she would let me touch it and look at it inside out so that I could understand how it was made. But I was embarrassed and I said, 'Oh no, no.' Besides, who in our city—country woman or gentlewoman—was ever going to ask me to make such a peculiar garment?

La Miss did not care about elegance, did not follow fashion, and often went out in warm weather without a hat; no one had ever seen her protect her skin with a parasol, and in summer she was always tanned like farm worker, even her hands because she only ever wore gloves in winter. She wore the same style of dress for years—the fabric was excellent quality and did not show signs of wear—for her, the important thing was that it was comfortable. She explained to my grandmother, as though to apologise for the fact that apart from her linen she never asked us to make her any clothes, that she bought them or had them made overseas. She travelled a lot, as I said, and not only in Italy. Every two or three years she went to England and from there she would take a liner to America. She would return after only two months. It was as though for her crossing the ocean was like popping outside the city walls for an Easter Monday picnic. Perhaps Ester picked up her passion for travel from La Miss.

None of us ever understood why La Miss never returned permanently to her homeland and instead remained in our city. My grandmother suspected that a love affair was behind it all. But through her work La Miss met so many men—aristocrats, bourgeoisie, artists, parish priests, artisans, poor unfortunates that she used as models in her paintings—that it was hard to tell if she had any favourite. She would receive them in her home without worrying about whether a chaperone was present. Her maid was married and went back to her own home each night to sleep. I did not much like this Filomena, perhaps because I was envious. Each year at the start of the opera season La Miss, heaping one scandal on top of another, would book a box all to herself and turn up night after night in her usual day clothes accompanied by her maid. The first time she arrived at the theatre with this escort people thought she had the maid come along for fear of the dark on the trip home, and that she would leave her to wait downstairs in the cloakroom. But then Filomena appeared alongside her in the box, dressed like the lower-class woman she was, and sat in her velvet-covered seat leaning out over the edge and looking all around through binoculars. Nobody had the courage to tell La Miss that her behaviour was inappropriate and offensive, as was her attire, suited to daytime and work, whereas at the theatre it was obligatory to dress elegantly. And if the maid loved music so much, her mistress could always buy her a seat in the gods. Not one of the upper-class men or women of the city had ever set foot in that box to pay her a visit during interval, not even out of curiosity. 'Ah, these Americans! They're real savages,' somebody commented on the way out, not even bothering to lower their voice. Miss Lily Rose probably heard, but she didn't give a damn. As for Filomena, I don't think she cared much for music, but she gave herself airs around all the other maids because of these incursions into the world of the upper crust. She was a very ambitious woman who adored luxury and would have loved to be able to indulge herself. She took certain liberties that only an American mistress would let her get away with—no woman from a respectable family would have tolerated such behaviour.

After my grandmother died, I took her place and continued to take care of La Miss's linen. I got it laundered and took it to my neighbour to be ironed; if there was a tear I would mend it, and I would sew buttons back on to bodices and shirts. For those few hours a week she would pay me three or four times what other ladies in the city would give me for two days' mending from dawn till dusk. According to Filomena, La Miss had no sense of the value of money. Filomena, who worked all day, every day, was also paid an exorbitant amount.

One day, as I was changing her sheets (this was a task that should have fallen to Filomena, but she didn't care to do it and would have left the same ones on the bed for two months straight), I noticed that an edge of the mattress was fraying and a tuft of wool was beginning to poke out. This was really a job for the mattress maker, but it was a small burst seam and I felt I could fix it myself. So, the following week I brought along with me the case in which grandmother kept a collection of needles of the strangest shapes and sizes, along with certain special types of thread that were not commonly used but were handy to have around the house. It was a hot day so I was not wearing a jacket, just a shirt with the sleeves rolled up above my elbows. I knew that La Miss had gone out herb-gathering on her bicycle and that Filomena was at the markets doing the shopping. It was easy to get into the house because they never locked the door; they just closed it with a latch. So I was not especially surprised to see someone as I crossed the living room, a gentleman with a cigar between his fingers who had just put a monocle to his eye and was closely examining one of La Miss's as-yet-unfinished paintings that she had left drying on the easel. I thought I recognised him as Barone Salai, a wealthy and respected middle-aged art collector who had been to the house on previous occasions. Perhaps he wished to buy the painting. Perhaps he was just curious to see how work on it was coming along. I thought nothing of it, greeted him politely and continued towards the bedroom, not bothering to close the door. I pulled back the sheet on the frayed side of the mattress, assessed the thickness of the fabric, opened the case and selected the longest, straightest, largest and sharpest needle, one with a wide eye. There were some curved needles in the collection and perhaps one of those would have made the job easier, but they looked too thin and I was afraid that they would not be strong enough, and I had no way of pushing one through the fabric. The thimble I had brought was not suited to that kind of needle. I searched the spools for a strong yarn, threaded it through the eye of the needle and leant over the bed. I poked the little bit of wool back in under the seam.

I had not yet pushed the needle through the fabric when someone grabbed me by the hips, and I felt the rough tickle of waxed whiskers and hot cigar-smelling breath on my neck. The man—I knew at once it was Barone Salai—did not say a word. He tried to lift my skirt and pull it over my head. This move had already been described to me a number of times by maids who had had to defend them-selves from their masters. It served to expose your behind, but also to impede the movement of your arms and cover your eyes so you couldn't look them in the face while they had their way with you. I was too fast, though: before the baron could throw himself on top of me and pin me down with his weight I leapt out of the way, accidentally hitting him on the chin with my head, tore my skirt from his hands and spun around. It was the first time I had faced that kind of attack. I remembered my naïve, cocky response to my

grandmother when she had tried to put me on my guard—
'I'd be able to defend myself!'—and I jabbed the needle
high into the chest of my attacker, just below his throat.
'Leave at once!' I ordered in a voice hoarse with emotion
and fear. 'Don't be stupid,' he replied in a mocking tone.
Who knows how many other times he'd had to overcome
resistance. He tried to pull my arms towards him, but my
hands were free, and I pressed on the needle. Not hard, but
enough to go through his cravat and shirt and touch his
bare skin. 'Leave at once,' I repeated. He had felt the steel
against his throat, but he was still laughing. 'What do you
think you're going to do with that little thing?' I pressed a
bit harder and a drop of blood appeared on the front of his
shirt. The baron pulled away, swearing, and it was only
then that he saw the needle in full it was the length of a
stiletto dagger. 'Don't touch me,' I said to him, and he
hurled an insult at me that I do not wish to record here.

I don't know how it would have ended if the sound of the
front door slamming had not startled us both. We heard
two people bantering: Filomena and—I soon discovered—
the tinsmith she had brought back with her so that he could
repair the kitchen tap. Barone Salai composed himself.
With a quick gesture he adjusted his cravat so that it covered
the little bloodstain, ran his hands through his hair and
returned to the living room without a word. I followed
him, still holding the needle, but he had already left.
Filomena was standing in the doorway of the kitchen.

'What are you doing?' she asked. I could hear the tinsmith banging away in the next room.

'That animal...' I said, my voice breaking.

And she laughed. 'Ah, he tried it on with you as well.' Then she turned serious. She stroked my cheek in a cursory way. 'Listen,' she said. 'You're fond of La Miss, aren't you?' I looked at her, bewildered. What did she have to do with anything? 'If you really care for her,' Filomena went on, 'you mustn't tell her anything about what happened.'

'But that animal,' I insisted, 'he wanders about the house, comes and goes as he pleases. He might try it on with her.'

'Don't be so naïve. And listen to what I'm saying. Don't mention it to La Miss. You'd be causing her pain.'

Her words had such a definitive tone that I didn't have the courage to insist. She stepped behind me and pinned my dishevelled plaits back into a bun. 'Off you go now, back into the bedroom to finish your work.'

But the following week, when I found myself alone with La Miss, I told her everything. To my surprise she was not outraged. Instead, she sighed and looked sad. 'You need to be careful,' she told me. 'Try not to be left alone with him. If you are, just go home, and don't worry about that day's work. I'll pay you regardless.'

I couldn't understand. On other occasions she had gone into battle in defence of the freedom and honour of women, especially poor women, and their right to be treated with respect.

I would have liked to talk to Signorina Ester about what

had happened and about this strange reaction from La Miss, but she was away travelling.

Now I was afraid to go into that apartment where the door was always open. If I could just walk in, so could anyone. I never knew in advance if I would find my mistress there, or Filomena, or if there would be nobody home. Or if I would find a murderer, a thief, or a gentleman convinced he could steal the honour of a poor defenceless young girl. Why didn't La Miss get into the habit of locking the door and giving a copy of the key only to people she trusted?

I was so worried that a month or so later, as I was lifting a heavy basket in which I had placed curtains, sheets and bedspread to take to the laundry, I was startled by a noise in the next room and I tripped over some fabric that was hanging out over the edge of the basket. I fell, dislocating my right wrist. This was a predicament. How long would I have to keep it bandaged, and be unable to sew? And who was going to do the cleaning in the building where I lived? Was I going to have to pay my neighbour to do it again? Would I be eating through all my savings?

I tried to wiggle my fingers, but they were swollen and painful. I'm not ashamed to say that, dejected, I burst into tears, and that was how La Miss found me when she returned home. 'What have they done to you?' she asked, very concerned, but not specifying who she meant. When she learnt I had fallen over all by myself, she was greatly relieved. She bandaged my wrist tightly and skilfully and sent Filomena to seek out the ice cart and buy a nice big piece that she broke up and applied to the injury. 'Forget about the linen. Filomena will take the basket to the laundry. You keep your arm in a sling and come back tomorrow, and I'll get you more ice.'

I had stopped crying, but such kindness—it was almost maternal—brought tears back to my eyes.

In the end, through daily ice packs and keeping my wrist completely still, it healed faster than I had dared hope. After a week I was able to sew again, though I still could not lift anything heavy.

But I was impatient. I had a little job I needed to do in the home of Signor Carrera, the engineer. He was from out of town and was working on the construction of the aqueduct. His wife wanted me to sew a Carnival costume for her seven-year-old daughter and they didn't have a sewing machine at home. I needed to bring my own.

I decided I could carry the little case in my left hand, and so I set off calmly, thinking about how to cut the shot taffeta for the trousers so that they would stay puffy like the picture in the book. Perhaps I would need to stiffen it up with some lining in tarlatan or sinamay.

The engineer's daughter was an odd creature, rather slight but pretty and delicate, and very fair, like a northern fairy, like the winged beings in the books of fables that Ester had bought Enrica in London. Her mother had asked her to choose from the images in a fashion magazine. I had assumed the girl would ask me to make her a princess costume. But instead that little eccentric became fixated with the cover of one of her father's novels, *The Pirates of Malaysia* by Salgari. She did not wish to dress as the Pearl of Labuan, though. No, she wanted a Sandokan costume: turban, tight double-breasted satin jacket with a sash around the waist in which to stash pistols and daggers, puffy trousers, and babouche slippers with curved tips. If she'd been my daughter, I'd have told her that it wasn't appropriate to go to the Children's Ball dressed as a boy, but her parents always let her get her own way. The mother had bought the fabric for the trousers and the sash. I was to make the turban and jacket out of her old satin dressing gowns.

I was walking along, bent over towards the left because I was struggling to carry the sewing machine, and I was thinking about the Carnivals of my childhood, when all it took to feel you were dressed up as a cat was a sheet with two little knots on either side of the head to look like ears. My grandmother used to dress up as a cat as well, and go with me into the piazza to throw confetti and toot one of those party blowers with the retractable tongue. She would be giggling like a little girl alongside me. This was a great social occasion for us, our only luxury.

I was so caught up in my memories that I only noticed the young man who had cut in front of me when he placed his hand on the case and lifted its weight from me. My first thought was that he wanted to steal it. I instinctively tightened my grip. A kind, polite voice said to me in correct Italian: 'I'm sorry, signorina—I frightened you. I only wanted to help you.' Signorina, me? I had to look up at him because he was tall. He really was a signorino: a fashionably dressed student, wearing clothes made to measure, a coat and hat, a silk scarf—the son of a respectable family. He was around my age, perhaps a little younger, clean-shaven, with lovely fresh cheeks, nice full mouth and beautiful clear, dark eyes. A line by a Persian poet Signorina Ester had got me to read flashed into my head: 'cheeks like a rose and the eyes of a gazelle'. But the poet had been talking about a girl. Nevertheless, I had to admit that this young man was not lacking in manliness. He could have been a cadet or young official in civilian dress.

I was embarrassed and did not know how to reply. I kept clutching the handle of the little case and our fingers touched.

'Allow me to introduce myself,' he said. 'My name is Guido Suriani, at your service.' He looked me in the eyes, waiting for me to tell him my name. But I remained silent. I didn't want to take any chances. I didn't know who he was. I had never heard that surname in the city, yet there were only so many families of his social class. He must be from out of town. And why was he treating me like I was one of his peers? Couldn't he see that I was a sartina? Was he making fun of me? Feeling wary, I said brusquely: 'It's fine. I don't need any help.'

'And yet you do,' he insisted. And to prove it to me he

lifted my sewing machine like it was a feather. 'I'll carry it, signorina. Where will I be accompanying you?'

I didn't say a word. I couldn't tear the case from his hand: I wouldn't be able to. I felt like crying but resisted the urge out of anger. 'If you don't give it back, I'll call for an officer,' I threatened. He laughed and let go. But at that point I was no longer able to hold it, my arm went soft, all strength had gone out of it, and I felt a strange languor. I had to let him take it back. Irritated, I gritted my teeth and walked towards the engineer's house with him following, holding the case.

At the front door we came upon the lady of the house. 'Good morning, Guido!' she said cordially to my companion. 'Are you back for the holidays? How's it going up there in Turin?'

I did not wish to hear anymore. At that point my strength had come back and I was able to carry the sewing machine. I reached out for it, he handed it over, and I slid through the door and up the stairs.

I thought about that encounter all afternoon as I cut and tacked the pieces of Clara's pirate costume. She remained by my side, as if we were joined at the hip, with her father's book in hand, watching to ensure I made everything exactly as in the picture. She was at the ready to pick up dropped pins, leaping into action like a miniature assistant, a *piccinina*, as they say in Milan. I got her to try on a wide yellow satin sash with tassels, which I had made out of an old curtain, and I thought of the signorino who had followed me. He was a handsome young gentleman, I couldn't deny it, and he seemed kind and well brought-up. He had behaved respectfully. But I had read so many tales in novels, and heard so many stories from my friends and from older women, about young men from good families who had courted and seduced a poor humble girl, deceived her with a thousand promises, got her into trouble and then abandoned her. There was even a novel by Carolina Invernizio, *Story of a Sartina*, that warned of just these sorts of dangers. I was perturbed, and afraid, in part because it was the first time in my life that I had been so struck by a young man. It was lucky that he was studying in Turin, I thought, and that he would be going back there after Carnival.

But he crossed my path several more times in the subsequent days. I was no longer carrying my sewing machine. The engineer's wife had convinced me to leave it at their house until I finished the costume, given that my right wrist was still a little weak—nobody would touch it, I could be sure of that; she would lock it away in a cupboard. On the street, Guido Suriani would greet me with a little nod, raising his hat. I couldn't tell if he was doing this seriously or as a joke. I kept on walking and did not return his greeting with so much as a glance. Yet I could not stop thinking about him.

Ester, the marchesina, had returned, but I didn't dare speak to her about him. After all, what advice could she possibly give me? It was obvious that there could never be

anything between me and this well-bred young man. I
didn't want her to think that I had got strange ideas into
my head. I have to confess that after I got over my initial
indignation, I did not even have the courage to talk to her
about Barone Salai. I was ashamed of what had happened,
as though it was my fault, as though I had provoked it. And
besides, the baron was held in great esteem throughout the
city and had a very important lineage. His family was not
one of the most wealthy, but their noble title had a long
history. He was the only heir. He had two older sisters,
deeply proud spinsters who had always prevented him from
marrying. Every time, it was deemed that the origins of the
chosen young lady were too humble to make her worthy
of becoming a Salai, even if she was a wealthy young
countess or the daughter of a marquis. He did not seem to
suffer loneliness. He was a skirt-chaser, everybody knew
that, but was also involved in many activities: he was on
the city board, on the administrative council of the
orphanage; he was adviser to the prefect, a court-appointed
expert, and for many years had been director of the city
museum.

I often met him at the home of La Miss, too often. He
would look at me shamelessly, as if to say, 'I'll catch you
sooner or later.' And if ever there was nobody else at home,
I would slip away immediately. When La Miss was around,
I couldn't help but notice that he treated her rudely, looked
down on her, ordered her about and criticised her. Why
didn't he just stay home? And why did she agree to receive

him? In any case, I had never put the mattress-maker's needle back in its case. I carried it with me at all times, slipped under the laces of my bodice, the sharp tip covered but always within reach. I would defend myself from the baron and, who could tell, perhaps also from the student if the need arose.

In a few days I had finished Clara's Sandokan costume. We hadn't yet got her to put the whole thing on; she had only tried on one piece at a time. That afternoon was going to be her chance to try the whole outfit, and if everything went well, I would be paid and sent on my way, with my sewing machine.

Her mother and I put the little girl on the dining table and took off her floral dress, so that she was just wearing her undergarments. I had made them too, like all of her underwear: a sleeveless bodice of 'egg skin' cotton with a Valenciennes lace trim and buttons around the waist to hold up a short pair of drawers, the sort little girls wore, so they could be unbuttoned and lowered quickly in case of urgent need. We got her to put on the double-breasted satin jacket with flared tailcoat and assorted fringes. Then there were stockings in the same colour as the puffy pantaloons, the pantaloons themselves, the sash around the waist and the slippers with curved tips—these, too, were covered in satin, stuffed with cotton and decorated with two rows of glass beads. And finally, we gathered her blond hair on top of her head and covered it with the turban. Clara stood quietly, happy to let us dress her. I was satisfied with my work, though I still found it strange to see that fragile little blond doll dressed as a ferocious pirate. When she was ready, her mother lifted her up under the arms and placed her on the ground. We all went into the parents' bedroom so the girl could see herself in the large wardrobe mirror.

'Do you like it?' her mother asked. Clara took one look at herself and burst into a flood of desperate tears, leaving us speechless.

'No, no!' she cried. 'I wanted this'—and she showed us the cover of the book that she had brought in with her.

'But darling, that's what it *is*,' the mother protested, disconcerted. 'You saw the sartina sewing it. She made it exactly the same.'

Clara was crying so much that the engineer came in from his study. And to my great surprise he was accompanied by my admirer, Guido Suriani, who had dropped by to visit him. But the girl's desperation was so great, and her cries so loud, that she was all we could think about. Her father knelt down in front of her. 'All right, my little doll: what's the matter? Tell Daddy. Whatever it is, we can fix it.'

'I wanted this,' Clara repeated through the sobbing, pointing at cover of the book.

'But that's what it *is*,' her mother insisted.

Guido's eyes followed the little girl's finger and saw that she was pointing not at the pirate's clothing, but at his face. He stifled a little laugh. 'You're right,' he said. 'But as your father said, this can be remedied.' And he asked her mother,

'Could I please have a cork and a candle?'

He sat in front of the vanity, put Clara, who had stopped sobbing, between his knees and dried her face. 'You'll see—we'll fix everything,' he said reassuringly. I liked that he was so comfortable with children. The mother, who had understood what was going on, charred the cork in the candle flame. Guido patiently traced some lines of soot on the little girl's face to make a nice pair of whiskers and a beard with sideburns like Cavour's, and darkened her eyebrows. He pushed Clara towards the mirror: 'How's that?'

'No!' the little girl shouted. Enraged, she whipped the turban off her head and threw it on the ground. She took off her shoes and hurled them at the mirror and then, in a frenzy, tore off all the other pieces of the costume. She was left wearing only her undergarments, her blond curls hanging loose over her shoulders, and clutching Salgari's novel to her chest. Against her pale, delicate skin her tear-smudged whiskers and beard made for a very strange effect.

'Claretta, dear! What's wrong?' her father asked in dismay.

Then an idea occurred to Guido. He approached the girl, took the book from her hand and pointed at the pirate's face, painted in tempera, as were all the illustrations in that series. It was dark, with hollow cheeks, an aquiline nose and sparkling eyes—a fierce, adult face.

'Is that what you wanted?'

'Yes, that,' said Clara.

'So, you thought that if you dressed up as Sandokan you

would also have a face just like his?'

The girl nodded.

Her mother said, 'But darling, he's an ugly brute. How did you think you could look like him?'

'A Carnival costume can't perform that kind of miracle,' her father added. 'And besides, you're much more beautiful. You're my precious little flower.'

Clara began crying again, but now she was disconsolate rather than enraged. Guido embraced her silently. We adults looked at each other perplexed. How to make sense of a child's reasoning, their desires and pain?

'There, there. You'll see, everyone at the party will be impressed—you'll have the best costume of all,' her mother said.

'I don't want a costume. I want to be a pirate,' Clara whispered into Guido's chest.

'Don't you like the face I gave you? I can do a better job with the make-up, if you can be patient.'

'I don't want a pirate face. I want to be a pirate. Like Sandokan. A real pirate. Forever.'

'When you grow up you can be a pirate, I promise,' Guido replied under his breath.

After witnessing a childhood drama that was incomprehensible to us adults but at the same time profound, it seemed natural that he should accompany me home, chivalrously carrying my sewing machine in its case. I was no longer afraid of letting him see where I lived. 'Tomorrow I leave for Turin,' he said as we walked. 'I'm studying at the university there. Engineering. But when I return, signorina, I would like us to see each other again. In the meantime I would like to write to you, if you'd let me.'

'It would be best if you didn't,' I replied instinctively. I was afraid of making a bad impression with my poor grammar. And besides, it was best to end the relationship straight away, as it promised nothing good for the future. I had my pride. But I also feared he might think I was refusing to write to him because I was illiterate. So many contradictions. He did not insist. He did not even make me tell him my name. But if he wanted, he could have found that out from the engineer's wife.

We said goodbye outside my building. And so, in my head, another dream rapidly formed. It was a noble building. He might think that I lived in one of the apartments higher up, not in the basement. But what was I thinking?! You could see at once that I was a sartina. Not only from my clothes: instead of a hat I wore a scarf on my head, tied at the back of my neck or under my chin. And it had been my sewing machine that had prompted our first encounter. How could I pass myself off as a young lady from a good family? And how could he possibly have serious intentions towards me?

No, no! as Clara had cried, this was not the kind of love story I wanted. Lies, deceit, disappointment, abandonment. In that moment, in my heart, I gave up all hope. I would always preserve the memory of his kindness.

'Thank you for everything,' I said, a little standoffish. I picked up my sewing machine and pulled the door behind me.

I never found out whether Clara could be convinced to wear the Sandokan costume to the Children's Ball that took place every Carnival in the foyer of Teatro Mascagni. I had another job that I urgently needed to finish—a layette for a baby that was to be born in April, whose grandmother wanted everything to be ready in time for the birth. Including squares of thick flannel that they would use to swaddle the baby's legs, because they were modern folk like the Artonesis, and would be wrapping stiff pieces of piqué only around the baby's chest and hips, to support its back. I sewed at home spending every day all alone, so I had a lot of time to think. Embroidering those little outfits, those christening garments and swaddles, I was surprised to find myself dreaming of my own child, a child that would have rosy cheeks and the dark, sweet eyes of a gazelle. But I quickly drove such thoughts away.

I continued to dedicate one day a week to Miss Lily Rose's linen. That gossip Filomena had informed me that La Miss had recently been in a terrible mood, that she would lock herself away in her room and cry, that she was unable to sleep and that she took a medicine the maid referred to as 'her drug'. When I happened to see her in the house, I too found her dejected and melancholy. She had lost so much weight that I had to take in her skirts and shift the buttons of her jackets. She ate very little. It was as though she had fallen ill, even though she still carried out all her usual activities as energetically as ever.

One day I noticed that she had a yellowish mark on her right cheekbone, like a fading bruise. She noticed me looking at it and hastened to explain to me, 'There's something wrong with the brake on my bicycle. I fell, a branch got stuck in the spokes of the front wheel. It is lucky I didn't dislocate a wrist, as happened to you.' Lucky indeed: during those days she was finishing off a painting on a religious theme, a large one, with a great deal of blue, and she was working quickly, with a palette knife and paintbrush.

'The dean of the cathedral in G— commissioned it,' she was kind enough to explain. 'I need to deliver it in time for the inauguration of the new chapel.' She had deadlines, just like me.

In her apartment there was the usual back-and-forth of people. Every so often Barone Salai turned up, behaving, as always, like he was the boss of everyone—he would criticise everything, look closely at the painting through his monocle, say the perspective was all wrong and the colours clashed. Unusually, however, La Miss refused to accept his criticisms, defended her work and one day in my presence even told him to go to hell.

When the painting was ready, instead of sending it on the mail train, La Miss decided to take it in person and have a brief holiday in G—, where she had a friend whose husband bred horses. 'Some riding in the open air will do me good,' she told us as she prepared her bags.

In the end her holiday was not so short. La Miss stayed away for more than a month and when she returned, she was completely changed. She was still thin, but her face had its colour back; she stood taller and was more serene. She had bought a new hat, very elegant, of a kind that hadn't yet appeared here, with roses made of silk, peacock feathers and cherries and other wax fruit. She had stopped taking medicine to help her sleep, Filomena told me, and since spring had arrived, she went on long bicycle rides every day. But she didn't return with her usual bundles of herbs in flower. In fact, she had asked me to help her pack the album containing her herb collection into a small trunk, along with some antique books, her camera and everything required for printing photographs; then she had asked me to arrange for the trunk to be taken to the post office and sent to the address of her bank in England. Filomena and I aired a thousand theories about what La Miss's intentions might be, and we were even more amazed when, one day, opening the drawer of her little table in search of a button that had come off her nightdress, I found a small revolver that would fit in a pocket or a lady's handbag.

La Miss happened upon us as, astonished, we were passing this dangerous object between us, but she did not get angry with us. She told us it was her fault: she should have kept the drawer locked. Luckily the gun was not loaded, but if we should ever see it lying around somewhere, we must not, under any circumstances, touch it. It took very little to fire a shot and kill somebody.

Filomena was bolder than me, and asked, 'But why do you need to keep a pistol in the house?'

'You're right to ask. And I never had one until now. I bought it in G— because I went with my friend and her husband on various excursions into the woods in that area, where they say there's a chance of running into brigands. What nonsense!' She laughed. 'We met a few rather primitive men, but they were shepherds, and all they wanted was to get us to taste and buy their excellent cheese.'

'But do you know how to use it?' Filomena asked.

'Yes, I knew how to use one as a girl. In America everyone takes a pistol with them when they travel. I have a gun licence, otherwise in G— they wouldn't have sold it to me. Perhaps it's best if I keep it in the bank, in the safety deposit box.'

Not much time would pass before we discovered that she had not done this.

A few days after the discovery of the pistol, La Miss called me aside and asked me if I wanted to have her bicycle. 'I can't give it to Filomena—her husband wouldn't let her use it. But you don't have a husband, and I've noticed that you often have to walk a long way to get work. It would be incredibly useful to you. It even has a lovely basket.'

For goodness sake, I thought: I'd be a laughing-stock throughout the city. Nobody would take me seriously. And would I have to wear those ridiculous trouser-skirts? But I couldn't say this to her. I couldn't repay her generosity with such an insult. 'I don't know how to ride one,' was the explanation I chose instead. 'I would fall off and injure myself. Thank you very much, though. Sorry, how come you've decided to give it away?'

'Don't tell anyone just yet, but next month I'm leaving. I'm going to America.'

'Like two years ago. You're off to visit your sister, right? But then when you come back, your bicycle will be waiting for you down in the storeroom.'

'This time I'm not coming back. I have to move out of the apartment. I've already given notice, and I want to give away everything I can't take along with me.'

I was so upset that La Miss took me by the hand and got me to sit down next to her. 'I've stayed too long, really,' she said. 'More than ten years. And it wasn't worth it. I had to make this decision sooner or later. My friend in G— convinced me that the time has come. But I'm happy, you know? Leaving here is like starting a new life, putting all my troubles behind me.'

I wasn't close enough to her to be able to ask what these troubles were, nor did she tell me.

'I'm very sorry. I'll miss you,' I stammered.

'You needn't worry about the job,' La Miss said, squeezing my hand tight. 'I've arranged for my bank here to transfer to you every month the amount that I pay you now, as though you were still coming and looking after my linen. I've rounded it up to forty lire, so the calculations will be easier for them.'

This was more than double what she was paying me. All that money for doing nothing! I couldn't believe it— nothing like this had ever happened to me.

I plucked up the courage to ask, 'And for how long?'

'Forever. A small allowance. I've made the same arrangement for Filomena. That way you'll both have fond memories of me.'

I was speechless. And I thought of my grandmother's assessment—that La Miss was much richer than she seemed, and that she was a true lady.

Then she said to me: 'That corset I normally take travelling, the one I can hide money and documents in—it's old, the pockets are all torn...'

'Shall I repair it?' I asked.

'No. I need you to make me a new one, more durable, and with larger internal pockets. This time I need to carry with me all the dollars and pounds sterling that I normally keep in the safe.'

I was not surprised by this. It was an article of underwear, if you could call it that, that I had already made for a few elderly ladies who liked to travel. A bag could easily be snatched and was best used only for coins, a handkerchief, smelling salts—items of little value that it was necessary to keep close at hand. The corset was ideal for valuables. It would take a physical attack, in which the victim's clothes were torn off, before a thief could seize its contents. And this could not happen if one took care never to be alone in an isolated place.

My grandmother had made La Miss her old corset many years earlier. I had seen it occasionally when I was reorganising her drawers, and it was indeed in a rather poor state. And so, with money given to me by La Miss I went off to buy durable fabric, cotton tape, new hooks and new whalebone. I took out the paper pattern that I kept with all the others, cut and tacked the fabric, and took it to La Miss for measuring.

'That's good. But I need more pockets,' she said.

'If you fill it up too much it will become as stiff as a coat of armour,' I pointed out.

She laughed, 'A warrior's armour. I'm going to need it this time. It will be quite a battle to tear myself away from this place, away from—' She stopped herself. Then she stood up and started pacing nervously around the room. 'Enough!' she said, without looking my way, as though she was addressing the furniture and walls. 'Enough! It's over. Where has all my patience got me? He can't marry me, he says. And why not? What obstacles are in our way? Doesn't he judge me worthy? He can't marry me? He should have the courage to say he doesn't want to, that he's ashamed of me. But I'm the one who is ashamed of him. What does he think, that we're still living in the Middle Ages, in times of slavery? Does he want a secret concubine? Well, I'm a free woman. I can't abide that kind of jealousy. And I've got better things to do than stay here and be insulted. It's a big world; I'm still young; there are so many great things to see, to achieve. Does he think he's cut my wings? Well, he'll see if I still know how to fly!'

I looked at her wide-eyed, still holding the corset in my hand. My grandmother was right, then. There was a man behind all this. But who? Was I so naïve that in all those years I'd never realised? Filomena probably knew.

La Miss sat back down by my side. The outburst had calmed her down, and her eyes were lit up. 'I've got so many plans, you know? Things I've always postponed, friends I haven't seen for a long time. Before setting sail for America I want to visit Scotland and the Isle of Wight. The light there is very special, and my friend Ellen is expecting me so she can show me her darkroom. There's this new technique, portraits like in painting—I want to learn how to do it. I've wasted so much time...'

'You've done lots of great things here too,' I pointed out timidly.

She hugged me. No signora had ever done this. Except for Signorina Ester occasionally. They were two special women.

'Listen to me,' La Miss said in a serious tone. 'You're young, and you might happen to fall in love. But don't ever let any man be disrespectful to you, or stop you doing what you think is right and necessary, or what you like doing. It's your life, yours: remember that. Your only duty is to yourself.'

Strong words, the words of un'americana...

A woman must sacrifice herself, must suffer, and you can't have people talking behind your back. That was what I'd always been taught; that was how all the women I knew behaved. Was it not a huge sacrifice to give up my dreams about Signorino Guido? I thought of him with great fondness, and with regret, as though towards a person I would only ever see again in heaven, if it existed.

I reinforced the corset as La Miss had requested. I added more pockets. She'd lost so much weight lately that even after she had filled it right up with banknotes and coins she still had a slim silhouette. We did several trials. Once she had a jacket on you couldn't tell she was carrying all that money. She had been to the bank and withdrawn all her cash, and it was a tidy sum. I was amazed that with so much money in the house she still didn't lock the door.

Day after day she kept giving her things away to people who came to visit. News of her departure had spread through the city. The people who had visited her over the years dropped in to say goodbye. Barone Salai came too, one day when I was helping La Miss lay out her clothes in the vertical trunk that would be travelling with her. There were other people in the room as well, but when the Baron started pontificating everyone went quiet out of respect. He knew he had an audience and articulated every word as though he was an actor on stage. La Miss listened distractedly, continuing with her work.

'So you've decided,' said Barone Salai, looking disapprovingly at the bare walls, which still bore signs of the paintings that used to hang on them. 'A bad decision. You'll regret it.'

'I don't think so,' La Miss replied calmly. 'I'll be happy to see my home again, my sister, my friends.'

'You're leaving your best friends here,' the Baron said.

'That's not how they've behaved. I finally understood that.'

'You don't understand a thing. You're a stupid woman.'

'If that's what you think, you won't miss me.'

'No, that's right. I came to say goodbye because I'm leaving too. Three days before you. I'm going to Paris.'

'Have a good trip. Enjoy yourself.'

I couldn't help but think of Le Chabanais. Since the Provera scandal I was no longer innocent on such matters. The Baron, I thought, would certainly have no trouble finding the five-hundred-franc minimum fee.

After he left we continued packing her clothes, and then her hats into hat boxes.

The eve of La Miss's departure arrived. The luggage had already been sent to the station. All that remained in the apartment were a few pieces of furniture in the bedroom and the drawing room that the owner wanted to keep for himself. Filomena and I had finished sweeping the floors in the empty rooms, and she had left for the day. She would return before dawn with her husband and a hired carriage to accompany La Miss to the station. I stayed back a little longer to check that everything was in order. I did one more round of all the rooms. La Miss was anxious to leave the apartment just as she had found it. When I said goodbye she gave me a hug, a generous tip and a card on which she had written her address in New York. 'If one day you should think of emigrating, you must write to me,' she insisted. I cried a little. She did not. She was too happy, too excited, to become sentimental. Her jacket for the journey was ready, as was her corset, already filled with banknotes and coins.

'Promise me that tonight, at least, you'll lock the door,' I begged her.

'All right, I promise. But you go now. It's late. Good luck.' I dried my eyes on the corner of my apron as I walked down the stairs. Although she didn't want me to, I had decided that the next day I would go and wait for her at the station so I could say goodbye one last time.

That night I couldn't sleep. I would nod off for a few minutes, begin dreaming and wake up with a start. I dreamt of my grandmother, who was looking at me with a concerned expression, as though she wanted to warn me of danger. 'I know, I know,' I wanted to tell her, 'don't worry—I'll give no more thought to Guido Suriani.' But I kept waking up before I could utter the words. Until, finally, I decided to get out of bed. I lit a candle and picked up a book. The house was cold. I wrapped a shawl around me and sat by the window waiting for the light of dawn, so I could get dressed and go out as I had planned.

But the sun had not yet risen when I heard knocking on the window shutters that overlooked the street. It was Filomena.

'Come! Run!' she whispered in an anguished tone.
'Something terrible has happened. The police are there.
They want to talk to you.'

'Where? What happened?'

'At La Miss's place. She's dead.'

It felt like my heart had stopped. In a flash I put a skirt
and a bodice on over my nightgown, pulled my shawl
tightly around me because I felt chilled to the bone, and
ran after Filomena.

They found her, the officers wrote in their statement,
wearing a travel jacket made of grey gabardine, with a
strange corset underneath stuffed with Italian and foreign
banknotes, especially dollars. In one of the pockets, on the
left-hand side, was a considerable amount of sterling in
silver coins. With a bit of luck one of the coins could have
stopped the bullet that struck her heart. But no. Miss Lily
Rose Briscoe had been truly unfortunate, in life and in
death.

When I arrived at the apartment several police officers
were there, as well as Dr Bonetti, who lived opposite. The
eldest officer took me to see La Miss. She was in her
bedroom, laid out on the bed, with a sheet pulled up to her
chin, her hair neat. She looked like she was sleeping. Her
gabardine coat, corset and undershirt had been placed on
the nearby armchair.

'Do you recognise her?' the man asked kindly, holding
me by the shoulder in case I fainted. I'd seen myself in the

mirror of the chest of drawers: I was whiter than the sheet. But I did not faint. I felt like I was inside a glass ball, as though I was elsewhere watching the whole scene, myself included, from a great distance.

'Of course I recognise her,' I said. 'It's Miss Lily Rose Briscoe. I work—worked for her for the last ten years.'

'The maid says you were the last person to see her alive yesterday. Is that true? What time did you leave?'

'At eight-thirty. But what happened? She was absolutely fine. Did she have a stroke? Such a young woman. Was it her heart?'

'Her heart. Right. Didn't the maid tell you anything? She shot herself.'

I collapsed into the armchair, on top of La Miss's clothes, and felt her corset full of money poking into my back, the coins bumpy.

'It's not possible,' I said. 'I don't believe it. A thief must have got in. There was a lot of money in the house.'

'And there still is. Nothing is missing, according to the maid. Come through here and check for yourself.'

I followed him into the drawing room. It was an indescribable mess. La Miss's suitcase lay open and her things were scattered all over the place—on the floor, on the chairs, everywhere. Pages torn out of a book. Large and small banknotes. Chairs overturned. The velvet tablecloth with tassels was lying on the floor, as was the crystal vase full of jonquils, now lying in a small puddle of water. And at the foot of the armchair, the pistol.

'Don't touch that!' the officer ordered. 'We're waiting for the inspector to arrive.' They had drawn a white chalk outline around it.

'But it's obvious that someone got into the house. They fought,' I pointed out. It seemed very strange to me that before killing herself La Miss, all alone, would wreak such havoc.

'The door was locked. And there's no sign of forced entry through the windows. We've checked everywhere,' the officer said.

'La Miss sometimes had crises, attacks of hysteria. She'd throw things around, tear up books, break glasses,' said Filomena, who was standing by the door wringing her hands. I looked at her, astonished. In all those years I had never witnessed one of these crises, nor had I ever heard tell of them. 'I never told you because she was always embarrassed about it afterwards,' she explained to me. 'It would happen when she abused her drugs.'

'Don't talk like that. It was medicine to help her sleep. And she hadn't taken it in months.'

'What would you know? The officer found a dirty glass and the open bottle on her bedside table.'

During all this, the doctor had not said a word. I knew him; when my grandmother was still alive, we had turned overcoats for his wife once or twice. They were respectable people, the Bonettis, but had too many children to be able to afford to buy new clothes often.

'Did l'americana seem agitated when you left yesterday? Had she been complaining about anything?' the officers asked.

'No. She was relaxed. Happy. She had no reason to kill herself.'

'She wouldn't have come to you to talk about it,' Filomena said, interrupting me.

I couldn't understand her aggressive manner. My head began to spin. Someone got me a glass of water.

Meanwhile, the inspector had arrived, along with a police photographer. He got everyone to repeat how it happened. Filomena had found La Miss. She explained that her appointment with her employer was for six in the morning: the train was to depart at seven. But she had woken at four from a nightmare in which La Miss, in tears, was calling for her. 'I don't usually believe in that sort of thing—I'm not superstitious. But this dream was so strange. It still felt real even once I was awake. I got out of bed and, without disturbing my husband, I came to have a look. I live just around the corner.'

I was reminded of how at the same hour I'd dreamt of my grandmother looking concerned. She had not come to warn me about the student, but about La Miss, I thought to myself. And I felt immediately embarrassed—this was not the kind of nonsense to be relating to the police.

Filomena had run to La Miss's home and, unusually, had found the door locked. She had a copy of the key; she opened up, came inside and noticed the confusion at once.

One of her employer's shoes was lying on the ground, upside down, near the wardrobe. La Miss was in the drawing room, sitting in the armchair, head thrown backwards, eyes closed, unconscious. She was gasping for air.

'Was she wearing her nightdress?' the inspector asked.

'No, she was wearing her travelling clothes.'

'It was four in the morning and she hadn't yet gone to bed?! Or was she already up out of bed and dressed for the day?'

Filomena shrugged. She wasn't responsible for La Miss's strange habits. She'd seen a lot worse than that, she implied. She'd got quite a fright, and instead of going straight to her employer's aid, she ran across the street to knock on Dr Bonetti's door and had returned with him.

La Miss no longer seemed to be breathing, but there was no blood around, the doctor explained, so initially he thought she had fainted or had a heart attack that might still be treated. The two of them lifted her onto the bed, the doctor undid her jacket to allow her to breathe more easily and that's when they came upon the corset. He unhooked this as well and to his great astonishment discovered a bullet hole in her left breast. He held a feather to Miss Briscoe's mouth. It did not move. However, her body was neither cold nor stiff, he explained. This was why, at first, he had thought she had only fainted. How long had l'americana been dead? Difficult to say. Five minutes? Ten? Twenty? No more than thirty, but he couldn't say with any certainty because the large porcelain stove was lit and the drawing room was very hot.

'When I found her, she was still breathing—she was gasping for air,' Filomena repeated. 'And it didn't take you any more than five minutes to get here.'

'But how is it possible there was no blood?' the inspector asked.

'It can happen,' the doctor explained. 'Especially if the bullet also went through the lung, because then the blood can collect in there. The autopsy will tell. But that won't change much.'

Though Filomena was convinced it was a case of suicide, she was careful not to say so, in order to protect La Miss from scandal and from the church's condemnation. Dr Bonetti had sent her to fetch the police. One of the men, upon entering the drawing room, noticed that l'americana's revolver lay at the foot of the armchair, next to the jonquils. The inspector got the maid and me to say in our statements that we had seen it before, that La Miss had bought it recently and that she kept it in the drawer of her bedside table. 'So she could shoot herself when she got the urge,' Filomena commented in a disapproving tone that I found offensive. If her employer was still alive she wouldn't have dared speak like this. I couldn't understand how Filomena could be so convinced that it was a case of suicide. Just because the door was locked?

The doctor was not so sure. He took the inspector into the bedroom, picked up her jacket and corset from the armchair, and showed them to him. I followed, so I saw them too. They were intact. There was no hole, no blood-stain, not even a small burn. How had the bullet got through to her heart?

'La Miss was very fond of that jacket,' Filomena said, cutting in. 'She must've unbuttoned it and moved it aside before shooting herself.'

'And then done it back up again? And what about the corset? It's very stiff, and it closes with a row of hooks. I had trouble undoing it,' the doctor said.

'But she was practical. And she didn't die at once—when I found her she was still breathing. She might have buttoned it back up again,' Filomena insisted. The inspector wrote everything down. He asked us to look around carefully and to let him know if anything was missing. He wanted to know who else had the keys. Nothing was missing, and only Filomena had a set of keys.

That her clothing was undamaged was just too strange, however. The doctor refused to sign a suicide certificate. The inspector decided to open an investigation and got the apartment all sealed up. Filomena protested—she wanted to save Miss Briscoe's reputation; she was afraid of rumours. Not to humour her but to avoid warning the guilty party, the inspector decided to put out the news that La Miss, on the eve of her departure, had died of a heart attack, and he asked us to keep quiet about what had happened.

This meant the church gave permission for a religious funeral, which was attended by all the most important figures in the city—highly placed families, people who knew La

Miss well, along with those who only knew her by sight. They came more out of curiosity, I think, than affection—in order to check up on one another, and to see who turned up and who didn't. Barone Salai was not there, naturally, but everybody knew he had left for Paris. Yes, he was one of the most frequent visitors to the home of La Miss, but nobody expected that he would return from so far away for her funeral. At the end of the procession was a large group of poor people like me, humble folk, those who had worked for La Miss, and whom she had trusted and treated cordially, never 'keeping her distance' as the middle classes would have liked. Poor La Miss was buried in our cemetery.

Today nobody goes to visit her grave, not even Filomena and yet, like me, she continues to receive her allowance every month—and hers must not have been small like mine, because she no longer works as a maid and she gets her clothes at Belledame, though you can see from a mile away that she's not a lady. In fact, not only do I not know how much her allowance is, I don't even know what monthly salary La Miss paid her when she was alive or if she left her something in her will. However, every time I go to visit Nonna I also take a flower for l'americana. I stop in front of that gravestone, recall her fondly, and think, 'Oh, if the dead could talk!' Even after all these years, I do not believe she committed suicide.

Two months after her death the investigation was closed. The two most important witnesses were Filomena and me.

And somewhat less important was Dr Bonetti, who had not spent much time around La Miss and could not say he knew her well.

My statement and Filomena's contradicted each other. I declared that, yes, La Miss had in the past had crises of melancholy and depression, and that at those times she needed to take medicine to help her sleep, but that she had always behaved reasonably. And in any case, those moments of crisis belonged to the past. Since her return from G—, La Miss had been well, serene; not just serene, but happy, full of big plans. She was eagerly anticipating her imminent trip and her return to her homeland, where she would embrace her sister once more. I was certain, I would swear to God, that she had no thought of suicide. I believed, I insisted, that she had been killed by someone. Someone who had burst in on her in her nightdress, shot her and then put her into her clothes. Her nightshirt had never been found, the officers objected. It wouldn't take much, I replied, to scrunch it up—it was made of light cambric—put it in a pocket and take it away.

But the door was locked. She might have opened it, if it was somebody she knew. Or perhaps it was such a frequent visitor, somebody so trusted that they had another copy of the keys.

'These are just theories, not facts. Tell us only what you know for sure, what you saw,' they admonished me.

Filomena declared under oath that La Miss had always had a very nervous disposition, that there were often scenes, that she took drugs, always, right up until the end. That in her presence, she had often threatened to kill herself at the slightest thing. Especially over love affairs. She had frequent liaisons. No, she was not respectable like Italian ladies. She was *un'americana*—they have a whole other set of morals over there. La Miss often fell in love with men who were unworthy of her, from the lower classes, and she even paid them and showered them with gifts. Then she would regret it; she would feel betrayed, ashamed, and want to die. She had bought the pistol for that purpose and had confided in Filomena about it. 'I should have taken it from her, I know. I should have thrown it away, got rid of it. But I didn't believe those threats and besides, she was my boss.' They asked her if she could name these lads. She replied, 'Not all of them. Besides, they'd deny it. And none of them had the keys, I'm sure of that.' She declared that La Miss was obsessed with the cleanliness of her clothing, and that she would do anything to avoid getting it stained or dirty, even getting undressed, shooting herself and getting dressed again. She said I didn't know La Miss well, I couldn't know everything about her; after all, I only saw her once a week, and didn't live alongside her every day like she did.

Couldn't the investigators see that Filomena was lying? Why was she lying—to protect somebody? But who? I had no idea, and I couldn't come up with any theory. I was certain of one thing: that the story about La Miss and the young men, that she would pay them, was invented. How could Filomena make such terrible accusations against someone who could no longer defend herself, someone who had always been so good to her? But how could I prove her wrong?

The doctor declared that when he arrived La Miss was dead—for how long, he couldn't say. She was dressed from head to toe, her travel jacket buttoned up to the neck. And her jacket and underwear were intact, with no sign whatsoever of the gunshot. The money in her corset was untouched. He maintained that it was unlikely that the poor woman had the time and strength to get dressed or even to button up her clothes after the shot had reached her heart. But he could not completely exclude the possibility. At the point of death people could do the most incredible things. He knew this from experience.

The investigators believed, or wanted to believe, Filomena's story and the doctor's doubts. They told me I was too overwrought, and that they had received information about me: they knew I read novels. They advised me to keep my imagination in check.

The death was filed as a suicide. The bishop at that point behaved generously, not demanding that Miss Briscoe's grave be removed from the cemetery. If you go looking, you'll still find her there.

The seals on the apartment were removed, and the owner asked Filomena and me, since we had worked there for so many years, to do the final clean and put everything back in order, removing all trace of what had happened. After which, he would get the rooms painted and look for another tenant.

To be able to sweep more easily, we moved the few pieces of furniture remaining and mopped the floors. One of my tasks was to take care of the little room next to the bedroom. There wasn't much to do apart from clean the floor. The room had been cleared some time earlier; the night before the tragedy I had checked it one last time, and had seen that it was empty. So I was astonished to see something sparkling on the ground in the corner, amid the fluff that had accumulated during those two months in which the place had been all closed up. I bent to pick it up. It was a gold-framed monocle, its velvet cord ruined by dust.

I called Filomena in. I held it out to her in the palm of my hand. I didn't know what to think. 'All sorts of people came to this house,' she said. 'It was worse than a brothel. Who knows how long that thing was lying there and we never noticed.'

'I'd have noticed,' I protested. 'That last night, before I said goodbye to La Miss, I saw very clearly that there was nothing in here.'

'You read too many novels. What's got into your head—who do you think you are? Don't you remember what the sergeant said? Try to keep your imagination in check or you'll end up in trouble.'

She took the monocle from my hand and threw it out, along with the rest of the rubbish.

My Tin of Illusions

'WE POOR FOLK need to help each other out,' Nonna always used to say, 'because if we wait for the rich to come to our aid in times of need, we'll be in trouble.' For her part, she never refused to share a piece of bread, even if it was the last we had, with a neighbour who was struggling, or to stay awake watching over a sick child while its mother finished a job that absolutely had to be done by the next morning. She had a large circle of friends in the neighbourhood, women on their own like her—elderly women who had lost their family in the epidemic, young widows with little children, or young mothers who had husbands they couldn't count on because he drank or couldn't hold down a job. There was nobody to whom she wouldn't offer a shovelful of charcoal, a piece of advice, a bowl of soup, a scrap of fabric to patch a skirt that was falling to pieces. She was reluctant to seek help herself, because she knew their abject misery, and besides, she had her pride: ever since she was young, it had meant a lot to her to be able to look after herself and her own. I had picked up from her the same need for independence—I absorbed it from her example without ever realising it. If it was absolutely essential for me to ask a favour of somebody, I tried to repay them as soon as possible. For example, in the case of my neighbour who lived off what she could earn taking in ironing, when every so often I needed to ask her to cook me some soup, or clean the stairs on my behalf, or send her little girl to make a delivery, anytime I couldn't pay her I tried to get her some work, or I would pass on to her an old piece of clothing that had been given to me by one of my clients.

Zita and Assuntina were truly poor. There had been no man on the scene since their husband and father, respectively, had been killed in a brawl between drunks. Mother and daughter lived in a *basso*, a damp hovel below street level with no windows, which you reached by going down three steps. In such a perpetually dark environment it was not easy to iron the linen of the upper classes and deliver it back to them immaculately white, unsullied by soot, and not burnt by the sparks that went flying when you took the hot iron out of the embers. Garments that also needed to be starched, like men's shirts, were a real problem. Zita needed to have at least three irons always at the ready on the stove so that she wouldn't waste precious time waiting for one that had cooled down with use to heat back up again. If she'd had a courtyard with a water source, where she could keep a washtub, she'd have been able to offer a full service and earn a little more; instead, she had to collect the wet linen from the washerwoman.

She had a few regular clients, most of whom I had got for her—including La Miss, who had been her most generous client—and that was how she made ends meet. Only just, though—often she and her daughter ate only stale bread without so much as a drop of oil. For them, dried beans with cabbage or roasted eggplant, which we townspeople called 'poor man's meat', was the kind of luxury they could only afford on a Sunday. If I hadn't, as I said, passed on and altered for them a few old clothes from the ladies I worked for, both mother and daughter would have gone around dressed in rags.

After La Miss died there was a kind of imbalance between us, an unpleasant situation. Zita now had to manage without the income that, although only a modest sum, she had counted on, whereas I, after certain bureaucratic processes had run their course, began to receive my monthly allowance of forty lire from the bank. Naturally, this was not enough to live on, but it made things a lot easier, giving me a chance to breathe in a way I had never imagined, particularly because I didn't need to do any work to earn it.

Because of the delay, the first eight months' worth arrived all at once at the end of December—three hundred and twenty lire, a real fortune, which tempted me to indulge in the most ridiculous dreams. I would be able to buy a subscription to the opera—just a seat in the gods, but I would be able to see every opera, and not have to rack my brains trying to choose the one or two I could afford tickets for. Or I could enrol in evening classes and learn to write well, so that I wouldn't be ashamed if I needed to write a letter. I could also learn a bit of history, some geography, some arithmetic. Maybe I could even get my primary-school certificate, even though it would be of no use in my work. I didn't know if my allowance would be enough to pay for school, or if I would have time to attend—that's how unrealistic a plan it was—but receiving all that money at once went to my head. I also had more modest desires. To take a trip on a train, for example. I had never set foot on one, though I'd seen them arrive and depart many times. Just a short trip. Perhaps just as far as G—. I knew you could get there and back in a day and not to need to spend money staying the night. Or perhaps I could get as far as the port city of P— and finally see the sea. But then I would need to stay the night. Would there be enough money for a modest hotel? I was afraid to go alone to one of the cheap little *pensioni* I had heard Signorina Gemma talk about—people couldn't be trusted; what if some unknown man got into my room? Perhaps there was a convent in P— where I could stay the night. Yes, except how would I convince the nuns that I was a respectable young girl and not some madwoman off looking for adventures?

While I was building all these castles in the sky it also occurred to me that I didn't deserve this money, as I was doing nothing to earn it, and that I ought to be sharing it with Zita. But I confess that I quickly drove away such thoughts: it wasn't hard to find justifications. La Miss had left that money to me; I'd be offending her memory if I gave it to somebody else. She knew that other women washed and ironed her linen, that I wasn't the one doing it. Why didn't she leave them an allowance as well? Because she didn't know their names, a little voice in my head hinted, because she had never seen their faces, because I had always taken care of everything. So what? The city was full of poor people. Was I now supposed to share everything I earned through hard work with a bunch of strangers? Wasn't it enough that I had clothed mother and daughter from head to toe, altering hand-me-downs that Signora Carrera, the engineer's wife, had passed on? Thick, warm clothes: Assuntina no longer needed to protect herself from the cold with a little knitted shawl like the other little girls in the alley. Instead she had a woollen coat with velvet lining, like the daughter of real signori. Originally, there had been beautiful frog fasteners on the front but I removed them when I took it in, as this seemed an inappropriate level of elegance for the daughter of a woman who made her living taking in ironing. Assuntina liked that coat so much that she wore it only rarely, to keep it nice. She preferred to wrap herself in one of my old shawls, perhaps in part so that she didn't look too different from the other little girls in the alleyway. I also managed to get her a pair of winter shoes in good condition, only two sizes too big, which with a pair of woollen socks fitted her perfectly and would last through to the following year. Zita couldn't stop thanking me; she'd have liked at the very least to repay the hours I'd spent unpicking and altering, sewing hems, shifting buttons. But I knew she didn't have a penny and so I would say magnanimously, 'You'll be able to make it up to me some time.' I hoped I'd be able to convince the engineer's wife to get my friend to do her ironing, thus replacing the work she had lost with the death of La Miss. But for the moment the signora had a washerwoman who took care of ironing as well. She was happy with her and saw no need to change.

That winter had been long and cold. Assuntina had fallen ill with pneumonia and the doctor said it was a miracle she had survived. Now that the better weather had arrived, she was back outside playing on the footpath, with a red scarf that had belonged to Clara wrapped tightly around her neck. She did the occasional delivery for me and I would give her a few coins. At the Saturday market I bought her a gift—a jar of honey for her cough.

I was in such a muddle over how to use my allowance that I ended up deciding to postpone any decision and ask Signorina Ester's advice when she returned from her ump-teenth trip. I locked away the three hundred and twenty lire, plus the money that was now coming in every month, in my savings tin, which I was now calling the wishing tin, and concentrated on working. Luckily, there was no shortage of orders—my clientele had gradually increased—

Signora Carrera had spread the word and a lot of people were now asking for children's clothes, not only costumes for Carnival or for performances, but also school smocks, shirts, shorts, jackets with frog fasteners, and undergarments. If I wanted, I could have specialised. But my experience with Nonna, that time we gave up all other work to concentrate on the Artonesi layette, made me wary. There were some families I'd been working for over many years, families made up only of the elderly, who paid well and on time. The Delsorbos, for example. They were extravagant people; Nonna didn't like them, though she had never wanted to tell me the reason why. She had been in domestic service with them many years earlier, before I was born, but only for a few months. She discovered something she didn't like and had preferred to leave. But she still accepted sewing jobs from them: she couldn't afford to turn them down. The Delsorbos had always behaved well towards me. Not like those ladies who, all smiles and simpering, would say when I finished a job, 'Come back in a week and I'll give you what I owe you.' And when I returned, would snort, 'Gosh, so eager!' And then would make me come back three or four more times before they paid me. I knew they'd pay up eventually, but meanwhile the grocers had stopped giving me anything on credit, and I needed paraffin and candles. What's more, I was sure they had the money, right there in their purse, so why make me suffer? Why treat me like some annoying beggarwoman harassing them? To keep me in my place?

Not the Delsorbos. They would pay me the agreed sum on the very day I finished a job. Quirica would give me the money wrapped in leftover pieces of fabric. Not many people did this. To me, those offcuts were precious; there were lots of things I could make out of them, from simple patches to pincushions and pockets hidden inside skirts, and if I patiently sewed them together, matching textiles and colours tastefully, I could even make them into cushions, quilts, bedspreads. 'Take them, take them!' Quirica would say. 'What do you think a couple of poor old biddies like us are going to do with them? Can't you see the state of our fingers?' Hers were deformed by arthritis, but she moved around the kitchen as though she were still young, and she ironed Don Urbano's shirts like not even Zita would be able to do at her very best. Quirica was the 'old servant'. This was what she called herself, though out of respect I would never have used the term in her presence. I don't know how old she was. She had already been in domestic service for several years at the time of the unification. There was also a 'young servant' in the Delsorbo household, Rinuccia, who was at least fifty. Her hands, too, were in such a bad state that she couldn't handle a needle.

The household observed a strict separation of servants and signori, as though they lived on two different planets. The borders between the two territories had to be crossed by the maids when they did the cleaning, served at table, and opened and closed the shutters, but once these tasks had been carried out the two women retired quickly to the other side of the corridor, to the area with the linen room, wardrobes and an ironing board, their bedroom, the kitchen and the pantry. They spent their lives in the kitchen, which smelled of smoked sausages, burnt wood and menthol, because Quirica suffered from asthma and was constantly smoking special cigarettes that helped with her breathing. They never left the house except for Sunday mass; daily groceries and any other goods that were required were delivered to their door by shop boys.

Their employers, on the other hand, never crossed that corridor. They had at their disposal a large drawing room, a dining room, a study for Don Urbano, several bedrooms and a bathroom with running water, equipped with all modern conveniences. There were only the two of them left now: the very ancient mother, Donna Licinia, who was almost a hundred and had been a widow since time immemorial, and the son, Don Urbano, who was the wrong side of seventy. Once upon a time there had also been a daughter, born many years after her brother, but she had married somebody from out of town and had gone to live elsewhere. The mother had not suffered greatly over this separation, Quirica told me, because her son and heir had always been her favourite. In fact, he had never been permitted to marry, so that she would not be left alone. Don Urbano had had various fiancées but Donna Licinia had put an end to the match every time.

'What about grandchildren?' I asked. 'Didn't her daughter give her any grandchildren?'

'Donna Vittoria, may she rest in peace, married late; all her children were born sickly and didn't survive,' the old servant explained. 'But she never resigned herself, or at least her husband didn't.' And Donna Vittoria had fallen pregnant one more time, past forty years, and died in childbirth. The baby, unlike his brothers and sisters, was born healthy and thrived. His grandmother, Donna Licinia, would have liked to have him to herself, so she could bring him up as a Delsorbo, but the father of this motherless child was against it and the disagreement drove the two families apart. Once he grew up, the lad had got into the habit of visiting his grandmother and uncle every so often; he was affectionate, handsome, polite, intelligent, and the two old folks were very proud of him. Quirica was too, and she was certain that grandmother and uncle had both chosen him as the beneficiary of their wills. He was, after all, their only heir.

The Delsorbos were of aristocratic stock, from an ancient line. They didn't have titles like count or baron or marquis; the only embellishment they could use was the descriptive term 'nobleman' or 'noblewoman', and the title don before their name, but due to the antiquity of their bloodline and their wealth they considered themselves superior to all the other nobles of the city. Quirica, too, was convinced of this, and proud. She had been born in an extremely poor village of the interior and at fifteen had come to work as a maid for the Delsorbos. Her devotion to the family was religious, and she reeled off their genealogy to me as though reciting pages from her missal.

I was never summoned to sew at the Delsorbo home. Quirica would hand me the fabric for sheets and undergarments for me to take home, where I would carry out the work and then deliver it once it was finished. On a couple of occasions, though, they had asked me to do a little bit of upholstery—the lining of armchairs and cushions, the pelmet for some curtains, a damask bedspread for the guestroom. They weren't afraid to entrust such precious fabrics to me, as my grandmother had won their trust with her honesty and expertise as a seamstress, and even many years later that worked in my favour. In those circumstances, I needed to take measurements, and that meant crossing the hallway border and penetrating the signori's quarters. Dark rooms, with the shutters always closed, red velvet all around, heavy silverware, enormous paintings in frames of the finest gold. A couple of times I had glimpsed Donna Licinia through a half-open door—seated in her armchair, as rigid as a statue, thin, wizened and dressed in black. She had never stopped wearing black, Quirica explained to me, though more than fifty years had passed since she became a widow. However, even though she never left the house, every day Donna Licinia would put on all her pearl jewellery, the only kind permissible during mourning—pendant earrings, a high collar with an amethyst clasp, a brooch on her chest to keep her fichu in place, and a four-string bracelet. She looked like Our Lady of Sorrows, one of those

Madonna statues they have in the cathedral that they only pull out on Good Friday, with seven swords to the heart, and decked out in all the finery the faithful can offer.

Don Urbano, on the other hand—he had greeted me cordially, even though he didn't know who I was—was an elderly potbellied gentleman, not tall, dressed in the latest fashion. Around the house he wore a Garibaldi-style velvet smoking cap but when he went out he put on a straw hat in summer and a bowler hat in winter. Unlike his mother and the maids, he was out all the time, sitting in the glass cage of the Crystal Palace smoking a cigar, visiting the most important families in the city, at the noblemen's casino playing cards, at the hippodrome for the horse races, at the theatre, at the café chantant. He was what I later learnt the French call a *viveur*. His mother gave him complete liberty now that he too was old and no longer talked of marrying, and she didn't even protest when he stayed out the whole night. Where—in an expensive hotel? At the house of friends? Was he having a secret affair? In telling me this, Quirica would wink, as though it went without saying where her boss spent those nights, but I couldn't begin to imagine and I didn't care. 'The richer they are, the madder they are,' my grandmother had taught me, and also: 'Every madman is crazy in his own way.' Why try to understand something that had nothing to do with me?

After Carnival, Signorina Ester had returned and had sent for me so that she could give me the little gift she brought back for me every time. Nothing valuable, just something to show that during the trip she had thought of me. This time it was an album with hand-coloured photographs of the most important monuments in Europe. We talked of this and that; she called in Enrica so that I could see how much she had grown, and said that I would soon need to lengthen all her pinafores. I summoned up the courage to tell her about my desire to make a trip to P—, if only I could find somewhere safe to stay the night without spending too much money. Signorina Ester said she thought this an excellent idea, and a distant cousin of hers, a nun, worked at a home for the scrofulous that her order had built right on the seafront. She could ask her to put me up not just for one night but for three or four if I wished, without charge. The nuns of P— could not refuse such a request. Every year her father made a generous donation to the home.

Once Signorina Ester decided on something, she didn't spend long thinking about it. She wrote to her cousin and ten days later she called for me so that she could show me the reply. The nuns would be very happy to host me, and I could bring a friend. 'Perhaps they think it's not prudent for a young girl to travel alone,' Ester said, and laughed. For a week I would have at my disposal a small guestroom with two beds. And if I wanted, I could have my meals with the patients in the refectory. That way I would only need to pay for the train ticket.

A friend? I had no friend my age who could leave her work or who could afford the ticket, and I wanted to enjoy the experience alone. I wanted to walk along the beach contemplating the horizon and, as I had seen in a painting, collecting seashells and daydreaming while gulls flew overhead. Dreaming of what? Of whom? Dreaming was very dangerous, this I knew: I couldn't afford to dream. And besides, wasn't the very sight of the sea the realisation of a dream?

I had a job that was going to take a few more days to finish. I decided that I would set off the following Monday and return on the Thursday, and I wrote to the nuns to this effect. I was quite emotional as I packed the straw bag in which I would carry my things: a change of underwear, combs and hairpins, soap, a shawl that could double as a blanket, my sewing pouch and a few handkerchiefs to work on, just so that I wouldn't be left twiddling my thumbs if it was rainy. I must confess that before packing the handkerchiefs, I had at first put in a novel, but then I thought that this might not make a good impression on the nuns— some sewing would be better. I would have to content myself with the missal as reading material. So as not to turn up empty-handed, I also took along, wrapped in tissue paper, two doilies I had made using a new stitch I'd read about in a magazine.

Sunday arrived. I was excited, impatient. I had checked the train timetable a thousand times, and had bought my ticket three days earlier. I got the house in order, carefully scrubbed the kitchen sink and swept under the bed. With a start I realised that I had been so caught up in preparations that I had not arranged for anyone to replace me cleaning the stairs. That was all I needed—for my trip to the seaside to end in eviction! Fortunately, I still had time to fix this; there was no risk that Zita would refuse the job and the unexpected extra income.

I rushed across to her place. The door that led onto the street was wide open to let a bit of air in. Assuntina, who had started school that year—though she had hardly ever attended, because of her pneumonia—was sitting on the step in the draught, the red scarf wrapped around her head. She was tracing lines in her exercise book with some difficulty. And she was coughing.

A phrase flashed through my head that I'd heard Signora Carrera say as she was taking Clara's woollen jumper off before putting her in the bathtub. 'You're as skinny as an Indian fakir,' she had said, tickling the little girl's tummy. Clara had sneezed. 'Ha, there you go. You know what? At the end of the month, school or no school, we're going to go visit Nonna. You need to breathe a bit of sea air—it'll do you good.'

It would do Assuntina good, too. Before I had the chance to change my mind, I blurted out: 'Tomorrow I'm going to P— for a few days. Do you want to come with me?' The nuns wouldn't protest: they had offered hospitality for two. And train tickets were half price for children.

Zita didn't know how to express her gratitude. Both for the cleaning job and for the invitation to her daughter. They had never travelled by train either, or seen the sea. The mother would have liked to join us, I could see that in her eyes. But she couldn't leave her work, couldn't skip deliveries, or she'd lose customers. And besides, who would mop the stairs and hallway of our building? The owner didn't mind if occasionally I got someone to stand in for me, but if she'd found a single muddy footprint on the marble steps, a single cobweb on one of the ceilings…I didn't dare think about it.

And there was the cost of the ticket to consider. Zita knew she couldn't ask me to pay for her as well as for her daughter.

She thanked me with tears in her eyes and prepared a few things for Assuntina, which she popped inside a cushion cover, since they didn't have any straw baskets like mine. She wouldn't let her daughter bring along the velvet-lined coat, for fear that she would ruin it; instead she packed her heavy shawl, which would also mean that she wouldn't get any strange looks travelling with me. She was even thoughtful enough to prepare us two packages to eat on the train: chickpea and onion farinata, and bread. The trip would take more than five hours and I had not given any thought to our need to eat.

On the Monday we set off at eight in the morning. We had arrived half an hour early at the station and taken our spots on the wooden seats in third class, which were already almost all occupied by people travelling for work. We, on the other hand, were going on holidays, I thought proudly, like real signori. Who knows if my grandmother, in her most secret thoughts, had ever dared to wish for, even imagine, such a thing?

As we waited for departure, I placed my bag in my seat and leant out the window to watch the remaining tardy passengers hurrying towards the carriages. To my astonishment, I recognised Filomena and her husband, dressed like signori—she was wearing a big hat—followed by a porter carrying two large, heavy suitcases, brand-new. Where were they going? I saw them board the first-class carriage. I had always known that Filomena loved life's luxuries and envied the rich who could afford them. Was it possible that she had decided to spend all her money on that charade? But this was none of my business. Just as it was none of hers that I had decided to treat myself to a little holiday by the sea.

The stationmaster raised his paddle; the train emitted a long whistle. When the locomotive began to move, puffing steam, Assuntina squeezed my hand tight. Since her mother had woken her that morning, she had not uttered a word. She hadn't cried when they said goodbye; she pretended to be busy checking that her bundle contained everything she needed, that her primer and exercise book were kept separate from her food package so that they didn't get greasy.

Now we were travelling. The countryside passed by on either side: trees, cows at pasture, strange granite formations, donkeys loaded with baskets and saddlebags, artichoke and watermelon plantations, farmers hard at work. My little travel companion stared out at all this, her eyes wide, her nose glued to the windowpane. For her, a city girl born and raised in the alleyways, everything was new, especially the vast sky over the fields, the white clouds that were travelling just like us but much higher up, the cawing birds, the brightness, and the juniper bushes bent over by the wind. I had occasionally left the city, but I had never gone far, only ever on foot or on a donkey-drawn wagon to visit some acquaintance of my grandmother's in the country, and more recently to visit the Proveras. But this time was different, if only because of the speed—the trees that seemed to be hurtling towards us, the rapid changes in landscape that you only ever glimpsed, because no sooner had you spotted a yoke of oxen or a hawthorn bush than, whoosh, it had already disappeared. I was happy I had followed my impulse—this was not a waste of money; travel broadens the mind. Signorina Ester had been right.

We arrived in G—. From what we could see out the window, the city was not so different from our own, though if you were to wander its streets, crossing from one end to the other, it would be clear that it was larger. But we did not get off the train. It only stopped in the station for ten minutes, during which nobody left our compartment and no new traveller entered. I was watching through the window to see who alighted, as I was curious to see where Filomena was headed, but I didn't see her. Puffing steam—every time, Assuntina looked at that white smoke like it was some kind of miracle—the locomotive recommenced its journey and in a few minutes we were in the country once again.

After a few hours we came within sight of the sea, still just a narrow dark-blue strip on the horizon. I knew it from the many paintings I had admired in the homes of Signorina Ester, La Miss and other ladies I worked for. And from illustrations and photographs in magazines. I wondered whether, up close, it was really so blue; did it move, would there be waves and would the crest of the waves have white foam like in paintings of naval battles? And would there be sandy beaches with seashells? I had promised Assuntina seashells. I had told her that she'd be able to collect as many as she wanted and bring them home. The people sitting next to us in the compartment were used to the spectacle and hardly looked out at all. Instead they were trying to defeat boredom by striking up conversations with their neighbours. I responded to their questions in monosyllables to discourage too much familiarity. Right now, I was happy to be travelling in company—Assuntina's presence protected me from being pestered, even though she, completely absorbed by what she saw out the window, behaved as though she didn't know me, as though she was deaf and mute. One woman had asked me if she was my daughter and, so as not to have to go into an explanation, I had said yes and Assuntina had not reacted, not even with a conspiratorial smile.

She did not even smile when finally, at a curve in the tracks, the sea leapt out at us very close, immense, more green than blue, and twinkling in the rays of the sun. I hadn't imagined it like that, alive, like the spine of some huge sleeping animal, even though there was no longer any wind and the surface had barely a ripple. Without turning around Assuntina said under her breath, 'You can't see the fish.' But the woman sitting next to me heard her and laughed. 'Not yet. But when you go on a boat you'll see them, oh yes, you'll see them, all right. And then, if you dive in, you'll be able to catch them in your hands, that's how many there are. You know how to swim, don't you, little one?'

Assuntina didn't reply, she just looked at me, her eyes like two saucers. A boat? Diving in? Swimming? We hadn't spoken of any of this, only about seeing it, seeing the water. I could tell that she didn't want anyone to notice, but she was frightened as well as fascinated. I sat her in my lap, felt how thin and small she was under her woollen dress and shawl, and thought about how the sea wind might blow her right away.

'It's still too cold to get in the water,' I told her, 'don't worry.' And I took my lunch out of my basket and encouraged her to do the same.

It was early afternoon when we arrived. As I stepped off the train I looked around for Filomena with some curiosity, and saw her and her husband heading towards the carriages waiting to take passengers to the port. So they were taking a ship, travelling far away, perhaps overseas. She could stay away, for all I cared; I wouldn't miss her—I had not appreciated her behaviour during the investigation, or the lies she had told about La Miss. And to what end? So that the inspector would find her more interesting?

As for Assuntina and me, everything went smoothly, despite my fears. A nun came to meet us at the station and accompany us to the home, which was right on the beach. From our little room in the guest quarters, looking out over the sea, you could hear the coming and going of the water like a gentle breath, even with the French doors closed. That sound kept us company every night of our holiday. During daylight hours, we were always out in the open air, and when night fell we warmed ourselves in front of the big stove in the large hall of the women's refectory, along with the nuns and the patients. There were all ages, but many were little girls, all dressed in an identical grey-striped smock and with shaven heads; I don't know why. After our first meal in company, Assuntina found her tongue, and began to bombard me with questions about everything she saw. She responded politely to the nuns and the other women, while with little girls, it wasn't long before she was once again that bold little devil from the alleyways, with her thousand street games— playing tag, skipping, throwing stones, but also spitting and swearing. I had to take her away into our room and give her a good talking-to—if she made a bad impression on our hosts, we would have to return immediately to L—. She made promises, and even cried a little, but she couldn't help herself: having so much space at her disposal, so much fresh air…it was as though she was drunk on it all.

Every so often, seeing her so wild and unmanageable, I would regret bringing her along with me. Before agreeing to take me in, the nuns had asked Ester for information about me, and they knew I was not married. They thought Assuntina worked for me, that I had brought an apprentice along with me. This was because of the burn marks she had on her hands. Among other tasks, little girls who worked for dressmakers were required to keep the irons always at the ready. When they saw her appear in the refectory with her primer and her exercise book, they were astonished. I had to tell them about Zita and our neighbourly relationship, and about how Assuntina, who was not related to me, needed to recover from pneumonia. 'Truly a good deed!' the mother superior said warmly. 'But just a few days won't do her much good. You can tell her mother, though, that if she makes a request to our house in L—, bringing along a medical certificate and explaining the situation, she can send her to stay with us for free for the season. I examined her neck—she's not scrofulous yet, but she's well on the way. In fact, you know what—you can leave her here with us so that she doesn't have to make the trip twice. I trust you. You can send me the documents in the post.'

I could see that Assuntina was happy. The meals in the refectory were abundant and she was eating heartily. She was sleeping happily in a soft, warm bed next to mine, and had already made many friends. I told her about the mother superior's proposal and asked her if she wanted to stay. I would explain to Zita why I had left her in P—.

She looked cross. 'You said we'd be going back on Thursday.'

'Yes, but we can change plans.'

'No. I don't want to. I want to go back home, back to Mamma.'

'Mamma would be happy for you to stay. It would do you good, your pneumonia wouldn't come back.'

'If I stay they'll cut my hair. I want to go back to Mamma.'

There was no way of convincing her, and I didn't want to take responsibility for forcing her without first speaking to Zita. So I went to the station and bought our return tickets for Thursday afternoon as planned.

Apart from my constantly feeling nervous about Assuntina's unpredictable behaviour, the holiday had gone well, though it hadn't been as exhilarating as in my dreams. I had strolled along the sand and breathed in air that smelled so different from city air. I had even collected seashells. But this had not given me a special happiness; nothing had changed inside me. There was always that niggling thought that would pop into my head and that I would hasten to drive away: Signorino Guido was certainly not thinking of me, and I must not think of him. He would only hurt me.

The day of our departure I woke a little before dawn, suddenly, as though somebody had touched me on the shoulder. The bed next to mine was empty. The French doors leading to the beach were ajar, and a cold draft was coming in.

Assuntina! I got out of bed, wrapped my shawl around me and hurried out onto the wooden walkway that separated the building from the beach, looking towards the sea. There she was, the disobedient little wretch—I would break every bone in her body when she came back to the shore: I'd beat her to a pulp. I had never reacted so violently to anything, not even that time I'd had to defend myself from Barone Salai. I felt a sense of tragedy, of fatalism. 'This time she'll fall seriously ill—she's going to die on me,' I thought furiously. 'What will I tell Zita?'

I saw her flannel nightshirt—an old one of Clara's that I'd taken in—lying on the sand. No shoes—she had thoughtlessly gone out barefoot, and now she was splashing about in shallow water with her hair fanned out over her shoulders. The light of the last few stars was reflected in the black water. I threw my shawl on the ground so it wouldn't get wet, pulled up my skirt and ran like a fury into water that came up to my knees, grabbing Assuntina by the hair.

'Do you want to die?' I shouted, shaking her. 'You'll catch your death!'

It was cold, and the girl's wet, slippery arms slid out of my grasp, but I could feel she had goose bumps. I dragged her to shore and wrapped the shawl around her.

'What on earth were you thinking?'

'I wanted to see if you can catch fish in your hands.'

I couldn't slap her because I had my hands full keeping hold of her. I carried her into the bedroom and threw her on the bed. Because the shawl was now wet, I started rubbing her dry with the sheets. She kept quiet. What worried me most of all was her wet hair. Fortunately, the nuns were already in the chapel for matins. The fire had been lit in the kitchen and the nun in charge of cooking let us in and set us up near the door of the stove, in front of the glowing embers. She wrapped a warm towel around the girl's head and gave her some boiling milk to drink.

'It's not the first time this has happened,' she said under her breath to reassure me, and gave me a glass of milk too.

'That was a nice little performance,' I said to Assuntina sternly. 'It's just as well you'll be leaving after lunch, otherwise you'd be looking forward to a week locked in your room with only bread and water. And what was so nice about that black water, anyway?'

'Nothing,' she replied in a surly tone. 'There weren't any fish.'

'I can well believe it!' the nun replied. 'They're still asleep at this hour.'

When prayers were over the other nuns joined us. The mother superior wanted to examine the girl and afterwards reassured me: 'She's warm, but not feverish. She's not coughing or shivering. Let's hope you got her out in time. But you're right—it's better that you take her back with you. I'd rather not take on such a big responsibility.'

Assuntina was put into bed under a mountain of blankets, with two hot water bottles at her feet and a lit brazier by her side, and that's where she stayed until it was time to leave. They even served her lunch there—a nun came and fed her. I was so angry that I wouldn't so much as speak to her, and she was sulking too. The only words she said when I approached to touch her forehead were, 'I don't want you. I want Mamma.'

When the time came she got out of bed, dressed in silence, packed her things up in a bundle and followed me to the station, also in silence. On the train she sat as far away from me as possible, leant against the wooden backrest, and pretended to sleep. We were alone in the compartment. I listened in anguish to her breathing, but as the minutes passed, hearing that it was regular, with neither coughing nor wheezing, I slowly began to relax. But I no longer felt like looking out the window to admire the landscape.

When we arrived in G— it was almost dark and the station gas lamps had already been lit. I opened the window and leant out to have a look. There was more activity this time: porters carrying luggage and calling out to each other, travellers of all classes greeting friends and relatives, people spruiking hot fritters dusted with sugar at the top of their voices. The nuns had given us bread rolls with cheese and a bottle of hot milk with honey for Assuntina. I thought I might buy her a hot fritter as a peace offering, and leant out further to call the vendor over. But it was too late, the train had already begun to move. That was when I thought I saw him. It was just an instant, as he leapt onto the first-class carriage: a young man in a camel overcoat who was the spitting image of Signorino Guido. But of course it wasn't him. What would he be doing in G—? Wasn't he supposed to be in Turin?

My heart was beating like crazy. I shut the window and sat down. I felt cold. I wrapped my shawl around me and tried to calm down. And so what if it was Guido? Nowhere was the distance between us more evident than on a train. First class. Third class. Further apart than the earth from the moon. I must never forget that, never.

Once my heartbeat had returned to normal I glanced across at Assuntina, who still had her eyes closed: perhaps now she really was sleeping. Rocked by the movement of the train, without realising it, I too fell asleep.

I was woken I'm not sure how much later by a kind, not unfamiliar voice saying, 'Can I do anything for you, signorina? Are you quite comfortable?' I saw a hand holding out a travel pillow, one of those they rent out in first class, and I looked up. It was Signorino Guido, sitting alongside Assuntina in the seat opposite mine.

'It's lucky I saw you at the station, looking out the window. I would never have expected you to be on this train. Are you coming from P—? Have you been to the seaside? You've both got a nice bit of colour. Is this little girl your niece?'

I was grateful to him for not asking, 'Is she your daughter?' Assuntina was so small and delicate that she didn't look her age. For all Guido knew, I could have had her at the age of sixteen: I wouldn't be the first. Only I could know that I had kept my heart, and my body, intact for him up until that moment. And I would never confess this to him.

'No,' I replied, 'the daughter of a friend.' I didn't ask why he was on that train, and how come he hadn't stayed in first class. There was no need.

'My uncle has had a turn,' he explained at once, 'and my grandmother sent a telegram asking me to come. It's given her a fright. I hope it's nothing serious. They're so alone, poor old things; I'm all they've got.'

'I'm sorry,' I said. 'I hope your uncle gets better soon.' I still didn't have the faintest idea who his uncle and grand-mother were. I hoped, though I would never have admitted this to myself, that they were middle-class people who owned a business or worked in an office, who were making a thousand sacrifices to allow him to keep up his studies and to dress in a way that would not make a bad impression on his wealthier fellow students.

'Can I spend the rest of the trip here with you?' Signorino Guido asked.

'I'm not the boss of the train,' I said bluntly. 'But you'd be more comfortable in first class.'

'Then I wouldn't have the pleasure of your company.'

What could I say? 'The pleasure is also mine'? Or, 'Do me the pleasure of leaving'? I kept quiet. I was torn between the joy that this unexpected encounter brought me and distrust. What could he want from me? Why had he come looking for me? Had he known that there would be nobody else in the compartment? Did he want to take advantage of me—lure me into some kind of trap? Just as well Assuntina was there.

He settled into his seat with total self-assurance and continued speaking without appearing at all uncomfortable about my silence. 'Fortunately, classes finished last month. It's still ten days or so until my last exam. In four months, I'll graduate. I'm preparing the final chapters of my thesis and need to work flat-out. But at my grandmother's house they won't let me work in peace. So, if it looks like my uncle's condition is not as serious as they say in their letters, and he has good care, from the day after tomorrow I'll be spending at least a few hours in the reading room at the city library. From nine to twelve. Won't you come and meet me? Do you know where it is? It's free entry. We could go down to the patio and chat without interruption.'

'We have nothing to say to each other.'

'Don't be like that. Why don't you trust me? I would never be disrespectful towards you.'

I knew that the library patio was not a solitary spot; there was a constant coming and going of people. If he wanted to lure me into a trap, that wasn't the place to do it. What's more, people would see us together. Wasn't he embarrassed by me? A student with a sartina? People would rush straight to tell his grandmother, his family. All these thoughts crowded into my head.

'So? Will you come?' he asked, stretching out his hand

to brush mine. I didn't pull away, even though I was ashamed of my rough skin, ruined by needles and burns from the iron. I looked at Assuntina. Her eyes were closed but I was sure she was awake and listening to us.

'I've thought of nothing but you in all these months,' Guido said.

You'll forgive me, reader, for slowly beginning to think of him simply as Guido, forgetting or wanting to eliminate the distance presupposed by Signorino.

'And you? Have you thought of me, at least occasionally?'

I didn't know how to answer; my lips were trembling. I didn't want to burst into tears.

'Please, I beg you,' Guido said. 'Come. The day after tomorrow, in the morning. It will be quieter on a Saturday, won't it? Or if you can't do that, come on Monday. At whatever time you wish. I'll wait for you every day, every minute.'

I didn't promise. But nor did I pull away my hand, which he was squeezing ever more tightly. We sat in silence as the train continued its journey. Darkness had fallen by now. How much time went by? I was incapable of measuring it. I was incapable of thinking of anything: all I could do was hold back the tears burning my eyes.

And there, off in the distance, were the lights of L——. We were arriving. I stirred, and stood up. I woke Assuntina and wrapped the shawl tightly around her, tying it at the back. I wound her red scarf twice around her neck. She was docile and silent and let me dress her, but eyed Guido with an enquiring look.

'She mustn't catch cold,' I explained to him. 'Last night she fell in the sea, and she's been recovering from a nasty bout of pneumonia.' I realised it was the first full sentence I had uttered since we left P—.

'If you'll allow it, tomorrow I'll send my uncle Urbano's doctor over to have a look at her,' Guido said.

And still that name meant nothing to me. It's true what Nonna used to say—no one is deafer than someone who doesn't wish to hear.

At the station Guido insisted on accompanying us home in a hired carriage, one of those that wait in the piazza outside the station for the last travellers of the night. His beautiful leather suitcase contrasted with my straw basket and Assuntina's little bundle. There was no need to tell him my address: he remembered it from that day he'd accompanied me home with my little sewing machine in its case.

He helped us down. At the sound of the carriage Zita came out onto the street and looked on in astonishment. 'Mamma! The fish wouldn't let me touch them but I brought you three seashells,' Assuntina exclaimed, her voice a little hoarse from her long silence. Or perhaps, I thought anxiously, as a result of her icy dip in the water.

Guido squeezed my hand tightly and, trying to meet my gaze, though I kept looking away, he whispered, 'All right—the day after tomorrow I'll be expecting you in the library.' Then he climbed back into the carriage and said

to the driver, 'And now to Palazzo Delsorbo, in via Cesare
Battisti! As fast as you can, please. My grandmother will be
anxious about the delay.'

'And there'll be no end to it if you get Donna Licinia
angry,' the cabbie said with a laugh. He evidently knew her.

That name resounded in my ears like a cannon shot, a death
sentence pronounced by the most merciless of judges, a
curse invoked by a cruel and powerful sorceress. How was
it possible I hadn't realised this in all these months? I hadn't
wanted to learn anything of Guido's family, defending
myself from the truth, allowing myself to be deceived by
that surname from another part of the country, Suriani. I
hadn't wanted to realise that 'my' signorino wasn't named
Delsorbo because he was the son of Donna Vittoria; the
orphan Quirica had told me about; the only grandson; the
only heir of that proud, arrogant family who considered
nobody to be worthy of them, neither counts nor barons,
princes nor kings. Never mind a poor sartina paid by the
day. And it was certain that Guido—Don Guido, I should
say—was aware of this. He knew perfectly well that we had
no future. Why had he lied to me? Why had he deceived
me? Was he that good an actor? Did he want to have a little
fun with me? Was he a pleasure-seeking egotist like his
uncle, Don Urbano?

I cut short Zita's thanks, opened the main door, entered
my flat and threw myself on the bed in tears. I cried and
cried and cried, until I lost all strength, until my mind

became all muddled and I fell into an agitated, anguished sleep, visited by dreams and by dark, gloomy images, threatening and unsettling, like shadows underwater.

As soon as I woke, still wearing my travel clothes, with my eyes so puffy I could barely open them, it all came back to me and I swore to myself that I would not go looking for him in the library, not the next day, not ever.

I washed my face in cold water, untied my hair and pulled the comb through it, tearing mercilessly at the knots, and then went to look in the mirror. I could barely recognise myself. The colour that a few days of sea and wind had painted on my cheeks looked odd to me, like something that didn't belong, a mask someone had put on me by force. In my heart I was as pale as a ghost, a dead woman. Something inside me had died forever. Trust? Hope? It all seemed like a nightmare. Had I really spent four days in P—? Had I really been on a train, and on that train had I met and squeezed the hand of the man I thought was my love? My one true love, as all the songs put it?

I snapped out of it: somebody was knocking at the door. I was dressed, though looking rather scruffy, so I opened it. There was Zita, holding her daughter by the hand, and behind them an elderly gentleman with a grey beard, wearing an overcoat with a fur lapel.

'He's come to examine Assuntina,' my neighbour said. 'The young man from yesterday sent him.'

'Good morning. I'm Dr Ricci,' the stranger said. 'The younger Delsorbo asked me to come, the grandson. His name's not Delsorbo, I know, but for me it's as though he were Donna Licinia's son.'

I felt the urge to reply, 'What does the young grandson want from me? Tell him to go to hell! I don't want anything to do with him.' But my upbringing got the better of me, and obliged me to grit my teeth and ask politely, 'How is Don Urbano doing?'

'Badly. I fear he hasn't long to live. Don Guido can't leave his bedside. He asked me to tell you that. He won't be able to go and study in the library. His uncle might pass away at any moment.'

'I'm sorry,' I said, even though I cared little for that rich, arrogant old man who had lived his life to the fullest, suffering neither sacrifice nor displeasure.

'However,' the doctor continued, 'he asked me to come and take a look at this little girl.'

'Ah, did he?' I replied. I was struck, despite myself, that the liar had remembered his promise. 'And what do you think?'

I could see for myself, to my great relief, that Assuntina was well—she wasn't coughing and she had a nice colour. She was rather timidly huddling up to her mother, distrustfully scrutinising that unknown man who, as Zita later told me, had lifted up her layers of clothing and put his ear to her back, rapped his knuckles against it, got her to cough and count, palpated her neck, and felt her tummy. It was the first time in her life that the little one had been examined so carefully.

'She's quite well, considering the circumstances. Keep her nice and warm,' Dr Ricci replied. Then he added, directly to me: 'I would like to speak to you alone.'

A private message from Guido, I thought, my heart in my mouth. But no matter: I had decided—I was not going to be deceived by his insincere attentions. There was a saying about people from Turin that Nonna used to quote: *torinesi falsi e cortesi*—courteous in their customs, but never trust 'em. A characteristic that liar must have picked up while living there. But my own good upbringing obliged me to take my leave of Zita and her daughter, and listen to what the doctor had come to tell me.

Once we had closed the door behind us, I looked at him defiantly, ready to reject any offer or request he might make. I did not expect him to want to talk to me about Zita.

'I also took the liberty of examining the mother—your friend, if I've understood correctly,' he said. 'And her condition worries me greatly. Her lungs are completely shot. Did you know that? Final-stage tuberculosis.'

I had never given it any thought. I had known Zita forever, and she had always looked like that—consumed by her work, terribly thin, perpetually tired. I knew that she coughed a lot, every so often she spat up a little blood, but I saw her working energetically; she had never once spent the day in bed, away from her ironing board. I thought they were just seasonal disturbances. I felt a bitter sense of guilt. Instead of dreaming of the opera, evening school, travel, I should have given her all the money from my allowance, and all the money in my wishing tin, so that she could rest a little, eat meat once a month and not go around barefoot.

'You should convince her to be admitted to hospital,' the doctor went on. 'Not that they'll be able to cure her, given how far gone she is. But they could provide some relief, and it would be best for her to stay away from her daughter, if she hasn't already infected her.'

'She won't want to go to hospital,' I objected. And I couldn't blame her. Poor people went to hospital to die: I'd never heard of anyone who'd made it out alive. Rich people, as everyone knew, were treated at home, like Don Urbano, or they would go to a sanatorium in Switzerland or one of the large hotels on the Riviera.

Dr Ricci shrugged and gave me a few pieces of paper. 'I've written a referral to the hospital here. Use it as you see fit. And this is a prescription for the pharmacist. At least get her to take the medicine. And the little girl needs to be kept away from her—sent off to the country or to the sea, if possible. It's a miracle if life in that damp little hole hasn't already made her sick in the chest.'

Did Dr Ricci have any idea how many people in the city lived in bassi like theirs, how many children? I wanted to snap at him that not everybody could afford nice dry apartments in via Cesare Battisti.

Now he was holding out a sealed envelope. A message? I did not want to read any message. But in fact it contained money. 'To buy the medicine,' the doctor explained. 'It's very expensive and you need to give it to her twice a day. Don Guido says...'

I interrupted him, refusing to take the envelope. 'Don Guido should worry about his uncle,' I exclaimed. 'We can manage fine on our own. Thank you.' Who wanted charity from that liar? He could keep his money and his noble family crest.

'As you wish,' he replied stiffly, offended by such ingratitude. 'I've told you. Here's the prescription for the medicine and the referral to the hospital. Now you do with them what you like.'

He said goodbye and went on his way, careful not to dirty his shiny boots in the mud on the street.

Against all my expectations, Zita agreed to be admitted to hospital. I had been so caught up in my fantasies I hadn't realised that my friend had become quite exhausted. She was so weak that she struggled even to stand; she was very thin and her eyes were always watery, her cheeks always burning. Her only concern about going to hospital was the thought of leaving her daughter alone. But when I told her that during her absence I would have Assuntina to stay at my place, she agreed. She heated some water, took a bath in the tub and put on the best underwear she owned, without too many holes or tears. I lent her my flannel nightshirt. Assuntina and I accompanied her to the hospital. When the people at reception read Dr Ricci's letter, they immediately assigned her a bed in the ward for patients with tuberculosis. It would not be possible to visit her because she would be in isolation. Before she went through that glass door, not knowing if she would ever come back out again, Zita urged her daughter to be obedient, to help me wash the stairs and to behave well at school. She didn't want to kiss her. The doctor had frightened her with his talk of contagion. Assuntina showed no emotion. She stared at her mother earnestly, but did not cry. She clutched my skirt with her right hand, and with the left she fiddled with the button on her bodice. I cried a little. Probably more from remorse than sorrow. It was only later, after I'd given Assuntina her dinner and put her to bed, in the smaller bed that had been mine when Nonna was still around, that I stopped to reflect and realised what a responsibility I'd taken on. If Zita died—or, rather, when Zita died—would I have the courage to take the girl to the orphanage?

On the way back from the hospital, with Assuntina still clutching my skirt, I had stopped by the butcher's to buy a chicken thigh to make broth, then I'd got the milk bottle filled with two litres of milk and had also gone to the bakery. Because the envelope in the first drawer of my dressing table was now empty, before leaving I'd had to take some money from my wishing tin—which now I would be better off calling my tin of illusions—and I noticed that the coins and banknotes destined for super-fluous things were not as many as, in my absurd dreams, I had imagined them to be.

The next day I got up early as usual to mop the stairs and the hallway, and after Assuntina had left for school, her hand held tight by a bigger girl from the alley, I got the place in order, went to check that the door of Zita's basso was locked, and pulled out a set of sheets I was working on. I had agreed to embroider the edges with buttonhole stitch, but there was no great rush with the order. As I pulled the needle through the fabric, knotting the thread at the top of the curve of each scallop, my thoughts raced freely. It seemed that in the past week my life had changed completely. But in reality, the only real changes were the colour in my cheeks, which would soon disappear, and the presence of Assuntina. She, too, would not be around for long, though there was no way of predicting how long. Everything else had just been shattered illusions. Dreams that vanish into thin air at sunrise.

A Narrow Bridge Over the Abyss

EVER SINCE NONNA died I had lived alone. Not that I minded. At night when I locked the door and took off my shoes, I felt free, in command. Even when my resources seemed about to run out and there were no orders on the horizon, I had never thought of renting out one of my two little rooms, of taking in a boarder. For one thing, I wasn't sure the owner of the house would agree to it. But it had not even entered my head to ask for permission to have Assuntina stay with me. The old lady knew Zita and the child. She knew they were good people, polite and clean, even though they lived in a basso— which in any case she owned, as she owned the entire building—and Zita had always paid the rent on time. More than once she had sung Zita's praises, noting how she kept the place in order despite having to go to the fountain in the nearby piazza to get water. She had been there when Assuntina was born. She wouldn't have the heart to ask me to send her away now, I thought, out onto the street.

For me the presence of Zita's daughter meant quite a change, and I felt the weight of it, and sometimes the inconvenience. I was unaccustomed to having not even a moment alone and I had no idea how to take care of a child, though for her age Assuntina was very independent and tried not to cause me any trouble. She had always liked my house, especially the room my grandmother called 'the little parlour', where she would receive clients. Assuntina was fascinated by the two small chintz-covered armchairs, by the tall, narrow mirror you could tilt at different angles, and above all by the sewing machine. Compared to the windowless basso with no dividing walls in which she had always lived, coming to live with me was like moving into a palace. She enjoyed opening and closing the windows and the shutters, closing the kitchen door to isolate the smell whenever we cooked cauliflower, and using the toilet down in the courtyard, throwing down great bucketfuls of water that she didn't need to go to the fountain to collect. Residents were able to get water from a little spigot in the courtyard. It was over the marble-grit washtub, which had a sloping, ridged bench alongside, where I would do my washing. This, too, was a source of great admiration for Assuntina, who was constantly asking me for handkerchiefs to wash. She would scrub them so energetically they tore.

A few days went by. While the little girl was at school I would stay home sewing and brooding over what had happened on the train. I was still angry with Guido, even though I was consumed by tenderness whenever I remembered the look in his eyes and the sound of his voice.

I was finishing off the scallop pattern on the last sheet when, around one-thirty, there was a knock on the door. I was somewhat disappointed to find it was Rinuccia, the Delsorbos' 'young servant'. I stiffened, ready to refuse to receive any message. And there was a message, but it was from Donna Licinia.

'Don Urbano is dying,' Rinuccia informed me. From her tone I could tell she was unaware of my relationship with Guido, and that I had already been informed of her master's illness. 'Quirica won't leave his bedside—she's desperate.' *Thou good and faithful servant*, I thought instinctively, remembering the Scriptures. But why was Rinuccia talking about Quirica's sorrow? How could that possibly be of interest?'

'Donna Licinia must be desperate,' I retorted. 'It's terrible losing a son. Especially at nearly a hundred years of age.'

'Donna Licinia wants you to come and sew silk braiding onto the pall. Since Donna Vittoria's death, the edging has become frayed. If not tonight, then certainly tomorrow, they'll need to have everything ready for the viewing of the body.'

She stood there with her hands under her apron, waiting for me to put down my sewing and prepare to follow her. She didn't have the slightest concern that I would refuse. I had always gone when they called, and this time it really was urgent.

How could I tell her I didn't want to go, without having to explain what had happened between me and Don Guido?

'I've taken in a little girl,' I said. 'I need to wait for her to come home from school. I can't leave.'

'Donna Licinia won't be happy to be kept waiting,' Rinuccia said, vexed and astonished that the lady's orders were not being followed on the double.

I was hastily trying to think of another excuse I might use to avoid going. If I refused without good reason I'd be making myself a powerful enemy. Donna Licinia would spread the word that I was unreliable, that I was fickle, that you couldn't depend on me, and God knew I needed work, now that I had Assuntina to take care of.

'Come, get a move on,' Rinuccia urged me in a stern tone. 'Your goddaughter's returning, can't you hear her?' The alley was echoing with the voices of young children taking over the footpath en masse, some of them calling out at the top of their lungs, 'Ma, I'm hungry!'

Assuntina crossed the threshold with her red scarf wrapped around her head and her little rich girl's coat buttoned right up to the neck. She was following the doctor's recommendations to the letter, and the coat covered her up much better than her old shawl. She put her primer and exercise book on the chair and looked enquiringly at Rinuccia.

'I have to go out for a job,' I told her at last. 'There's some bread and cheese in the pantry. Are you able to heat up a cup of milk? Stay inside until I get back.' Out of prudence I put around her neck the piece of string with the spare key attached. 'Don't open up for anybody. And don't touch the sewing machine.'

I pulled the door behind me and followed Rinuccia down the street. On the way to via Cesare Battisti I thought about how I should behave when I saw Guido. I decided I'd pretend not to know him. He certainly wouldn't dare talk to me in front of his grandmother. I no longer felt desperate; I had regained my courage. More than anything, I felt resentful, almost angry. Look at the situation that lying signorino has gone and got me in—nobleman, my foot.

Rinuccia let me in by the service entrance as usual and took me through to the kitchen. There we found Quirica crying, her hands wringing the large red damask pall whose edging I was to sew.

'She sent me away,' she sobbed. 'Donna Licinia told me I had to leave, that Don Urbano should only have his family by his side at the end.'

This was surely to be expected, I said, trying to console her.

'But his cousins from F— were in there,' Quirica said. 'They arrived yesterday evening, like vultures. They haven't been in touch in more than ten years. They've never given a damn about Don Urbano. And yet she let them stay. And then there was the doctor by his bed. And the priest. It was only me—why did she have to drive me out like a mangy dog?'

'Stop it—they can hear you in there,' Rinuccia said brusquely. But the door separating the signori's quarters from the servants' was shut and did not let any sound through.

I was beginning to hope that I might be able to finish my work and leave without encountering any of the family. With a bit of luck Guido wouldn't even hear about my visit. And if I remained in the kitchen there would be no risk of meeting him, as would happen if I went to work alone in the sewing room. The presence of the two maids was reassuring.

I took the large rectangular piece of precious fabric from Quirica's hands and checked the edging. The silk braiding had come off in several places, and in others it was worn. It couldn't be mended: it needed to be replaced. The women must have realised this, as they had bought new braiding; there was also a spool of cotton in a matching colour and a pincushion. I sat down with my back to the door and began carefully unpicking the old trim, mindful not to ruin the damask, which was very old. It was not a difficult job, but it was slow and required concentration. A sewing machine wouldn't be any use: the braiding needed to be sewn by hand with tiny invisible stitches. I knew, having witnessed viewings in other important households, that Don Urbano's bed would be taken into the drawing room and the pall would be draped over it. The body, washed and dressed in the best clothing, would be laid on top, and people would come to pay their final respects.

I sewed for some time. Quirica, exhausted from crying, had nodded off, her head resting on the table. Rinuccia was reciting the rosary under her breath. The hands of the clock hanging next to the door were moving terribly slowly. Every so often my thoughts ran to Assuntina, and I hoped she had not gone out into the street to play, that after finishing her homework she had sat down to a quiet pastime, perhaps flicking through old illustrated magazines that I kept in the drawer.

At last I finished. I knotted and cut the thread, tucking the ends out of sight, put away my needle, and folded the pall over the back of a chair. Rinuccia was heating the iron, so that she could give it a quick going-over, when there was a light knock on the door. I jumped, fearing it might be Guido; because I was right next to the door of the pantry, I slipped in there.

But it was Dr Ricci. 'It's all over,' he announced. 'You may go into the bedroom to prepare the body.' Quirica lifted her head from the table and brought her hand to her mouth to stifle a cry. Rinuccia said, 'Ave Maria.'

As soon as the doctor left the room Rinuccia began heating a large pot of water on the stove, even though Don Urbano was hardly going to care if he was washed in cold water. Quirica straightened her clothes and hair, dried her eyes, and went into the bathroom to get a razor, foam and shaving brush. 'His cheeks must be as smooth as silk,' she said. The prospect of being of service to her master one last time seemed to have calmed her down a little. I wrapped my shawl around my shoulders. 'I'll head off then,' I said, taking my leave.

'Don't you want to come in and see him?' Rinuccia asked. 'If you wait a little maybe you can give us a hand dressing him.'

'No, dead bodies make me uneasy. And besides, I've got the little girl at home, remember? Pass on my condolences to Donna Licinia.'

'Wait a minute, then.' We hadn't talked about payment and I would even have left without asking about it just to get away quickly. But Quirica had already thought about it in the morning. As usual she had rolled up a banknote, placed some coins inside, and then wrapped the whole thing in the leftover pieces of new silk braiding along with the older bits I had unpicked. 'If you come by tomorrow you can say goodbye to him. By then they'll have decided the date and time of the funeral.' She took it as a given that I wanted to attend.

I thanked her and hurried down the hall towards the service entrance, greatly relieved that I had managed to avoid the encounter I had feared. But it was too early to celebrate. The hall was long, poorly lit by a single little window onto the stairs, and full of recesses where there had once been large built-in wardrobes. I was walking so fast that I didn't notice somebody half hidden in one of those spots, and when the person stepped out I crashed right into him.

'I'm sorry,' I said, instinctively stepping back. I recognised him at once.

'What are you doing here, signorina?' Guido asked, astonished. His face was distorted from crying, and his eyes were red from the long vigil. I later learnt that he hadn't so much as touched his bed for two nights straight. He had sat by his uncle's side holding his hand until his last breath, forcing himself to hold back his tears. When Don Urbano breathed his last, he stepped out of the room: he needed some time alone, not talking to anybody; he needed to let it all out, to cry. He had gone to take refuge in the servants' corridor, thinking he would find nobody there.

'What are you doing here?' he repeated incredulously.

I didn't stop to explain. Instead I said, 'I'm sorry about your uncle.'

He tried to dry his tears. 'He was a good man. I'll miss him greatly. First my father and then...' His speech was broken by sobs.

I don't know how it happened. We were standing opposite each other, close, in the shadows. With one hand I was holding the corners of my shawl over my chest, while the other was clutching the roll of fabric with my payment inside. I didn't know what to say and he wasn't asking anything; he was just watching me. His pain appeared sincere: he was defenceless, like a child. Full of compassion, I instinctively reached out and brushed his cheek, and he opened his arms. I found myself clutched to his chest, my face buried in his neck, which was wet with tears. I did not pull away. Rather, I let go of my shawl and hugged him tightly back.

'Don't cry—please don't cry.'

He kissed me on the side of the head, on the temple. I looked up at him.

At that moment the door that separated the two sections of the house opened, and Donna Licinia appeared. Guido had his back to her but I saw her clearly and she saw me: she saw us. She said nothing. She stepped back inside but banged the door loudly. Guido jumped and let go of me.

'Forgive me,' he said. 'I'm sorry—I didn't mean to.'

I picked up my shawl, ashamed to look him in the eye. 'I'll leave,' I murmured in a quiet voice that did not seem like my own, and headed towards the door. He followed me.

'After the funeral,' he said, 'I'll need to stay on in L— for a few days. I want to see you. I'll wait for you every morning in the library.'

I left and hurried down the stairs. Outside it was almost dark, but my house was not far away and I walked quickly down the street, almost without thinking about where I was going. I felt pity and tenderness for Guido's pain, a kind of torment, but also a strange exultation, unfamiliar joy, a confused hopefulness. And at the same time, uncertainty, fear, doubts, and icy dread of that black silhouette standing in the doorway. Had she recognised me? What would she think of me? I was so agitated that I almost forgot about Assuntina, who needed her dinner—if possible, something hot. And who might have got into some kind of mischief while I was gone.

I was panting when I arrived home. As I stepped inside and took off my shawl I realised that I was no longer holding the roll of money and scraps of fabric. I must have dropped it in the corridor at the Delsorbos'. I was upset, then immediately felt ashamed to be thinking about such a vulgar little thing. After all, it wasn't a large sum of money. But every penny counted, especially now that I needed to think about Assuntina, and my tin was growing emptier by the day.

The little girl realised that something unusual had happened. She looked at me inquisitively but didn't ask anything. She had set the table, sliced the bread, and peeled and cut the potatoes, celery and carrot for the soup. 'I didn't manage to light the stove,' she confessed. 'It's not like Mamma's.'

'I'll show you now.' From time to time I would need to leave her alone. If I was called to sew in somebody's house I wouldn't be able to take her with me.

I added some chicory to the soup, along with lentils I had left soaking, and made a large batch—enough to last us at least three days. I took two eggs out of the pantry and fried them up with a little onion.

When we sat down at the table I made an effort to talk with Assuntina, asking her what she had learnt that morning at school and whether she had done her homework. She answered in monosyllables and seemed very tired. So different, I thought, from the uncontrollable little rascal at the seaside. She had lost that impudent manner, that confidence and vivacity. She had no doubt spent the whole day thinking of her mother, and wondering about her own future. But she asked no questions, demanded no explanations. 'Poor thing,' I couldn't help but think, 'who knows what awaits her?' I'd had my grandmother by my side, at least.

Although I was sorry to have lost the payment for an afternoon's work, the next day I was certainly not going to return to the Delsorbos' house. I did not wish to see the body, listen to visitors' chatter, embarrass Guido or have to face his grandmother. Nor did I wish to know the date and time of the funeral. I knew there would be a huge crowd in attendance—friends, relatives, people of every class, even the most humble, if only out of curiosity to see Donna Licinia, who had not left the house since the death of her daughter. But I had no intention of attending.

Over the next few days I stayed at home sewing. I needed to finish embroidering the edging on the sheets and lengthening four pinafores for Enrica. This was simple: I just needed to unpick the hem and let it out by one or two folds of fabric. The folds had been made in part for decoration, but above all for that very eventuality. Signorina Ester, though rich, followed the rules of common sense and thrift. Her daughter's little smocks were worn right up to the end, until the fabric was almost threadbare and the corners of the pockets were coming undone, or they had become so tight that they could no longer be buttoned up at the back.

Sewing at home allowed me to take better care of Assuntina, preparing her hot meals and helping with her homework. I worried about her health. Every day I felt her forehead to see if she had a temperature, and I would wake in the night to listen to her breathing. But my little guest was in good form—her cough had even gone away, as though three days of sea air and that cold dip that had so alarmed me truly were a miracle cure. What gave me pause for thought was her radically different behaviour. She was now a sensible, obedient and silent child: too silent.

I spoke about it with Signorina Ester when I went to drop off the pinafores, and she asked me to stop for a cup of coffee and a chat. I hadn't told her anything about Guido, but she guessed that something was different in my mood. She was too delicate and respectful to ask me about it directly; she was waiting for me to talk about it, and I did not have the courage. She was so far from suspecting who I was thinking about that, after saying she shared my concern about Assuntina and writing a letter to the matron at the hospital (someone she knew, who I could ask to pay special attention to poor Zita), she began telling me, as though it was just a curious anecdote, about the Delsorbo funeral and Donna Licinia's reaction to the reading of the will. As I had expected, many citizens had attended the funeral: the procession was extremely long and the cathedral full to bursting. The aristocracy was lined up in the first pews and then, working back towards the exit, were officials from the regiment, industrialists, upper-bourgeoisie, civil servants of the kingdom, office workers, shopkeepers, servants and day labourers. It was murmured, and Signorina Ester told me this with amusement in her eyes, that among the crowd standing at the back there were even a couple of residents of the best brothel in the city, along with the proprietor, who had allowed them out for the occasion. Right to the end, Don Urbano had been one of their most affectionate clients.

'He'll have found a way to have fun even in paradise,' she commented with a laugh, even though the dead man's habits went against her principles. 'Unless he's gone to hell. Not for his pleasure-seeking lifestyle but for the trick he pulled on his mother. It seems Donna Licinia was furious and fired Quirica on the spot.'

'What's Quirica got to do with anything?'

'In his will Don Urbano did not leave everything to his mother and nephew, as was expected. He left a large part of his wealth to the woman referred to in the house as the "old servant".'

On rare occasions signori might make a bequest to their servants. But a large part of his wealth!

'And he didn't leave anything to Rinuccia?'

'Nothing. And that's the curious thing—though Quirica had been in domestic service for the Delsorbos for half a century and they only employed Rinuccia much later, after the cholera epidemic. In any case, the stickybeaks won't need to wait long to learn more details. Don Urbano's will is going to be made public by the notary before the end of the month.'

Signorina Ester seemed more worried about Assuntina than I was. 'This is too great a responsibility for you to take on,' she told me. 'It'll get worse with every day that passes. Are you sure the girl doesn't have any relatives who can take care of her?'

'Zita never spoke of any. If she had anybody, she'd have asked them for help a good while back. There were times when they were close to dying of hunger. No, after her husband was killed, the two of them were left alone.'

'And the girl knows it. She's hoping her mother will return, but she's old enough to understand she needs to expect the worst. Poor little thing! But you mustn't feel obliged to take her on. You're too young, you're on your own, and you need to earn a living.' She looked me in the eye, as though assessing my capacity to tackle the situation. Then she said, 'Don't worry—when the time comes, I'll help you find an acceptable arrangement for your ward. In fact, if you don't think you can manage it, we can start right away to look for something for her.'

'Thank you, but I prefer to wait. Until Zita...She might even recover and come and take her back, don't you think?'

'No, I don't think so. It would be nice, but I don't believe in miracles. In any case, let's wait, as you wish. Can you manage? Do you need anything? No, not a gift—I wouldn't be so presumptuous. A little loan, an advance for future work.'

'I can manage for now. I have my savings.'

And so Don Urbano was buried in the family tomb, his will was made public, and the days of condolence visits came to an end. Guido had probably begun going to the library every morning. He was probably waiting for me.

After much hesitation, I decided to go looking for him. One day after Assuntina had left for school I dressed carefully and brushed my hair. I did not put on my thick dark woollen shawl, more suited to an old lady, but instead chose a lighter one with roses along the edges and silk fringes, which Signorina Ester had brought me from Rome. I even put on my grandmother's coral earrings and my best shoes. I tore a petal from the red geranium that I kept on the window and rubbed it on my lips to give them a little colour. I had read about this trick in a novel.

I hurried out and made my way to Piazza del Municipio. I had been to the city library a few times to borrow or return a book, but I'd never gone up to the reading room. I stopped by a bench in the piazza, behind a tree, to watch people coming and going. There were a lot, many of them young, not only students from wealthy families or minor officials but also office workers, some shop assistants, all respectably dressed. There were no tradesmen, no errand boys. Small wonder, as you only went to the library if you knew how to read. I was an exception among people of my class. The few women I saw going in were all of a certain age, and wore the severe, almost masculine clothing typical of middle-class women who worked outside the home—as teachers, or in public administration, the post office or the telephone exchange. None of them were dressed as humbly as I was. There was not even a maid sent by her mistress to return a novel. I began to feel embarrassed. What was Guido thinking suggesting we meet there, of all places, where I would stick out so much?

Then I saw them arrive. Two young ladies around eighteen years of age, accompanied by a young man who looked like a brother, or at least a close relative, and was treating them with great familiarity. Two rich, elegant signorine done up to the nines, their hair given extra body around their faces by means of horsehair rollers. They were wearing clothes suitable for an outing in town, and their jackets were very modern, with neither bustle nor train. They had almost certainly been made to measure at La Suprema Eleganza or Belledame Each carried a light-coloured lace parasol. Two young women who certainly no longer wore a corset. Their companion resembled Guido, in his clothing, his gestures, his manner of speaking, and he addressed them with great attention and respect.

I felt a knot in my throat. Envy? Awareness of just how different I was from these women? Of the abyss separating us? How could I compete with these two daughters of upper-class signori? How could I ever front up with Guido to meet their mothers, their families? How could I expect to be accepted by them, when I came from another world—I was born and lived among poor people, and that's where I belonged. I needed to earn a living day by day, and if I visited their homes I would need to come through the service entrance, and I would only ever be welcome in their salons with a tape measure in hand or wearing a maid's uniform and carrying a tray of pastries. If I were to turn up alongside a young man of their class they'd look at me in astonishment, with disdain, and would drive me away. My pride would not allow that. I turned on my heel and left, full of shame for my earrings and red lips and silk shawl and ridiculous dreams.

I did not know that Guido had seen me through the first-floor window and was coming down the stairs to meet me. I was walking so fast, blinded by tears, that I didn't realise I was being followed. By the time he reached me I had already turned down the Corso; he overtook me and blocked my way, arms wide like an officer stopping the traffic to let an ox-drawn cart through. 'Why are you running away?' he asked. 'I've been waiting two days for you.'

'Let me through. Can't you see people are looking at us?'

At that hour the Corso was full of people; it was fine weather and the cafés had put little tables out on the foot-path. The barbershop door was open and as they waited their turn, the clients were idly looking out at passers-by. Maids were returning from the market with bags of shopping; nannies were pushing prams towards the park; signore were ambling arm in arm and looking in shop windows; and florists and asparagus sellers, crouching down by their baskets, cast around for potential clients to whom they could offer their wares. This was not quite the predawn audience that used to witness Tommasina's triumphant return bearing the Atelier Printemps boxes, but there were nevertheless plenty of stickybeaks watching our encounter with interest and it was certain that they would go around talking about it.

'Let them look,' Guido said, putting his arm in mine. He brought my hand towards his face and kissed my fingers. I could feel myself burning up, and began to tremble.

'You're cold. Forgive me for keeping you out in the middle of the street like this. Let's go into this café. You need to drink something hot.'

I had never set foot in a café in my life. The tips of my ears were burning, and I hoped we would be able to slip into one of the inner rooms, which were more private. This would mean I was alone with him, but at that point I was no longer afraid of what he might say to me: it was more important to escape all the curious gazes fixed upon us.

But Guido did not enter the atrium of the Crystal Palace where the bar, cashier and entrance to the private rooms were to be found; he led me through to the glass cage on the footpath and got me to sit down at the outermost table, in full view of all the passers-by. He called over the waiter and ordered two hot chocolates with cream and a plate of pastries.

'Why did you run away?' he reproached me. 'If I hadn't happened to be at the window just at that moment, I'd have missed you.'

'We mustn't—' I began.

He interrupted me. 'But no, I wouldn't have missed you. I'd have come looking for you at home. But I'm glad you made the decision yourself. You, too, need to step forward. I can't go on chasing you forever.'

'Once you've returned to Turin you'll no longer need to chase me.'

'I'm very glad to have the chance to talk to you. I have so much to tell you.'

I kept my head lowered over my steaming cup. 'I'm very sorry about your uncle,' I murmured, 'and thank you for sending Dr Ricci. You shouldn't have gone to so much trouble.'

'I'm pleased the little girl is well. Let's not talk about that. We don't have long: I need to leave tomorrow.'

He took the hand in which I was holding my teaspoon, brought it to his lips and kissed it once again. He continued holding it tightly as he spoke.

'I do not wish to repeat that my intentions are serious— you should have understood that by now. I would like to get to know you better, spend time together; and you will need to get to know me. With the permission of your family of course. I shall come by this very morning to introduce myself.'

'I have no family,' I said, though I immediately thought

of Signorina Ester. I could introduce him to her, in the hope that she would understand me. Not today, though. Things were moving too quickly.

'I'm sorry,' said Guido. 'Yet another reason why I should take care of you. Unfortunately, I need to leave town, but we shall write to each other. Promise you'll reply if I write to you? Here's my address in Turin. Do you promise to reply? Promise?'

I was grateful that he was so sure I knew how to write. I promised, my voice very thin.

'I won't be able to come back for a while. My last exam is the day after tomorrow and then in four months' time I'll graduate. Between now and then my professor insists I go in to the university every day. But after that I'll be free. My grandmother wishes me to come and live with her in via Cesare Battisti, but I don't want to, especially after seeing how she treated Quirica. Luckily the poor woman has somewhere to live— Zio Urbano was generous to her; he was a good man. So no, I won't be going to Palazzo Delsorbo. My grandmother is old; she lives in another world. I can make the effort to understand her, but I can't agree with her. No. I couldn't bear living alongside her. I thought I'd rent a small apartment—we'll decide together when I come back.'

'An apartment? No, no, I...I'd never...'

'Don't be alarmed. I'll go live there on my own to begin with, until such times, until you...If, after getting to know me well, you agree to marry me.'

I started to cry. My tears fell into my cup of hot choco-late. I didn't care about the passers-by on the other side of the glass cage, who were staring at us as though they were at the theatre or at the zoo. I had a smudge of whipped cream on one cheek. Guido wiped it away delicately with a kiss as light as the wings of a butterfly.

When I arrived home Assuntina was already back from school. She realised at once that my mood, my entire being, had changed. I was trying not to let it show but I felt like I was floating between heaven and earth, walking as though immersed in a dream, like in a novel. It seemed to me that what had happened between Guido and me that morning was the product of my imagination—it couldn't be true. However, the ring he had given me was real; I needed only to bring my hand to my chest to touch it. At the table in the café he had slipped it onto my finger. He wanted me to wear it on my left hand, for all to see as evidence of the narrow bridge connecting the two sides of the abyss that separated us. A band of gold with two small stones, a sap-phire and a diamond, it had belonged to his mother, who had received it as a gift for her confirmation. It was a young girl's jewel, which for him held more sentimental than material value, but which for me, accustomed as I was to balancing my meagre budget every week, seemed enor-mous. I took fright. I was not yet ready to defy the city and its rules so openly. And alone, since he would be far away. 'I'll put it on my finger when you return from Turin,' I told him. 'In the meantime, I'll wear it over my heart.' I slipped it onto my grandmother's thin gold chain, which I always wore around my neck. It would be safe there, hidden under my shirt, away from curious eyes.

Perhaps if Assuntina had been able to see the ring, she'd have understood that my unusual euphoria was not because her greatest desire had been fulfilled. She wanted to believe that I had just returned from the hospital. 'Mamma's been cured!' she exclaimed, her face lighting up. 'When will she be back?'

'It'll be a little while yet,' I lied. 'You must be patient.' And I felt a twinge of guilt in comparing my own joy and hope with the black chasm that awaited her.

That afternoon I met with Guido again. We went for a walk along the avenue of plane trees. It was a work day and there were not too many people around, only nannies, little boys dressed in sailor suits on scooters and young girls rolling hoops. We talked for a long time. I can remember exactly what we talked about, but I prefer to keep it close to my heart. All I will say is that he gently stroked my hair and if, on the one hand, my shyness was slowly diminishing, on the other I became ever more aware of my own ignorance, which I sought to hide, and ever more resolved to improve myself, to study so that I might fill in all the gaps. I did not want him to be ashamed of me under any circumstances.

That evening Guido took me out to a small trattoria just outside the gates of the city. I had never eaten a meal in public. I returned home late, feeling guilty that yet again Assuntina had eaten alone. In the hope she would forgive me I showed her the ring hanging on my grandmother's chain.

'Who gave it to you?' she asked.

'Somebody who cares for me.'

'And why aren't you wearing it on your finger?'

'Because I'm afraid somebody will steal it.'

'Is it worth a lot?' She was not able to distinguish the diamond and the sapphire from the pieces of coloured glass she had seen on the fingers and around the necks of shop girls in our neighbourhood. 'If you took it to the pawnshop what would they give you for it?'

'I will never take it to the pawnshop.'

'Do you care for this person more than you do for me?'

'What are you talking about, silly! It's different.'

Assuntina sighed. I had not expected her to be so sentimental. She wanted to try on the ring, which naturally was too big for her, but then she didn't want to give it back. We fought over it playfully for a little bit, and in the back-and-forth the chain, which was very thin, broke. It was my fault—I shouldn't have let her touch it—so I didn't scold the little girl. Actually, I thought I'd been lucky. The chain could have broken out on the street somewhere, and the ring could have fallen without me realising and I'd have lost it forever. I'd be better off attaching it to a strong shoelace, but just then I didn't have anything appropriate in the house. So, after Assuntina had fallen asleep, I climbed up on the chair and slipped the ring into my wishing tin, first giving it a little kiss.

The next morning I got up very early and, after cleaning the stairs, went to the station to say goodbye to Guido. I had decided it was more prudent to leave the ring in the tin until I was able to procure a lace that was strong enough, but I didn't tell him this. I accompanied him all the way to his first-class carriage—I felt safe in his presence, and more self-assured than I would ever have imagined. People were looking at us. Although I was wearing my best clothes, perhaps they thought I was a maid accompanying her little master to help with his bags. But other people knew us, and when he stroked my face and hair, embraced me tightly, kissed me and dried my tears, they could not hide their astonishment and made loud, nasty comments.

'They'll run off and tell your grandmother,' I said.

'Let them. She'll find out sooner or later. She's going to have to come to terms with it.'

I would have preferred for this to happen while Guido was still in town, so that I didn't have to face it alone. But there was no turning back. He said, 'I'll write to you as soon as I arrive. And you must reply by return post.' Then he took my hand and placed it on his heart. 'Will you promise me something?'

'What?'

'When I return, I want us to stop being so formal and talking in such a roundabout way. Can we speak as equals?

Will you promise me that?'

It was not going to be easy, I knew that already, but it was necessary. I promised.

After the train had left I headed for the hospital. It seemed pointless to go back home to cry. 'Don't be sad,' Guido had urged me. 'Four months will pass quickly. Think about my return. Think about how we will no longer need to be apart.'

The hospital was on the outskirts of town, so it was quite a walk, which gave me a chance to reflect, to put my thoughts in order, though they were running off in all directions. The people who had seen us at the café, under the plane trees that lined the avenue and at the station would not only go and tell Donna Licinia—they would talk about it all over the city. I was sorry that Signorina Ester would come to learn of this through gossip, and I regretted not having said anything to her myself, as forewarning. Perhaps I still had time. I decided to go visit her that afternoon.

At the hospital I sought out the matron, for whom I'd been given the letter of introduction. I found her—a middle-aged woman, polite and helpful—just as she was about to go home after her shift. Although she was tired, she agreed to stop and talk to me for a while. She explained that, even though she had dedicated special attention to Zita, just as Signorina Ester had asked her to, there had not been much she could do for her. My friend was now at the final stage. She was no longer conscious. She might last another...She couldn't say for sure. Certainly no more than two weeks and possibly not even that. Did I wish to see her, to say goodbye one last time? With some precautions she could make an exception and let me enter the isolation ward, but I would need to promise not to get too close to Zita and not to touch her.

'Will she be able to recognise me?' I asked.

'No. We give her tranquilisers. She just sleeps.'

'Then I'd rather not see her.'

'As you wish.' She looked again at the letter. 'I see there's a young daughter. And that something will need to be arranged for her—the best we can manage. I can help you with that. We entrust the orphaned girls our patients leave behind to the Institute for the Child Mary. It's a good orphanage—it includes a school, and those girls who wish to can study to become kindergarten teachers. The buildings are spacious, clean and dry. They have a flower garden and a vegetable garden that the little girls take care of. In the summer they take them to the beach for a week, to their sister establishment in P—. Believe me, this is the best there is in the city. They receive many requests. It would be wise to book a spot for your ward immediately. So that when the time comes...If you like, I can go with you. The bureaucracy is a little complicated for people who turn up at their doors for the first time. What's more, you'd need to be able to read and complete the forms. You're going to need help.'

She thought I was ignorant, illiterate. I didn't correct her, as her assistance would be invaluable. I thanked her for her time. I would have preferred not to have to decide so quickly, but I understood that it was pointless to wait. And it would be pointless to speak first with Assuntina and ask her if she agreed. After all, what choice did she have? And besides, taking action would help take my mind off Guido.

When we were out on the street, in the light of the sun, the matron looked at me more closely. 'But I know you from somewhere,' she said. 'Where could I have seen you?'

'In the Artonesi home?' I ventured, hoping that any rumours about what I was certain the city's gossips were now calling my 'affair' with Guido had not yet reached her ears.

'No, no. Somewhere else...Turn around, lift your chin. I've seen those earrings before. Ah, that's it! At the theatre. You sit in the gods, don't you? So, you like the opera. I do too. My husband introduced me to it: he's part of the claque. Last Christmas he gave me opera glasses. It's a whole different experience when you can see the singers' faces clearly.'

I gave a sigh of relief. We spoke about our favourite composers. She adored Verdi; I loved Puccini. How I had cried over the young artists in *La Bohème*, their poverty made them seem like my brothers and sisters—and now Zita was dying of consumption like Mimì, who was not quite a sartina but almost, an embroiderer...All that was missing from that freezing garret so close to the moon was a little girl who needed a home.

My companion began rattling off the names of all the signori who had boxes at the theatre, people who, thanks to her opera glasses, she was now able to observe in such detail that she considered them old acquaintances. At a certain point she sighed and said, 'What a pity! Last year we lost the American lady, La Miss. Her maid still comes—she has no shame!—but now she sits in the stalls. And we won't be seeing Don Urbano Delsorbo next season. He was nice. But what an eccentric old man! Have you heard about his will?'

I swallowed and shook my head. 'No,' I said rather brusquely, hoping she would let the subject drop. But she pulled a folded-up newspaper out of her bag. 'Read this! Oh, sorry, let me read it for you.'

I did not correct her this time either. I listened to her words without comment, initially worried not so much about the content of the article but about what she would think the next day, or in the following days, when she learnt that my lack of interest in the will and in the Delsorbo family was not sincere, that I was pretending. She would be scornful, and would see me as a liar, a hypocrite, a conniving social climber. Would she continue to help my friends? Was I harming Zita with my silence? Was I jeopardising Assuntina's future? Secrets and lies are like snakes: you never know where the body ends and the tail begins, where they will take you—that's what Nonna used to say. But what could I do at that point but listen? And anyway, I truly was interested to hear the story.

—

Don Urbano's will had finally been made public by the notary's office. He had written it with his own hand and had included some inexplicable sentences, quite outside the typical legal formulations, alongside what were already rather unusual provisions. These were so bizarre that the newspaper considered them of great interest to the reading public and had decided to record them in full. It was peculiar enough, the journalist wrote, that the old libertine had left one of his maids—the older one, while the other got nothing—a two-storey residential building in the city's historic centre, as well as a five-storey building in the more modern neighbourhood, a nice piece of land and a great deal of money. And that he had entrusted his nephew, the heir he had deprived of that portion of his estate, with watching over his beneficiary, looking after her interests, helping her to rent out the apartments at a good price and to set herself up in whichever one she chose to live in. But Don Urbano had also wanted to justify this unusual decision. 'Quirica Grechi,' he had written, 'was extremely young when she came to serve in our house. She has always done everything that was asked of her with great dedication and affection, quietly and discreetly. She was so generous as to give up her own personal life, never having a family of her own. She endured disdain and ingratitude, and has never received a just reward for everything she did for us, for me. I ask her forgiveness for this. I wish to make an act of reparation here, and may God too forgive me. What I am leaving to her is merely the smallest part of that to which she is justly entitled.'

I recalled Guido's words in the corridor: 'He was a good man.' Though I still didn't understand what Quirica could have done that was special enough to deserve such preferential treatment and such an apologetic tone. All live-in maids give up their own personal life, and in exchange receive a salary and the security of a roof over their head. I had not forgotten that my grandmother had given up just such a salary and security to be able to keep me by her side.

The matron, too, found such gratitude exaggerated. 'Next people will be asking their servants' forgiveness for giving them work!' she said. 'So much praise, too! So what if she'd been faithful and discreet? That was part of her duty. And if her salary was too low, that was her fault for not coming to a clear arrangement at the beginning and not asking for a raise later on. And so what if her masters treated her disdainfully? She could have resigned and looked for a better family, one that was less arrogant. Besides, everybody knows that the masters give the orders and the servants put up with it. I don't understand all these regrets and justifications from Don Urbano. The stuff was his and he could leave it to whoever he wanted. And that's that.' She snickered a little nastily: 'But I get why his mother is angry. Essentially, he's accusing her of never having paid that jewel of a maid enough. He's accusing her of such arrogance that, on the point of death, he has had to make amends. Was it really necessary to write that in a public document? Surely it's better to air your dirty laundry at home, don't you think?'

She looked to me for confirmation. I stammered, 'You're right.' And I thanked the heavens that we had arrived at the orphanage, and my companion needed to fold her newspaper back up and put it away in her bag.

The Institute for the Child Mary may have been the best orphanage in the city, but it didn't look too special to me. There was a low building with land around it divided into garden beds, with a few trees and bushes, some rows of peas and lettuce, but no flowers. A high fence separated the garden from the street and all the building's windows had bars. Inside, the reception was spartan, with yellowish walls, a table, a filing cabinet and two chairs. On a shelf there was a statue of Our Lady of Sorrows with seven swords to her heart. There was also, under a bell jar, a cradle decorated with gilded lace where a wax figure of the baby Mary lay, wrapped from neck to toe in gilt swaddling clothes.

Continuing to pretend I did not know how to read or write, I let the matron ask for information and fill out the forms. The nun informed us sternly that there was a long waiting list—there were always more little orphan girls in the city than places available, and we would need to join the queue. I felt a sense of relief. I could wait before telling Assuntina what had been decided for her. But the matron approached the desk and said quietly, with a knowing smile:

'Signor Artonesi's daughter, Signorina Ester, asked me to pass her greetings on to you, sister. This little girl is very close to her heart.'

'My greetings to her too,' the nun replied, not lifting her head from her papers. She took our forms, which she had put at the bottom of the pile, and placed them on top.

'If you'd like, you can visit the refectory. It's lunchtime.'

She accompanied us into a large room full of tables that looked much like the one at the home for the scrofulous in P—. Here, too, the girls wore a grey striped uniform and had shaven heads.

'Why is their hair cut so short?' I plucked up the courage to ask in a whisper.

'Because of lice,' she replied. 'And so as not to encourage vanity.'

I said goodbye to the matron, thanking her profusely. I headed off to the Artonesi home full of doubts. I was questioning, above all, the steps I had just taken. Had I been too hasty in making arrangements for Assuntina? Had I been too shy in making clear my intentions, and allowed myself to get railroaded into something I didn't want? And what should I tell Signorina Ester about Guido? Just what everyone had already seen, and she might soon hear on the grapevine, or should I tell her how things really were, talk to her about our engagement, show her the ring? But she didn't want to talk of love ever again. She might be upset that I hadn't asked her advice from the beginning. But we weren't close friends, equals, like two signorine from good families who have been confiding in each other since school days—I would never dare think such a thing. I had never forgotten that she was a signora and I was a sartina. Signorina Ester never mentioned Marquis Rizzaldo to me, even though I had known him. It was only through the town's gossips that I knew that, like her, Enrica's father was always off travelling, in Persia, Turkey, Arabia. But perhaps she would have been able to advise me from the very beginning on how to behave with Guido, since she knew the noble families of L— so well.

I could have saved myself all this agonising, because when I arrived at the Artonesi home and asked for the lady of the house, the housekeeper replied that she had headed out early in the morning. She had gone with her father to visit the brewery and would not be back before dinner time. I left her a note, saying that I had dropped by to tell her something important, something wonderful, and that should anybody tell her anything bad about me, she was not to believe it. I said I would explain everything the next day.

It was well into the afternoon by the time I got home. Assuntina had eaten alone yet again. By now she had learnt how to light the stove, and she had left my lunch warming on the embers. I hadn't the courage to tell her anything about her mother or the orphanage, and she didn't ask. She told me that Rinuccia had come looking for me, and that I was to go at once to Palazzo Delsorbo.

'She said *at once*: "As soon as she gets back she has to come over and see us."'

Even though I was expecting this, it took my breath away for a moment. I knew sooner or later I was going to have to face Donna Licinia, but I'd hoped to have a little more time. Rumours travelled so fast in our city.

'I can't go at once. I'm too tired,' I said, sitting down at the kitchen table. I had been on the go since before dawn. I took off my shoes. I took off the earrings that I'd put on to accompany Guido to the station and that I had then forgotten about. I thanked Assuntina for keeping my lunch warm and she promptly brought it over to me—a plate of food with another covering it, along with a glass and a fork. It was cauliflower with olives left over from the day before, and I began eating heartily.

I hadn't yet finished when there was a knock at the door. It was Rinuccia again. She immediately got stuck into the little girl: 'Didn't I tell you it was urgent?' I could feel my anger rising. Did they think I was at their disposal day and night?

'Urgent? Do I need to urgently sew another funeral pall?' I asked sarcastically. 'Whose turn is it this time? Your mistress's? Or is she eager to return to me the money that I left behind there the other day?'

'Don't try to be funny. This is no laughing matter, you stupid girl. Donna Licinia is furious. Come on—hurry up.'

I put my fork down calmly and deliberately, went to the sink to wash my hands, loosened my bun and then carefully tied my plaits back up, and looked under the chest for a more comfortable pair of shoes. I shook out my heavy shawl, the dark one, and placed it over my shoulders. Rinuccia was bursting with impatience.

'Have you finished your homework?' I asked Assuntina. 'Do you want to come with me?'

'No, no. She wants to talk to you alone. And come on—hurry up!' Rinuccia snapped.

I gave the little girl permission to go and play for an hour or so on the footpath with her friends, provided she didn't do any skipping or work up a sweat, and then I followed the 'young servant'. She was so agitated that I felt a little sorry for her. After all, none of this was her fault, and she deserved sympathy for being left out of Don Urbano's will. And for being left alone to do all the work in that enormous house, alone with that arrogant, overbearing mistress.

'So now that Quirica has left, doesn't Donna Licinia intend to employ another maid? Perhaps somebody younger?' I asked as we walked along.

'She wants to talk to you about that too.'

'To me? What's it got to do with me?'

'How should I know? I'd like to know what you did the other day over at our place to make her so angry. Ever since then, even before the reading of the will, she's been beside herself. And since last night, she's been even worse.'

So, her informers had wasted no time in apprising her. I resolved not to submit to an interrogation. I would not give her my version of the facts, and I would not apologise, if that was what she wanted. I wouldn't give her the satisfaction.

I was just a poor sartina and she was a grand signora. But she was not my boss.

Material Evidence

MY GRANDMOTHER HAD always taught me to respect the elderly. She'd never needed to tell me this in so many words; she had shown me through her behaviour that old age, with its weight of experience, and the courage, knowledge and sheer endurance that had enabled a person to overcome so many problems, sorrows and obstacles to survive to that point, was something to admire, to honour publicly, to aspire one day to emulate.

Life had taught me to respect the rich, whatever their age, character or actions. Being rich made them stronger than us, capable of crushing us, destroying us with a click of their fingers. The rich were not necessarily to be admired; we could certainly judge them critically, even disdainfully. But we could never express this. Especially not in their presence. We always had to be respectful around them.

Donna Licinia was old and she was rich, and I could not

allow myself to forget this.

I did not expect to find her so calm, so composed, sitting bolt upright in her red velvet armchair by the window.

'You kept me waiting. Where were you?' she asked, without so much as a greeting, the moment I appeared before her.

'At work,' I replied without further explanation. It was hot in the parlour and although she had not invited me to do so, I took off my shawl and placed it on a chair. I stayed standing, however, because that was what you had to do in the presence of signori. She sent Rinuccia away, ordering her to close the door behind her. Now we were alone.

'I saw you the other day, in the corridor.'

'I know.'

'You're a cunning one. You worked a nice little number on that simpleton of a grandson of mine. You haven't got any strange ideas in your head, have you?'

I did not reply, but I held her gaze.

'No, I don't believe you have,' she continued. 'You're a sensible girl. You might have beguiled him, but you know you'll never get anything out of him.'

I remained silent.

'You do know that, don't you? Your grandmother was no fool. She would have taught you that people like you need to know their place.'

Still I said nothing.

'But you're ambitious, aren't you? Like all those nasty little girls from the back alleys—you get around in filthy rags, the lot of you, but you long to dress like signori, to wear a hat, carry a fan and mince about in front of our sons so you can dupe them into giving you the family jewels. Or perhaps marrying you. You haven't dragged a marriage proposal out of my grandson, have you? He needs only to clap eyes on a skirt...Worse than his uncle. Weak, and an imbecile. But don't believe a word of it. Don't get your hopes up: Guido knows perfectly well who he is, and who you are.'

'You're right. I think he does know that. And he doesn't care.'

'Oh, really? He doesn't care? I care. Don't you know I can ruin you? That I could report you for soliciting? There's no shortage of witnesses. You thought you were too smart, didn't you? Leading him on like that in front of everybody. Why did you have to drag him into the glass cage of the Crystal Palace? And get all lovey-dovey in public? What were you trying to prove?'

'Listen, why don't you ask your grandson all these questions? Why don't you ask him when he returns? Why don't you write to him?'

'Because Guido has gone soft. Because he needs to study and not think about this sort of nonsense. And because it's much better if you and I reach an agreement. I'm sure we'll come to an understanding in the end.'

'Reach an agreement about what?'

'I have a proposal to make to you. Listen carefully.'

'Go ahead.'

'You know Quirica is gone. Rinuccia can't manage on her own. I need another maid.'

'You're right. And it's not going to be easy to find one.'

'I've already found one. I need a girl who's young and healthy. I want you to come and work here.'

'I'm a seamstress.'

'Pah! Will you listen to her, the great couturière! For a little bit of mending here and there. Your grandmother was an excellent maid. You know she worked here for a few months, when Vittoria was little. I never understood why she wanted to leave. But she must have taught you how to do the job.'

'She taught me how to sew.'

'You stubborn girl. If it means so much to you I'll give you some sewing to do. I couldn't care less. And I'll pay you a good salary. How much do you earn a month at the moment?'

'I'm sorry, but your proposal doesn't interest me.'

'Oh, but it does interest you. You rather like Guido, I've noticed. And he likes you. You know that as soon as he graduates he'll come and live here with me. That would be the ideal solution.'

I couldn't understand this. She'd just said she wanted to report me for soliciting.

'Don't play the saint now—don't pretend to be so naïve. You understand perfectly. Naturally, you will need to undergo a medical examination first. A discreet one. Dr Ricci will do it. He's already told me that you seemed healthy to him, that you probably don't have any shameful disease, so you're not likely to infect him with anything.'

Shameful disease? Infect him? I was beginning to understand, and a shiver ran down my spine. I'd heard stories like this. Stories of young servant girls employed by the family matriarch to provide an outlet for the urges of the young signorini of the house. Country girls chosen carefully from among the most naïve and inexpert. Virgins, to be sure they did not have any of those sorts of diseases. And I was beginning to understand Don Urbano's words in his will. Poor Quirica! She couldn't have been more than fifteen when they went to the country to collect her. And then she'd fallen in love with her young lord. She was still crying over him half a century later! She had spent fifty years as a slave, as the 'old servant', enduring contempt and arrogance from her mistress. And her suffering had increased when, later on, with his mother's permission, Don Urbano had been allowed to seek an outlet in brothels—after laws were introduced requiring prostitutes to undergo medical examinations, they were no longer so dangerous. Just as long as he never married. So that was where the gentleman spent the night when he was not sleeping at home. Even Signorina Ester knew this. It was a miracle they hadn't fired poor Quirica at that point, given that she was no longer needed. Now I understood why my grandmother had not wanted to remain in domestic service in that home. She was an honest woman; she would not have been able to bear seeing such shameful behaviour day in, day out. And what about

Rinuccia? Who knows if Rinuccia knew about it. She had been employed much later, after the epidemic, when it was probably all over between the two of them. But had she sensed something? Had Quirica confided in her?

So many questions. I didn't want the thought, the doubt, to creep into my mind. But I couldn't avoid it. Did Guido know? Did he suspect?

I felt the red damask walls begin to spin around me. I became unsteady on my feet and needed to lean on the back of the chair so I didn't fall over. No. Not Guido. He hadn't grown up in this house. His father had argued with his mother-in-law, Donna Licinia, and refused to let her bring Guido up. He had taught the boy a different set of values. Guido was respectful. He wouldn't have given me his mother's ring if he thought he could buy exclusive rights to my body with the salary of a servant girl.

All these thoughts ran through my head at lightning speed. Donna Licinia was watching me, waiting for an answer.

'So? Doesn't that sound like a good solution to you? We would all be much more comfortable.'

I picked up my shawl. 'You disgust me,' I'd have liked to say to her, but shyness and my upbringing prevented me from doing so. Instead, I repeated, 'I'm not interested: I've already told you that. Good evening.'

'Do you think you get a choice, you stupid girl? Have you not realised I could destroy you?'

I did not reply. I put on my shawl and made my way to the door.

'Wait! Before you leave, listen to what I have to tell you.'

I stopped with one hand on the doorknob.

'If you don't wish to accept my peace offering, that means you want war. Who do you think you are? You'll lose that war. Can't you see that I'm stronger than you? I have a lot of connections. In the prefecture, in the police force, in the courts. These are all people with the power in this city. Watch out. It will only take one word for me and you're done for.'

'I haven't done anything wrong.'

'You tell that to the police officers who come to get you when I report you as a prostitute. All it would take is an anonymous letter, you know? But I won't lower myself to that. No, I'll say that you tried multiple times to seduce my grandson, and that I have witnesses. And I'll find some other men who will say that you followed them down the street, that you made indecent proposals to them.'

'The only indecent proposal is the one that you have just made me, Donna Licinia. Aren't you ashamed of yourself?'

'Be quiet. It was an excellent proposal. And you still have time to accept it. You don't want to? Well, then, you little saint. You'll need to explain what resources you're living off, how you can afford certain luxuries, where you get your money.'

'What luxuries? Everybody knows that I live off my work.'

'A sartina getting around in fancy clothes made of English fabric, with an apartment all to yourself, and a bastard daughter you send off to school instead of to work, and who knows, perhaps some valuable little trinket...I saw that Guido has taken his mother's jewellery out of the safe, who knows what he's done with it...But I don't want to sit here wasting time. You can discuss all that with the officers. You know the law, don't you? You'll have to undergo a medical examination; you'll be unable to refuse, because to do so would be an admission that you've been infected and you'd end up getting booked anyway. I will speak to the doctor in charge of public decency. You'll soon see—he'll be able to find some nasty wart down there. You'll end up on the police register, with your own official whore's permit, working in a house of ill repute. And after two weeks they'll take you off to another city, with all the other little trollops, to entertain a new selection of clients. It won't take much for me to be rid of you. When my grandson returns, he won't know where to look for you.'

I was almost choking with indignation and at the same time was astonished that she was using such vulgar language. I didn't believe a single one of her threats. She only wanted to frighten me. Who knows if those laws she was talking about even existed. And in any case, I had done nothing wrong. 'Do no wrong, have no fear,' Nonna used to say. In silence, I opened the door and left.

Rinuccia was just outside trying to listen in. 'You didn't come to an agreement?' she asked. 'You've made a big mistake. She'll make you pay for it.'

'Why are you sticking your nose in?'

'I'm telling you for your own good.'

'You and your mistress can go to hell!' I said. I ran down the corridor and out the service door, slamming it behind me.

I was beside myself. If it hadn't been so late, I'd have run straight to Signorina Ester's to give vent to my feelings. It would have to wait until the next morning. In the meantime, as I walked towards home, I went through each of Donna Licinia's threats in my head, one by one, both the explicit and the veiled ones, in an effort to calm myself down, to convince myself that they were absurd and that no one would believe them. As if Assuntina was my bastard daughter! Everybody in the neighbourhood knew her mother. Her schoolteacher could testify to this. And the women of the neighbourhood would also be able to say that the fabric of my best clothes had come from Signorina Ester's hand-me-downs, which I had taken apart and sewn back together myself in a more modest style, just as my grandmother had done many years earlier. I had altered clothes for them too, for a small fee, if I couldn't use them.

Yet something was bothering me, like the soft buzz of a mosquito—some other name, some other story...I couldn't remember what, or how, but there was a vague memory. It was too muddled. Or perhaps, after a day in which all manner of things had happened to me, I was the one who was confused, too tired to be able to grasp the link.

—

Assuntina had set the table and heated our dinner. She was scowling at me, as though she realised I had already taken the first steps to getting rid of her. My eyes fell on her plaits, as thin as rat tails. She had only just learnt to braid her own hair each morning and was so proud of them. I thought of the moment when they would be chopped off. We ate in silence and went straight to bed. She, as usual, plunged straight into a deep sleep. I tossed and turned between the sheets. I'd had to face too many things in a single day, one after another—too many bitter discoveries, too many emotions, too many choices—and I could find no peace. It felt as though Guido had departed not that morning, but a long time earlier. As though he had disappeared from my life forever, leaving me alone to face all that pain, all those regrets, all that impotent rage. He would already have arrived in Turin by now. Perhaps he was dining in a nice restaurant, in the company of his student friends, or in the home of some signori, sitting alongside their polite, elegant daughters, with their soft hands and generous dowries, so pleasing to his grandmother. Perhaps he had already had enough of me and the problems I could create for him, that I had already created for him. Perhaps he was regretting his promises and would not return. I cried until my pillow was soaked through and I finally fell into an exhausted light sleep.

I dreamt that my grandmother was trying to tell me something, like that night when La Miss died, but before I could understand the meaning of her words I woke with a start. Finally asleep again, I saw her take the chain from around her neck and wrap it several times around one finger. I felt a great relief. She had come to remind me of the ring Guido had given me, the ring belonging to his mother, and to tell me that his intentions were honourable—he loved me and would protect me from any danger. Consoled by this thought I managed to sleep for a few hours; it was a deep, dream-free sleep. But shortly before dawn, my grandmother returned. She was holding something made of heavy gold, a cigar case. She uttered just one word, 'Ofelia,' and disappeared.

I woke at once. That's what that hazy memory had been, that soft mosquito buzz—Ofelia, my grandmother's cousin, who had been accused of theft by her master. Donna Licinia's reference to her daughter's jewellery. The ring. If they really were coming for me, they would find it in my home. They wouldn't believe that I'd received it as a gift from Guido, and he wasn't here to confirm it. They would take me off to prison I needed to make it disappear. At once. I leapt out of bed. Without even worrying about waking Assuntina and revealing my hiding place, I pulled over the chair, climbed onto it and felt about in the little recess. My tin was not in its usual spot. My heart leapt into my mouth as though it wanted to escape my body altogether. The noise had woken the girl and she looked up at me from her bed, full of curiosity.

'Did anybody come into the house yesterday while I was out?' I asked her, my mouth dry with anxiety.

'No, why?'

'Did you close the place up properly, locking the door, when you went out to play?'

'I always do.'

'And then when you came home, did anybody follow you?'

'No. Nobody.'

I took a deep breath to calm myself down, stood up on tiptoes, stretched out my arm and poked as far back as I could...Aha! There it was, my little tin box. It was just a bit further back than usual. Who had moved it? Me, probably, a couple of nights earlier when I'd put the ring in. I brought it down with great relief, lifted the lid, and looked among the banknotes and coins. I looked and looked before I resigned myself. The ring was not there.

Assuntina had got out of bed and was standing in the doorway watching me, huddling in her nightshirt because of the cold. She did not seem worried. Nor did she seem surprised to have discovered my secret. She was watching me. There was the very slightest tremor in her right cheek, near her mouth, as though she was just holding back a sneer of...derision? Of revenge?

'You took it?!' I shouted. But how could she have managed to get up so high? I soon had proof, however. I hadn't noticed it the previous night, I was too tired, too upset, but by her bed was the little wooden stool that I normally kept in the courtyard near the clothesline. At risk of falling and cracking her head open, while I was at Palazzo

Delsorbo, Assuntina had placed the stool on top of the chair and climbed up. Otherwise, she would never have been able to reach the little alcove.

'Where is the ring? Where have you put it? Give it to me.'

'It's gone.'

Lord, I beg you, please, please don't let her have taken it to play knucklebones or hopscotch on the footpath. Please don't let her have lost it. Or have taken it to the pawnshop. But no, they don't accept valuables from children. And certainly not jewellery.

'Where have you put it?'

She looked at me defiantly. 'You love the person who gave you that more than you love me.'

Wretched child! I could've strangled her. I leapt down off the chair and grabbed her by the shoulders. 'So what? So what? Do I have to answer to you now? Where have you put it?'

She burst into tears, but continued to shake her head defiantly: 'I'm not telling.'

And she didn't tell me. I looked for it all morning, in the hope that it was still somewhere in the house. 'A house never steals, it hides,' Nonna used to say, and with a prayer to St Anthony she would always manage to find the lost item. But I didn't know if the ring was still in the house or if, while I was getting insulted by Donna Licinia the previous afternoon, Assuntina had taken it away somewhere.

She could have lost it down a drain, traded it or, lifting the marble disc that covered the opening, thrown it into the sewer where she and her mother used to relieve themselves when they lived in the basso. She could have cracked it with a stone. She could even have swallowed it just to spite me.

But something told me no, the ring was still somewhere in the house. Why else would my grandmother have come to warn me of the danger of them coming and finding it?

Assuntina was silent, still shivering in her nightshirt. She was expecting me to beat her to make her talk, and was prepared to resist me. But I didn't beat her. I felt a cold rage, different from the burning fury of that night when I had grabbed her by the hair and dragged her out of the dark sea.

'You're not leaving here until that ring turns up,' I said without touching her.

'I have to go to school.'

'Forget it. You not leaving and you're not getting dressed.'

In fact, the first thing I did was to take off all her clothes, unconcerned that she might catch cold, to look all over her body. I even let her hair down, though it was too thin to hide what I was looking for. I made her stand on a chair and ordered her not to get down while I shook out her bed, sheets, pillow, blankets and mattress. I ran the broom under the bed and lay down on the ground to check there was nothing on the floor. Then I picked the girl up and lay her, still naked, on the bed, covering her in a sheet which I tied to the two planks down the sides of the bed so that she couldn't move. Aside from the cold, she seemed almost amused, as though the whole thing was a game. She watched as slowly and with extreme attention I checked over every inch of the two rooms and the kitchen. The place was small, but full of furniture and objects: the little armchairs my grandmother kept for her clients, the tall mirror, various tools of the trade, my hand-crank sewing machine, drawers full of threads and buttons, the boxes where I kept offcuts and patterns; and then in the kitchen, pots and pans, cooking utensils, the coal scuttle, bottles of lye, bags of dried legumes and another of potatoes. A ring is so small it can be hidden anywhere, but I was determined to dedicate as long as necessary to the search, not eating, not drinking, on my knees on the ground and on tiptoe to open the highest cupboard doors, constantly praying to my grandmother and to St Anthony. Midday came. Assuntina, like me, had not eaten a thing. She must surely have been hungry and thirsty but she did not say a word.

'Tell me where it is! If you don't talk I'll take you off to the orphanage,' I'd have liked to threaten her. But I didn't have the courage. I needed to take her off to the orphanage regardless of whether she talked or not. But at that moment I felt no pity for her; her impassive gaze, which followed my every movement, was irritating me so much that I took her dress off the chair, shook it out, running my fingers over every seam and every pleat and under the collar to be sure that it wasn't hiding anything, and threw it on the bed.

Then I undid the knots on the sheet so that she could get up. 'Get dressed and go wait out in the street!' I gave her neither her underclothes nor her shoes. 'Out!'

'It's cold,' she protested. I allowed her to take her shawl, after shaking it out well, and closed the door behind her. I recommenced my search, delving into every corner with a paintbrush. I had once gone to deliver some work to a Jewish family during one of their holidays, and I had seen the women on their knees cleaning the floor, trying to flush out every little hidden crumb with the aid of a feather. They had explained to me that they needed to purify the home to celebrate I don't know what ceremony. The thing I was looking for was bigger than a breadcrumb, but I couldn't see it anywhere. Centimetre after centimetre, I continued to look.

About an hour later there was a knock on the door. 'Out!' I cried, thinking it was Assuntina wanting to come back in. But the knocking increased and a man's voice cried: 'Open up! Police!'

I froze and then got to my feet with my heart in turmoil. She had wasted no time, that old witch, she really had reported me. She had sent officers to my home. What could I do? I hurriedly put a skirt on over my nightshirt and went to open the door, straightening up my hair as I did so. Once I saw them I found I was no longer afraid. I felt a great calm, as though I was abandoning myself to my fate. Let it go however it was going to go. We are dry leaves at the mercy of the wind.

~

There were two of them. I knew them because they were the ones who had interrogated me when La Miss died. One was a good deal older than the other, with little hair and a big belly sticking out under the belt of his uniform. The younger one was smartly dressed, almost elegant. I remembered the first man for his kind, patient, at times playful manner; the second was cold, disdainful, severe, aggressive, his thin lips like a cut that often opened out into a cruel smile. Someone had told me that officers were obliged by law to work in pairs, and that they divided up the roles of good and bad guy like in the theatre. But it seemed to me on that occasion that the older man really was a gentle, compassionate fellow and that he would be reluctant to exercise force on somebody. He had comforted me in a paternal fashion when he saw me crying desperately over the death of La Miss. The younger one had insinuated that my habit of reading novels made me suspicious, a woman at risk, as the laws and the charitable ladies would put it, and so hardly a credible witness.

Assuntina was standing behind them, and she slipped quickly into the house and went to the kitchen to get a piece of bread. She then stood by the sink nibbling on it, closely watching everything that happened. I realised that I was at her mercy. If she told the officers where she had hidden the ring, I was done for.

'Were you in the middle of a big spring clean?' the older man asked, seeing the furniture all over the place. His attention was drawn to my sewing machine. He had evidently never seen one with a hand crank. He approached it, touched it, and tried to turn the wheel which, however, was locked in position. The young man looked around with enquiring eyes. He straightened up one of my grandmother's armchairs which I had turned upside down. He lifted the geranium pot from its saucer and looked underneath.

In the meantime, the older one had sat down at the kitchen table and pulled out some papers. 'Now then, girl, a report has been filed against you.' He said it with apparent reluctance.

I won't go into the details of the interrogation and what followed, because even after so many years recollecting it provokes great embarrassment in me, a burning shame, as though I really had done something to be ashamed of.

In short, just as Donna Licinia had threatened, I was accused of being a whore who plied that trade clandestinely, using my work as a seamstress as a cover. And of using my wiles to take advantage of a student from a good family in order to steal jewellery and other unspecified items of value from him.

The older officer told me at once he did not believe the first accusation—that of 'mere notoriety', as the document put it—in fact, he found it ridiculous, because he had known my grandmother and had been keeping an eye on me for years. He said he did so with all the residents of the alleyways, who were subject to all kinds of temptation because they lived too close to the wealthy. He knew which families I worked for, and that I was never idle, and he was familiar with my habits. The younger one had arrived at our local police station more recently, however, and my good reputation was not enough to satisfy him. He wanted to check, to hear from the witnesses named in the statement. Above all, he required me to undergo a medical examination. I don't know whether this was out of a wicked pleasure in imagining the procedure even though he wouldn't be able to attend, or if it was to humiliate me, to 'put me in my place' as he called it, to frighten me after seeing the dismay and terror in my eyes at the prospect.

'What are you crying for? If you're all right you have nothing to fear,' he said mockingly. He didn't seem to care that my modesty would be violated regardless. In fact, perhaps that was what he found so amusing: it excited his worst male instincts. Just as he got great pleasure, later on, in running his hands all over me on the pretext of looking for the stolen jewellery.

What saved me from the medical examination and, ultimately, from the first accusation was, incredible though it is to say it, the presence of my sewing machine. The older officer was almost more embarrassed than me by his colleague's manner and he tried every possible pretext to defend me, listing many points that would exonerate me, but which the other man would immediately demolish with his suspicions. At a certain point, when he had run out of arguments, the older officer brought up a very old verdict from his early years in the service, from way back on 11

February 1878. I remember that date and other details so precisely because that verdict saved me; it's the reason why I was not required to reveal my most private parts and have someone poking around in there, a man who, even if he was a doctor, might have been paid by Donna Licinia to lie. Those were not times in which a young, God-fearing, well-behaved girl could undergo such an outrage without being scarred by it forever, deep in her soul and in the eyes of others, whatever the results of the examination might be.

The older officer told his colleague that Article 60 of the Cavour law on prostitution in force at the time held that, 'Should a prostitute indicate her intention to abandon the trade, the brothel in question must promptly advise the Director of the Department of Health who will encourage the woman to act on these plans.' In addition to being encouraged to redeem herself, the prostitute needed to show that from now on she would be able to maintain herself through honest means, whether through marriage, by returning to the home of her parents, or by working in a job from which she could earn a living. But seamstress could hardly be considered such a job, the other officer objected, since the majority of the women working in bordellos (and they knew this from experience) came from the lower classes—they were maids or seamstresses, jobs which clearly did not provide them with sufficient resources to live an honest life. Perhaps this was true for those who sewed by hand, my defender replied triumphantly, but he recalled that when they handed down their judgment, the local authorities had authorised the removal of the prostitute Miss Such-and-such from the police register, admitting as the sole piece of evidence that she had ceased plying the trade that she owned a sewing machine.

He was so sure of himself in citing the facts, the law and the judgment, right down to precise dates and wording, and in underscoring the youth and inexperience of his colleague, that the latter could not counter his argument. I confess that I found his reasoning rather tortuous. Before I had even been proven to have engaged in prostitution, I was being declared worthy of abandoning it. I had never appeared on any such register, yet it now appeared was being removed from it. And all this because in my house I had a device that Signorina Ester had given to me. The logic was hardly impeccable, but since it worked in my favour, I was careful not to point this out.

It was not so easy to clear my name of the second accusation, unfortunately. That morning, before they came knocking on my door, the two officers had gone to the pawnshop to check that I had not already been there to get rid of the stolen jewellery. When the response was negative, they had begun interrogating several police informers and all the city's fences. None of them knew me; none had ever bought anything from me, recently or in the past. I must, therefore, still have the stolen goods somewhere on my person or hidden in the house. The younger officer searched me, as I mentioned. The other searched Assuntina, and although I had already ascertained that she did not have the ring, that was the moment of greatest apprehension for me.

They asked the girl how long she had been living with me and why. They knew who she was; they knew Zita, but her admission to hospital was so recent that they had not been informed of it. They asked the girl if she had seen me hide anything and, with the most innocent face in world, she said no.

The old man continued to hover around the sewing machine.

'Is it worth a lot of money?' he asked. 'I would like to give one like this to my wife.'

'I wouldn't know. I, too, got it as a gift.'

'From a lover?' asked the other one, his tone insinuating. 'Who's giving you such expensive gifts? And in exchange for what?'

'Marchesina Ester Artonesi gave it to me. You can ask her.'

He frowned and muttered under his breath, 'That good-for-nothing.' Then he asked me to open all the little nooks and crannies of the machine, and he poked his fingers around inside. He got me to turn it upside down to reveal all its inner workings, which were accessible so that they could be kept lubricated.

The other followed all these operations with interest. 'You can see that there's nothing inside. There wouldn't even be room for a necklace or bracelet.'

'Pity, eh?' the younger man replied maliciously. 'Then you'd have been able to seize it as material evidence, and

one way or another it could have disappeared from the
station and ended up in your wife's little parlour.' Then he
turned to me, his tone threatening: 'If you don't tell us
where you put the jewellery, things are going to turn ugly
for you. We're going to find it either way, can't you see that?
You'd be better off if you stopped wasting our time.'

'I haven't stolen anything. I haven't hidden anything.'

'Then you're going to have to come with us to the
station. We'll seal up the apartment and send our colleagues
to undertake a thorough inspection. We're in no hurry, but
we absolutely have to find this jewellery.'

I realised that they were afraid of fronting up to their
superiors empty-handed. Donna Licinia must have got some
of the city's most important figures involved.

They allowed me to get dressed, in their presence, and
to bring a change of underwear. 'Take your woollen jumper
and your heaviest shawl. It's cold in the lock-up,' said the
older officer. I asked if I could also bring along some
sewing, to pass the time. They told me that needles and
scissors were not allowed in the cell. 'Perhaps a book then...'
I was about to ask, but I remembered what the younger
officer had said to me during the business with La Miss, so
I kept quiet.

In the meantime, Assuntina had put on her shoes and
socks, taken the cover off the cushion and begun preparing
her own bundle of things.

'What are you doing? Are you coming to the lock-up
too? We don't want snotty little kids like you,' the younger

officer told her with a cruel laugh. The older one looked at him reproachfully. 'The child can't stay here,' he said, 'nor can she return to her own home. Her mother is in hospital, didn't you hear?' Then he asked me, 'Is there some neighbour who can take her in?'

'Take her to the Child Mary,' I replied. 'They're expecting her. I've already done all the paperwork.'

Assuntina looked at me in astonishment. Her expression was accusatory and reproachful for the manner of my betrayal, yet at the same time conveyed such deep desolation that I felt sorry for her, and all the resentment I had felt towards her over the ring melted away inside my chest.

I spent three days in the lock-up, during which time a team of five officers ran a fine-tooth comb over my apartment, carrying on methodically the search that I had barely begun. The only difference being that, unfortunately for them, they did not know exactly what they were looking for. In her statement Donna Licinia had only spoken generally of jewellery; she had not given a list or any description. She knew that Guido had taken his mother's jewellery box from the safe, but after so many years she could no longer remember precisely its contents and, most importantly, she was unaware that her grandson had only given me the ring, the humblest item of all, having more sentimental than monetary value. Whereas she was quite sure that I had got him to give me, if not everything, then certainly the most extravagant and valuable articles, those inherited from the

Delsorbo women, and she was insisting that the police find them all.

When I arrived at the station, the cell, which contained two bunks, was already occupied. I found a strange cellmate sitting on the bed by the window with a book in hand—a woman of around thirty, with fair hair, nicely dressed and well-mannered, who spoke with an out-of-towner's accent. I wondered what she was doing there; I expected her to treat me disdainfully, but instead she was kind to me, helping me set myself up, outlining the rules and customs of the place. It was not the first time she had spent a few days there, she told me. My astonishment increased when, by way of explanation for this familiarity, she told me quite openly, without the slightest embarrassment or shame, that she was a prostitute, a lady of the night who plied her trade in the city's top brothel, the most elegant one of all. And that, in order to visit her son, who lived with a wet nurse in the country, she had left her place of work for two days longer than the owner of the establishment allowed. This was the reason for her current arrest. On previous occasions she had ended up in the lock-up for violating one or other of the twenty-three rules that were written in her little registration booklet, just as they were written in those of all her fellow workers. 'Written rules,' she commented sarcastically, 'when not one of them can read. I'm a black swan, you'll have realised that by now.' She was originally from the north of Italy, and had come to our part of the country to 'work' under a false name, to avoid bringing shame on her family of origin. Seeing that I was looking at the book she was holding with great curiosity and trying to read the title, she explained that she had studied to be a schoolteacher and had started out working at a school up in the mountains, but the salary was very low, and then she had been seduced by the headmaster, a married man who tried it on with all the young teachers, and she had fallen pregnant…After the birth she had voluntarily registered with the authorities and been assigned to a bordello.

'That way I have a roof over my head and can maintain my son,' she said with calm cynicism, adding with a bitter laugh: 'And I'm still employed by the state, just like before. I earn only one-quarter of the fee the client plays, which is established by law. The rest goes in taxes, public administration, a cut for the madam, and expenses. But I have to pay out of my own pocket for the compulsory medical examinations. Luckily, I'm in high demand. Upwards of ten clients a day, you know? Blondes are not too common around here.'

She seemed amused by my astonishment at so many details I could never have imagined, and I could not hide my horror when I heard her talking about clients, fees and services.

'You know what?' she concluded. 'It's such a boring life. I don't know how I'd survive it weren't for my novels.' She passed me the book she was holding. 'This one is wonderful—I've just finished it. If you like, I can lend it to you. I noticed that you know how to read too. Or rather, when we both go home in three days' time, you can have it, as a gift.'

I was disconcerted. Like all young women who had been brought up in a respectable household, I had been horrified at the thought of women who sold their bodies. Once I was old enough and Nonna recounted to me the story of Ofelia, that horror had transformed into pity. This elegant, educated woman, who was not ashamed of her situation, did not want my pity.

The second day, we were joined by a drunk old woman who had flown into a mad rage and beaten up a cabman; she was released before nightfall. On the third day a vagrant arrived. It was impossible to guess her age; she was teeming with lice and her tattered rags were stiff with sweat. The soles of her bare feet had grown so thick that it looked like she was wearing heavy work boots. She stayed the night with us and I had to share my bed with her. The next morning, when all three of us were released, I returned home carrying the novel, which I had begun reading on the first day, a gift from the blond northerner, and scratching my head, which was riddled with lice, a gift from the vagrant woman that would take me several days and a great deal of effort to be rid of.

As I said, I began reading the novel in the cell, in part to avoid having to talk too much with its donor, whose brazen chatter left me embarrassed. The author was English, but the translation was fairly simple and I was able to read it without difficulty. It was engrossing, and told of a romance a little like mine—it was about a rich man who was in love with a poor and virtuous girl who returned his love but, aware of her own condition, was afraid even to admit it to herself. Unlike Guido, the man was a great deal older than her and had a daughter. Reading it helped me to keep my anguished thoughts at bay, along with the many questions that constantly assailed me. First and foremost, what had happened to the ring? Naturally I hoped that the police would not find it, but did that mean I must consider it lost forever? How would I ever be able to convince Assuntina to confess to me where she had hidden it, given that I had now betrayed her? And if I didn't find it, what would I tell Guido, who would expect to be seeing it soon on my finger? I also wondered whether news of the accusations against me had ended up in the newspaper; if so, some malicious person might have sent him a cutting in an anonymous envelope which at that very moment was making its way to Turin. I also wondered whether Signorina Ester would have read about it and what she would be thinking of me. I knew that during those three days under arrest no one was permitted to visit me, so I was not surprised that she hadn't come to see me, but what about afterwards?

There was too the risk that as the news spread by word of mouth, my reputation would be ruined forever. Even if eventually I was declared innocent, doubts would remain, and what kind of family would ever allow a suspected thief to enter their home to work? Yet another source of anguish was my landlady, who must certainly know of my arrest by now. Would she continue to think me an honest woman like my grandmother? Would she tolerate the confusion the police had wrought on the lower-ground floor of her building, the coming and going of officers, the fact that no one was mopping the floors and the entrance hall since they'd taken me away, with Zita no longer around to cover for me?

By day, reading helped to keep these fears at bay, but at night, once I put out the lamp, there was no way to stop the ugly thoughts returning, larger than ever in the dark. I lay awake on my bunk, pretending to sleep in order to avoid questions from my cellmate. I tried to summon sleep, but when it finally came it was restless, agitated, peppered with strange dreams. On the last night I dreamt that I had just one day to sew my wedding gown, yet I was in no hurry; I wanted to make it to the highest standard, as I had learnt from Signorina Gemma in the Provera household. I stretched a bolt of fabric over a large worktable. It was a silk shantung, soft but at the same time stiff, with a raised weft. It was a dense and opaque white that took on a pearly splendour in the light. I cut it freely, with no need for a pattern, along the lines of a design I had in my head, similar to Signorina Ester's wedding gown. I gathered in the sleeves and tacked them to the bodice, laid the skirt out on the bias, pinning the pleats so it would drape full and gentle around my hips. I brought it all together with tacking thread and tried it on: it fitted me perfectly. I sewed the pieces together with my machine, the hand crank magically turning of its own accord, leaving my hands free, the fabric gliding smoothly under the needle. And suddenly the gown was finished, fully lined and trimmed in every detail, with tiny buttons positioned all down the back, and hems sewn and pressed. I lifted it up and shook it out—the sleeves and skirt billowed, blooming at my fingertips like a flower at first light. And then I was wearing it, a gown fit for a lady, a fairytale princess; Guido would be so proud of my elegance. Only the veil was missing. I reached for a bolt of tulle trimmed with Valenciennes lace…and woke to the vagrant woman elbowing me in the back.

The next morning, after farewelling my cellmates and signing the necessary paperwork, I crossed the threshold of the police station to find Signor Artonesi awaiting me, accompanied by a man dressed in dark clothing, whom he introduced as his lawyer. 'They found nothing in your home,' the lawyer informed me. 'From the very beginning I insisted that one of my staff be present throughout the search. It wouldn't be the first time a crooked officer, paid off by the accuser, introduced something to the scene that he wanted at all costs to find. Your accuser was demanding that they continue searching, extending your time in detention, but I managed to prevent that. I had to go into battle against the prefect; whoever has it in for you is very powerful. But the sergeant in charge of the search had already given up; your apartment has been combed from top to bottom. All your acquaintances have been interrogated, any that were even slightly suspect in turn underwent careful searches. Where else could they look?'

I burst into tears, so great was my relief. Embarrassed, Signor Artonesi offered me his handkerchief. He had come to collect me in his carriage; he helped me up and escorted me home. In the entrance hall of my building, Ester was waiting with my landlady. My friend had managed to pacify her and convince her not to evict me; I still have no idea how. The 'marchesina' had once again deployed all her charm and eloquence. She had also paid for a team of three cleaning ladies to stand in for me from the first day, and had insisted relentlessly that the police officers repair any damage, dirt or mess they'd introduced into common areas of the building.

But there was nothing they could do for my apartment. It looked as though a cyclone had come through. 'The women will be back in the afternoon to give you a hand,' Ester said. 'In the meantime, let's check that nothing is missing.'

She followed right behind me as I looked in the sewing room, in the bedroom and in the kitchen. Two things weighed on my mind above anything else: my little tin and my sewing machine. The first of these I found lying on the kitchen floor in amongst a lot of other broken bits and pieces. It had been squashed, as though they had trampled it with their boots—perhaps enraged to have found only a few coins and not the jewellery they were searching for.

They hadn't taken the money, though. I found it in an envelope on the windowsill. The lawyer's assistant had sealed it with wax and demanded that the sergeant sign it. My sewing machine had ended up in the bedroom, goodness knows how. It was lying on the bed base, alongside the upturned mattress, but intact. The only damage was a few greasy fingerprints on its beautiful shiny surface and the needle, which had been bent. Someone had messed around with it, turning the handle without having the presser foot in position.

Signorina Ester picked up my grandmother's two little armchairs, cleared some space around them and asked me to sit down opposite her.

'I was intrigued by your note,' she began by way of explanation. 'You wrote that you had something wonderful to tell me and the next morning I waited eagerly for your visit. When it became clear after lunch that you weren't coming I began to worry, so I took the carriage and came over here. They'd taken you away less than an hour earlier; the women of the neighbourhood were all still out in the laneway talking about it. It will be some consolation to know that they were all on your side, furious with the police, and frightened to think that something like that could happen to them too. I hurried straight over to my father's office and asked him to do something. He called our lawyer, who immediately put in a request to be present for the search, and also advised us to gag the press. That would never have occurred to me. My father knows the director of the newspaper, who owes him a few favours. The man had already received an anonymous note that related the story of the accusations of theft and soliciting. We later learnt that it had been Donna Licinia Delsorbo who had reported you, and the letter to the newspaper probably came from her too. None of it makes any sense. The lawyer thinks that the whole scandal with Don Urbano's will must have caused her to take leave of her senses: she's almost a hundred years old, after all. In any case, you can tell me all about it. The director of the newspaper said that if the person accused of theft had been an important figure he would have been forced to publish the news. But given it was just a matter of a sartina—forgive him—and mere suspicion, at that, there was no need to spill any ink over it. So, luckily the news never got out. We're the only ones who know about it.'

She wouldn't accept any thanks. Didn't I know her better than that? Didn't I know that she could never hold back when faced with injustice? Even more so when the person involved was someone she cared for. I took her hand and kissed it.

'Come now, don't get carried away. It's not as though I'm Prince Rodolphe of the *Mysteries of Paris*,' she said with a smile. 'If I hadn't had the help of my father there would have been little I could do. I'm going to head home now— you try to rest. Come over to my place tomorrow after lunch, for a coffee. I want you to tell me everything, but today you're too tired.'

On her way out she told me that she had seen some envelopes in my letterbox in the entrance hall of the building. 'Somebody has written to you. If it's anything unpleasant, don't worry about it. Set it aside and we'll pass it on to the lawyer.'

But it wasn't anything unpleasant: quite the opposite. One envelope was from the bank and contained the twelfth instalment of the allowance from La Miss, which had been arriving regularly since January. The other was postmarked Turin. Before even opening it I kissed it. Then I closed and locked the door, sat on the edge of the bed, and began reading, my heart thumping. My first letter from Guido! And it was a letter so like him: kind, affectionate, sincere. I'm not going to repeat what it said. I still keep it among my most precious things. There was just one detail that made me a little uncomfortable, even though it was a sign of his attentiveness and his generosity. He had slipped a sheet of decalcomanias into the envelope, for Assuntina. 'From your travel companion,' he had written on the thin strip of paper that was not to be got wet. 'I'm sure you'll like these. The little girls of Turin are crazy about them.'

In my reply I was going to have to tell him that Assuntina was no longer around. That I was going to have to take the decalcomanias to her in the orphanage, where perhaps she was not even allowed to receive gifts. As for whether I ought to tell him everything that had happened in the meantime, about what his grandmother had done to me… This was something I still needed to decide.

I lay down on the bed with the letter held close to my heart and tried to sleep a little, even though it was daytime.

I was woken by the three cleaners sent by Signorina Ester, who were bearing lunch and fresh linen. I ate a little and then we set to work cleaning, picking up the debris and putting things back in order. Working with them helped to keep my worries at bay. Guido's letter, which I had slipped under my shirt, close to my heart, was a sweet and constant comfort.

By nightfall the place had almost begun to look normal again. My bed had been made up with the clean sheets Signorina Ester had sent. The women left, and as my evening meal I drank a cup of warm milk, before heating up some water so I could wash in the zinc tub. Three days in a cell, three days of anxiety, cold sweats, a filthy latrine, a bunk bed without sheets and a sink without water had left their mark. I greased my hair with petroleum and wrapped a towel tightly around my head. It would take several days for that treatment to rid me of the guests the vagrant woman had passed on to me, since I had no intention of cutting my hair. The four months I had to wait before Guido's return would not be sufficient for it to grow back enough to receive his caresses.

Finally I went to bed, exhausted, with one hand slid under the pillow clutching the letter, which to me was more precious than any jewel.

The next morning, as promised, I went over to Signorina Ester's house. I told her everything about Guido, apart from the story of the ring he had given me and that Assuntina had hidden. I don't know why, but I was more embarrassed about that than anything else. Even more than the obscene proposal that Donna Licinia had made me.

I thought that my protector, with her open and modern mentality, would be enthusiastic about my love story, that she would encourage me to fight to defend it. But instead she looked at me with concern. 'Are you quite sure of what you're doing? All told, you've only seen him a couple of times, for a few hours. You don't know him well enough. They're all like that when they're trying to get what they want.'

'He's never shown me any disrespect. He said he wants to marry me.'

'And that explains his grandmother's rage and her decision to do anything to stop him. But will he really marry you, in the end? Will he have the courage? Or will he pull out at the last minute, make some kind of excuse? Be careful not to be compromised; if he breaks it off, you'll be ruined forever. And even if he did marry you…Are you sure that once the initial enthusiasm has passed, he won't be embarrassed by you?'

She suggested I consider that in the end he, too, was a Delsorbo, that perhaps he was like Don Urbano. She said I should not forget what they had done to Quirica, and that maybe, if I had accepted his grandmother's proposal, he'd have been quite happy.

'Not at all!' I protested. 'You don't know him.'

'No, you're right. But you can't say that you know him deep down either.'

I didn't know what to say. Her advice, her concern, her distrust were all reasonable. But I couldn't help but think that her experience with Marquis Rizzaldo had forever shattered any illusions she might have had about love or marriage, any trust in the sincerity of men.

I believed in Guido's sincerity with all my soul. So I promised her that I would behave prudently, not least to avoid any further persecution from the authorities, but in my heart I resolved faithfully to await the return of my love, and in the meantime to better myself so that I would be worthy of him and he would under no circumstances ever be embarrassed by me.

Over the next few days I tried to resume my usual life. The owner of the grocery store had asked me to sew her daughter's linen and uniform for boarding school. She had provided me with patterns and fabric, which were strictly stipulated and not to be substituted. It was fabric of the best quality that could not be found in our town and instead needed to be ordered from G——. As it would not be long before the girl was sent off to school, I went to work at their house every morning. They had a lovely treadle-operated machine that allowed me to sew more quickly, and by setting up at their house I could measure the garments on the future boarder as often as necessary. I worked on the hand-sewn finishings at home in the afternoons. During this time, I had not been using my own sewing machine. I hadn't even looked at the broken needle to work out how it had bent or whether I would be able to repair it myself. I felt as though the police officers' hands had sullied it. Even cleaning their greasy fingerprints off with alcohol had made me feel disgust. Eventually I would have to see to it, I knew. But in the meantime, I had been using my client's treadle machine.

As I cut and sewed I couldn't help but think of the ugly grey striped uniform that Assuntina was currently wearing. One day, I had gone to see her at the orphanage, taking along the sheet of decalcomanias, but at the last minute I didn't have the courage to go in. I stopped in the large open area outside the institute and hid behind the statue of Garibaldi, watching the orphaned girls playing in the garden behind the railings. They were chasing after each other, skipping rope, arguing, squealing. I struggled to recognise Assuntina without her plaits, her bare head as round as a marble, shaven with a very short patch of hair on top, 'Umberto-style', as was typically used for little boys. She was one of the smallest, and she was sitting alone in a corner looking down and scuffing the ground with her shoe, like a puppy on a leash. She seemed even thinner and more fragile than when I'd picked her up and put her on my knee in the train, while her eyes seemed bigger than before, engrossed in something, and at the same time fierce.

I couldn't muster the courage to go in and ask to see her. Or even to go to the front desk and leave her the gift from

Guido. I returned home with a sense of such profound bitterness that for the rest of the day I could neither sew nor continue reading my English novel. Because there too events were unfolding in an unhappy way—the lover had turned out to be a liar, the marriage a sham; the poor girl had run away to save her honour and risked dying of hunger. Was all this a warning to me? To be on my guard, just as Signorina Ester had explicitly told me?

I was tormented by the thought of Zita and had not dared to ask the matron at the hospital for news of her. Was she still alive, and when she died what would they do with her? Would they carry her off to the cemetery, unaccompanied by so much as a dog, and throw her into the paupers' grave? Or worse still, would they hand her over to the university, so the professors could cut her up in front of the medical students to show them how we're made on the inside? I knew this was the fate of poor people without families, who had no relative to claim their body.

Spending every morning at my client's house, following the little girl's chatter as, torn between fear and excitement, she fantasised about her new life at boarding school—her new friends, the subjects she would be studying—helped me to dispel some of these melancholy thoughts. But when the time came to book a spot in the gods for the next season of the opera, I decided I would not go. I was spending all the money from my allowance, which I now kept with the rest of my savings in a fabric pouch hidden inside a picture frame, on school books: books about grammar, geography, arithmetic. Sometimes I borrowed them from the library, to save money. I had even managed to find there a book about etiquette, and another that showed you how to write all kinds of letters, especially love letters. The title was *The Gallant Secretary* and there was a model letter for every occasion. But the sentences all sounded ridiculous to me, false. Who would ever dream of writing such nonsense? The letters I received from Guido were completely different and reflected his spontaneous character, describing his daily life in such a way that I felt like I was there sharing it with him. For my part, I tried my best to respond in the same tone, even though I had little to relate, and he encouraged me, complimenting me on my progress, recommending I read this or that novel he had particularly liked, transcribing his favourite poems. He particularly loved a poet who wrote about poor people, Giovanni Pascoli. I, too, learnt to love his work.

Time passed slowly. I had finished sewing all the items the little girl needed for boarding school and she had departed, tremendously excited. One afternoon, as I was sewing the edging on a sheet destined for my own trousseau, a servant girl from the hospital knocked on my door. She had been sent by the matron to inform me that Zita had died and that they would be taking her to the cemetery the next day. Out of respect for Signorina Ester, they had spared her the Institute of Anatomy.

I decided to accompany her. She had been a good friend to me and I owed her that much. But my heart was so torn that I could not sleep that night, even though I was very tired. I lit a candle and picked up my English novel. I had almost reached the end—everything had worked out: the lying man's mad wife had died and now he was able to marry the poor young woman without deceit, and she had received an inheritance and was no longer poor. This was lucky, because I have never liked novels that end badly. Unlike in *La Bohème*, in this novel, just as in my own life over the past month, there was a young orphan girl who needed a home. I had been sure that, with the arrival of the inheritance and the marriage, there would be a happy ending for little Adèle too: a house, an affectionate father and stepmother she would now be able to live with. So I felt terrible when I read that the young protagonist had got rid of her by sending her away to boarding school. I don't know why this made me so angry. In the end it was just a novel, a made-up story.

I got up very early, did all the cleaning, wrapped my shawl around me and set off for the cemetery. Zita's coffin was not there. A little while later a plain-looking van arrived. No flowers, no wreaths, no mourners apart from the servant girl from the hospital, who handed Zita over to the under-taker along with a few sheets of paper. There wasn't even a priest to bless her. I was the only one there to say a prayer for her, and to stroke the wood of the coffin. Then they put her in a hole that had already been dug in the poor man's graveyard. So that I would be able to find her again, I memorised the position and the number written next to her name on the wooden cross. I was unable to cry: it was as though I was frozen inside. If I had pricked myself with a needle or my embroiderer's scissors, I wouldn't have felt the pain.

As always, I stopped briefly to greet Nonna and La Miss, who were buried not far away. But I was like a machine: I did it out of habit. My thoughts were elsewhere.

When I left, instead of making my way home I headed, on impulse, without thinking of the consequences, towards the Institute for the Child Mary. By now, the morning was well underway and the main door was open. At the front desk I asked after Assuntina. They told me they'd given her the day off school and she was in the chapel, where the priest was saying a brief funeral rite in memory of her mother. I would not have to be the one to inform her, then—this alone was a small relief to me.

Assuntina was sitting alone in the first few pew. About a dozen nuns sat behind her singing in Latin in reedy voices. The words were no doubt a plea for mercy on the soul of the departed. I waited for them to finish. Though I was grateful to the nuns and the chaplain for the small bunch of flowers on the altar, the incense, the Gregorian chant, I felt that Assuntina could not stay in that place any longer.

When she turned around and saw me up the back she looked at me defiantly. The nun alongside her had to push her towards me. I hastily tried to think of an excuse to take her outside. 'I'd like to take her to the cemetery to say a last goodbye to her mother,' I said. They gave me permission and entrusted her to me, insisting that I bring her straight back for lunch.

I had to drag her, holding on tightly to her clammy hand, as she kept trying to slip away from me. She was dragging her feet and following me against her will. She continued to scowl at me at the cemetery. Along the way I had pulled a few wildflowers off the bushes growing along the roadside, and now I gave them to her so she could place them on the fresh pile of earth. I said a brief prayer with her. More than a requiem for the mother, I felt what was needed was a prayer to the daughter's guardian angel. 'Be at her side, to light and guard, to rule and guide this child who has no one else left in the world.' Outside the cemetery gate, I took her by the chin and lifted her surly little face. 'You know what? I'm not taking you back to the orphanage. You and I are going home now.'

I would sign the release papers in the afternoon. I had no doubt that they would be very happy to free up a bed.

When she crossed the threshold of my flat Assuntina looked around her. Her tense, furrowed brow gradually relaxed. She knew nothing of the police search, and was astonished that some pieces of furniture had been moved and a few objects were missing. I didn't ask her about the ring. I confess that in that moment I wasn't even thinking about it. I was feeling deeply moved and at the same time worried about the responsibility which from that day forward I would need to shoulder. Signorina Ester would not be pleased with me. She had been so good to me, and I wasn't following her advice—I kept on disappointing her. And as for Guido, how would he react to my hasty decision? Should I have asked his opinion first?

The little girl slowly made her way around the apartment, running her hands over one object or another as though recognising them by touch, like she was blind. She opened the drawer where I kept the children's chronicles to see if they were still there. She saw the sheet of decalcomanias I had put in there. She didn't know what they were, but she was attracted by the brightly coloured pictures. 'They're yours,' I told her. 'Read what it says.' She slowly sounded out the words Guido had written. 'You'll have to thank him for the gift,' I added.

'Is he the one who gave you the ring?' she asked.

'Yes. You don't want to tell me where you put it?'

She didn't answer. She stood by her bed, looking puzzled and annoyed. The mattress, devoid of sheets and blankets, was rolled up and propped against a wall.

'We'll fix it up later. I didn't have time this morning. You can help me with the sheets,' I said. 'Do you want to go to bed already? Don't you want to eat something? It's well past dinnertime. You must be hungry. I'll heat up some soup for you, we can eat and then we'll go to bed. I'm exhausted too.'

'So can I stay?'

'Yes.'

'You won't send me away again?'

'No.'

That was all she said and, knowing her well, I didn't expect her to say anything more, or to thank me. But neither did I expect what she did next.

Averting her eyes, Assuntina walked decisively into the little parlour, went up to the sewing machine and with surprising dexterity opened the little door to the bobbin compartment, slid her fingers in, took out the bobbin case and held it out on the palm of her hand. Inside, instead of the bobbin with the spool of thread, was the ring.

It had been there all along. During my initial search I hadn't looked in that spot because I hadn't realised that Assuntina had spent so long watching me as I used the sewing machine, and that when she was alone at home she had practised taking it apart. The police officers, although they had examined the machine with great interest from the start, didn't understand how it worked; none of them had realised that section was hollow and could be slipped out. Perhaps they had tried but had not lifted the little lever blocking it which, unless you knew the machine, looked like a single solid piece or like it was welded on.

Perhaps that was what Nonna had been trying to tell me in my dream by winding the little chain around her finger. When the thread ran out you needed to pop the bobbin out of its case to refill it, but first you needed to get the case out of its compartment. After that you had to place the bobbin on the winder and fill it with new thread.

My grandmother knew that Assuntina had switched the bobbin with the ring.

Nonna, you know that difficult times lie ahead for me. Nonna, you must be my guardian angel: be at my side, to light and guard, to rule and guide.

Epilogue

SINCE THEN, FIFTY years have passed. I've seen two wars go by. The world has changed, but by the grace of God I'm still alive, I can see all right, and I'm still sewing, although only for the family these days. You'll be wanting to know, reader, what happened to me after the events you've just read about, and why I've related to you these stories of a time so distant that it seems even to me to belong to the life of another person, rather than my own.

As soon as he graduated, towards the end of July, Guido returned to L—. Only once we were together, and I could hold his hand and look him in the eyes, did I have the courage to reveal to him what his grandmother had done to me, and what she had done long before to Quirica in order to keep Don Urbano in the home. He had been unaware of that, as I had always felt certain was the case. I had never seen him so upset, so angry. He broke off all contact with Donna Licinia and went to live in a rented apartment. He chose it from among those that Quirica had inherited, and he decorated it in such a way that after our wedding we would be able to live there together with Assuntina, whose presence he had immediately accepted. When children came along later, we would move somewhere larger. Two rooms were to be for my sewing—he had not asked me to give up my work; he knew how proud I was of it. Thanks to Clara's father, he had found a job in the construction of the aqueduct.

I introduced Guido to my signorina Ester. She liked him and changed her mind about the seriousness of his intentions. However, she suggested that we move to G—, where we were not known, because things would be much easier that way. But Guido was proud too. There was no reason for us to hide, he said. From the beginning he had been honoured to be seen with me at his side.

Our mistake was not getting married immediately. He wanted a regular engagement; he wanted us to get to know each other, and take our time preparing for a big wedding that would show his grandmother and all the top families of the city that he didn't care about their prejudices and that the woman he had chosen was worth as much as their daughters.

Although I kept on living in my little rooms with Assuntina, we used to see each other every day. We were young, we loved each other, he desired me and I learnt to desire him in that way that novels never spoke about. I'd be doing him a disservice if I told you that I had to give in to his overtures, that I was carried away against my will by his passion. We were both carried away by reciprocal desire; we were of one mind, and in any case, the day of our marriage was now approaching. I had sewn myself a simple white gown, unlike the one I had dreamt about in prison; I still wasn't used to dressing like a lady.

Two days before our wedding, on his way to work, Guido was run over by an automobile whose owner had not yet learnt properly to control it. He died after a few hours. We were never able to say goodbye; he had no chance to worry about my future. What's more, neither of us knew it yet but we were expecting a baby. I only realised some months later, when I was already living with Assuntina in the apartment that Guido had rented from Quirica and that she had generously offered me for a price so low it was merely symbolic. And this was fortunate, because once my shame became evident, at least I didn't need to worry about accommodation along with all the other problems I had to face. If Guido had died three days later, I would have inherited his fortune and my son would not have been a bastard. But according to the law we were strangers to Guido, and all he possessed went to Donna Licinia, his only relative. Signorina Ester, who had stayed by my side and shown me great affection despite all the criticism in the city, offered me not only understanding but also the assistance of the family's lawyer; after all, in requesting the papers for marriage and setting a date, Guido had shown his intention to marry me. Proof of this were the banns posted on the door of the church.

You won't believe this, but although she was about to turn a hundred, Donna Licinia fought tooth and nail to stop me getting even a penny. There was no will in my favour and the case went on for years, so long that I tired of fighting, not least because in the meantime Quirica had died and, as she had no one else in the world, left everything she owned to me and my son. It was nothing compared to the riches of the Delsorbos, but it was enough for us. More than anything, I was sorry that the boy didn't have Guido's surname. He was a beautiful child, and so resembled his father—'cheeks like a rose and the eyes of a gazelle', I thought when I saw his face the moment he was born. I called him Guido. He did very well in his studies and now lives in America because over here the regime made his life very difficult, and afterwards he never returned. I gave him the ring with the diamond and sapphire, and he wore it for a time on his little finger, then found a wife and gave it to her. They have no children.

Donna Licinia died aged 104, still completely lucid. She too had no one left in the world, but she did not think of us; she did not think that my son was her only blood heir. She left everything to those distant relatives in F—, the ones who only appeared every quarter-century but who had swooped in to Don Urbano's deathbed like vultures.

As for me, at first I thought I would never find consolation. That I would never forget my great love and the tragedy of losing him. I kept studying to be worthy of Guido, as though it might still be possible to embarrass him in front of his peers. I continued to read, for my own pleasure and because it became easier as time went on. I helped my son with his schoolwork and learnt many new things alongside him.

But time, though it doesn't erase all memories, does make them fade. The pain that you think will break your heart becomes less bitter, and your regret is sweeter. Twelve years after the death of Guido I met a man who inspired affection and trust in me, and who respected me despite my poor reputation. He was a carpenter and his workshop was on the ground floor of our building. He was always in good spirits even though he too had lost a dearly loved wife, who had died in childbirth along with their first-born. After some time he asked me to marry him and he took care not only of my son but also of Assuntina, who had stayed on with me and to whom I was teaching my trade. He had even chosen to spend money and fight the bureaucratic battle to be able to give them both his surname. He was an excellent father to them, even though they were not of his blood. Not only is he a carpenter, his name is Giuseppe, like Jesus' father—perhaps that explains it. We live together, just the two of us now, and he is a great comfort to me. He's still working, despite his age. He says that craftsmen never retire; rather, they drop dead with their tools in hand. But I don't think he's about to die. He's still strong and full of energy; he can lift a window shutter with one hand.

I have learnt to love the smell of wood shavings, especially fir and pine. As a wedding gift, he gave me a treadle sewing machine that still works beautifully. I wouldn't know what to do with an electric one. We like going to the theatre, and are able to afford two seats in the stalls, but now we have a radio and we listen to the opera at home as well.

You'll be wanting to know, reader, what became of my friend and protector, Signorina Ester. She too, eight years after her first unhappy marriage, met a respectable man to whom she could entrust her own life and that of Enrica.

Marquis Rizzaldo, who through that time had continued travelling back and forth to the Orient, encountered a cholera epidemic in Constantinople, his second, and this time he did not come out alive. Widowed and free, at twenty-seven Ester married a young English engineer who had come to gain experience in the brewery, and had won the respect and friendship of Signor Artonesi. She married him on the condition that he never return to his homeland but rather remain in our city and help her father in his work. When the latter died a few years later, Ester did not entrust the management of her inheritance to her husband, as her aunts had expected—despite the many demands on her time, such as the upbringing of Enrica, who was eleven by now (the title of 'marchesina' had become hers, though nobody used it), and of the three children she'd had with the engineer. Instead, she worked side by side with her husband in running the mill and the brewery.

When the need arose, I continued going to their house to sew; I ate at their table and saw them behaving like two good friends, with no mawkish or sentimental behaviour. 'My signorina has given up on love forever,' I sometimes used to think. Other times, though, seeing them laugh together as they leaned over a catalogue to discuss the purchase of new machinery, I had the suspicion that the deep understanding I saw between them, their shared interests, that complicity and complete reciprocal trust, constituted a truer and deeper form of love than that talked about in romance novels.

Why did I want to write these stories of my youth? Enrica Rizzaldo, Ester's firstborn, asked me to. She teaches at the university now. She researches how our ways of living and working have changed. Now even people of little means buy ready-made clothes from the shops at a low price. Horrible clothes, if you want my opinion, always too wide or tight, too short or long, that pull at the armpits and bunch up over the shoulders and the hips. Few people go to a sartina these days, and they never call on one to go and work in their home.

Aged twenty, Assuntina, who had become a skilled seamstress, got a job as a pattern maker at La Supreme Eleganza. She preferred a secure salary over the uncertainty of working in people's homes. She too is married, to a man who works for the council, and they have three children. She's retired now and no longer sews. She spends all her time sitting in front of a new contraption, some kind of cross between a radio and the cinema, but small, a box you can keep in your own home. Her daughter Zita, who works as a shop assistant in a clothing store, would like to leave the children with her in the afternoon after they finish school, but Assuntina doesn't want them—she says they're a nuisance and won't let her watch her favourite programmes in peace. She says to bring them over to my place, because I have more time and know how to keep them entertained.

I'm teaching them, the boy and the girl, how to use a treadle sewing machine, and they love it. They even know how to sew on buttons, so that if they lose one they don't have to ask for help and can do the mending themselves. The girl has little patience, but the boy even likes sewing by hand. I haven't been able to persuade him to use a thimble but even without one he can sew the border on a handkerchief with tiny, precise little stitches, just like my grandmother taught me when I was his age. I've promised him that for Carnival I'll help him make an American Indian costume. We've based the pattern on a character from a film; you can't find anything that nice in the shops. His sister was jealous, so I've promised to make her a white cambric pinafore with cap sleeves, pleats down the front and a trim along the hem. 'Just like Beth in *Little Women*!' she says. Just like those I sewed for Enrica when she was little, I think to myself. I also think about how happy my poor friend Zita would be if she knew that Assuntina had given her daughter her name.

This new Zita's children are affectionate: they love me and call me Nonna. At night I make an effort always to sleep peacefully in my bed alongside Giuseppe, so that I never go visiting them in their dreams.

My Thanks

To Giulia Ichino, who fell in love with the sartina the moment she met her, and urged me to help her grow.

And to Francesca Lazzarato, who provided encouragement, criticism, excellent advice and beautiful suggestions, even though I couldn't follow them all. That would require another three novels. Though who knows...

Bianca Pitzorno was born in Sardinia in 1942. Since 1970 she has published seventy works of fiction and non-fiction, for adults and children. Her books have sold more than two million copies in Italy and been translated into many languages. *The Seamstress of Sardinia* is the first of her adult works to be translated into English. Pitzorno has also translated into Italian books by J. R. R. Tolkien, Sylvia Plath, Tove Jansson and David Grossman.

Brigid Maher is senior lecturer in Italian Studies at La Trobe University in Melbourne and has translated several works of contemporary Italian writing into English.